THE ART OF EVIL

THE ART OF EVIL

DARYN PARKE

FIVE STAR
A part of Gale, Cengage Learning

Detroit • New York • San Francisco • New Haven, Conn • Waterville, Maine • London

GALE
CENGAGE Learning

LIBRARY OF CONGRESS CATALOGING-IN-PUBLICATION DATA

Parke, Daryn.
 The art of evil / Daryn Parke. — 1st ed.
   p. cm.
 ISBN-13: 978-1-59414-786-9 (alk. paper)
 ISBN-10: 1-59414-786-8 (alk. paper)
  1. Government investigators—Fiction. 2. Women—Florida—
Fiction. 3. Serial murders—Florida—Fiction. 4. Florida—Fiction.
 I. Title.
PS3616.A7438A78 2009
813'.6 dc22   2009005175

First Edition. First Printing: June 2009.
Published in 2009 in conjunction with Tekno Books and Ed Gorman.

Printed in the United States of America
1 2 3 4 5 6 7 13 12 11 10 09

To John and Mable Ringling,
who followed their dream

AUTHOR'S NOTE

If you're going to have bad things happen in a real place, change the name. I have followed this sensible advice, offered via e-mail by a number of experienced mystery/suspense authors. For those who believe they recognize the location of *The Art of Evil*, let me hasten to say that certain changes in the Florida setting have been made to simplify the geography and to emphasize that the story and characters are pure fiction. For example, the "aerie" exists, but not as described in this book. It has been a perfectly mundane office for many years now. (The view, however, is as spectacular as described.)

Special thanks go to the Ritz-Carlton in Sarasota for allowing the use of the name and the hotel in a work of fiction. And to Shari Mitchell, Ron McCarty, Lin Vertefeuille, Fred Knight, and the other staff and volunteers at the John and Mable Ringling Museum of Art who answered countless questions, particularly those in Education, Archives, the Library, and Security. Thanks also to the circus buffs and performers who provided some of the circus background, including the story of the origin of the expression, "Break a leg." And a very special thanks to Tram Bosses Brad Helms, Ron Dawes, and Des Keenan and to the other members of the Tuesday afternoon tram crew—Robert, Marty, and Bob.

Daryn Parke

CHAPTER 1

There's something about a naked man seventeen feet tall. Even if he's bronze and pushing one hundred. I eat lunch with him twice a week, thanks to the machinations of my Aunt Hyacinth. More accurately, my great-aunt Hyacinth, the sister of my mother's mother, and the only person in our whole extended family who's never had to work a day in her life.

"Go visit Aunt Hy," my mother told me. "Florida's the perfect place to recuperate." She paused, pondering her next words, an unusual move for my mother who is seldom at a loss on any occasion. "Your Aunt Hy has always been a bit—ah—different," she confided.

As if I didn't know.

"But, lately," she continued, "well . . . I'd feel much better if you were down there keeping an eye on her."

There was more, I knew it. After all, when had Aunt Hyacinth not been strange?

"You know, Aurora"—I winced at my mother's use of the name she had inflicted on me in an excessive burst of romanticism some twenty-nine years ago—"your Aunt Hy is very wealthy and has no children—"

"Mom!" I cut her off, nearly strangling as I repressed a screech unsuitable to my proper New England upbringing. "Aunt Hyacinth lives in a condo at the Ritz. With a housekeeper and a maid. Believe me, she plans to spend it all."

"Nonetheless," my mother decreed, "you have several months

of recovery ahead of you and Florida is the ideal place to be. Aunt Hy tells me she'll be delighted to have you, so you might as well start packing. It's the perfect solution to your problem."

My problem. That's as close as we'd ever come to talking about my problem. My "accident." My probable career change. The great red blob in the middle of the white rug that everyone pussyfoots around and no one ever mentions. I guess I should have been grateful my parents recognized I wasn't yet ready to face the monster in the closet. Correction. My particular monster refused to be relegated to a closet. It hovered beside me every minute of every day, hissing in my ear, *Screwed the pooch, didn't you, girl? Messed up big-time. Pay for it the rest of your life, you will, Rory . . . Ro-ry . . . Ror-r-ry . . .*

Mom may have tippy-toed around the crisis in my life, but on the subject of my visit to Aunt Hyacinth she was inexorable. Okay, so I'd go to the land of the has-beens, the cast-offs, the seniors who alleviated boredom with endless rounds of golf and shopping while they longed to be back in the boardrooms and teeming activities of the North.

Or so I thought, while sunk in depression in my parents' Connecticut living room with its great bay windows overlooking Long Island Sound. Connecticut, the land of *real* people—the movers and shakers, from the rich-as-sin to university intellectuals, with a few *dons* and *capos* still clinging to the good old days. Florida, in contrast, was the end of the world. Exile. I'd be falling off the edge of the map, lost in the place that used to be labeled, "Here be dragons!"

Some dragons! White-haired seniors with quad canes or walkers, creeping along with oxygen bottles at their sides. And Rory Travis fitting right in. In fact, it was a good bet most of the seniors could outdistance my hobbling steps nine times out of ten.

Of course, I soon discovered my image of senior citizens was pretty far off the mark. Yes, Florida's seniors did play golf. Yes, they were avid shoppers, happily spending their children's inheritance. They also walked the beaches, swam, hiked, biked, enjoyed theater, concerts, sporting events, and put in a rather astonishing number of hours at volunteer jobs—from local hospitals to the sheriff's department, from libraries to museums. Sometimes they even allowed failures like me to join them. Which is how I ended up eating lunch under the watchful eye of Michelangelo's *David,* who was wearing nothing but his slingshot nonchalantly slung over one shoulder. (Yes, I know the marble original is in Florence, but the Bellman Museum's bronze reproduction is bigger and—um—well, even more startlingly anatomically correct.)

The minute Aunt Hyacinth noticed I was ready to do more than lie on the chaise on her balcony and gaze out over Sarasota Bay, she sent me off to the Bellman, where I promptly became the youngest volunteer on the roster. This, I must tell you, was not exactly a major accomplishment as Aunt Hy is a six-figure contributor to the museum's ever-struggling coffers, not to mention that it was August, a time when all those who could afford it had fled north for the summer. Tram drivers were in such short supply that on the day I reported for training, the Chief of Security was out on the run, driving a tram.

A tram at a museum? you ask. Sensible question. The Richard and Opal Bellman Museum of Art is actually three museums set on sixty-some acres of bay front just north of downtown Sarasota, Florida. Even the grounds are a museum of sorts, being chock full of exotic trees and plants, including a spectacular rose garden, an ear tree (honestly!), a sausage tree (definitely *not* edible), and those strange and mysterious imports from India—banyan trees—which are scattered like giant alien life forms in nearly every direction you look. So, between the Florida heat, monsoon rains, and flocks of visitors from all over the world, a fleet of trams is necessary, constantly moving people from the Art Museum to the Circus Museum to the Casa Bellissima, the Bellmans' spectacular winter home, set in the midst of more than a thousand feet of bay front.

I crumpled the brown paper bag that had held my E.T. bagel with veggie cream cheese and tucked it inside my mini-cooler. I finished my can of ginger ale while savoring the peace of the huge courtyard tucked between the long U-shaped sides of the Art Museum. Peace. That's why I was here. (Occasionally, dear old Aunt Hy displayed remarkably good sense.) Everywhere I looked, my wretched soul was soothed by beauty and serenity. The glory of *David*, the brilliant fuchsia of the bougainvilleas tumbling from enormous terra-cotta jugs, the life-size classical statues guarding the museum's roofline, the stately banyans putting down their octopus-like roots on the grounds outside, the acres of flowers and exotic greenery. The antique gilded wagons in the Circus Museum, the sparkling blue of Sarasota Bay, the magnificence of the Casa Bellissima—the Most Beautiful House—named in an obvious play on Richard Bellman's name. In short, the Bellman was exactly the oasis I needed at this time in my life.

Once again, my eyes strayed to *David*, my hero, proudly poised on the raised walkway at the west end of the courtyard. All two hundred glorious naked inches of him, looking out over the courtyard and Art Museum with all the casual elegance of an emperor surveying his realm. And, okay, I admit it, I wondered about the then-twenty-six-year-old Michelangelo and the glorious young man who had posed for him. Had they enjoyed each other when the workday was done?

I also wondered if God still made men who looked like that. Not to my personal knowledge, that's for sure. Not when I was working up north, and certainly not now, when I was a semi-invalid living in the land of senior citizens. Though, to be perfectly honest about my wistful fantasies, if I met someone who actually looked like *David*—that noble face, those springing curls, a body to die for—I'd probably turn and run.

But, no, girls with gimpy legs didn't run. Nor would running be necessary in the reincarnated presence of such a man. I could simply slip to the back of the crowd of women (and men) surrounding this phenomenon and fade into obscurity. Rory Travis—a woman of medium height, a figure that would never stand out in a crowd, bland coloring—skin too pale; hair, nondescript brown, medium length; eyes, blue with flecks of green. And a limp that verged on the grotesque.

I sighed, grabbed my cane, and hauled myself to my feet. My view of *David* was abruptly cut off by the roof of the loggia that extended around three sides of the courtyard. There was a time . . . yes, there was a time when all my perfectly ordinary parts came together in an attractive package. It seemed a very long time ago.

I hobbled to the edge of the loggia and took another peek at *David*. *Fool!* A woman of nearly thirty did not lust after a boy of . . . what? Seventeen? Eighteen? Surely, the model for *David* could not have been more than that. Yet that magnificent hunk of bronze was *safe;* I could lust after him all I wanted. This boy, forever immortalized by Michelangelo, did not mind my sickly complexion, my limp, my heavy heart. I could look my fill and he would still stand there, arrogantly overlooking his kingdom, just as Richard Bellman had placed him some seventy-five years ago.

I picked up my cooler and made my way up the shallow steps to the elevator. I'd already checked in with Security on the lower level, so the only preparations remaining for my tram run were a trip to the Ladies' Room and pouring quarters into the drink machine, which dutifully plopped down an ice-cold bottle of water. It was late September, and September in Florida is exactly like June, July, and August. Blazing hot, with afternoon thunderstorms likely. The only difference from the previous months was that, by September, everyone is thoroughly sick of the unremitting heat alleviated only by total immersion in refrigerated cars and buildings.

My tram, however, was not air-conditioned. And its rain protection consisted of plastic curtains that rolled down and zipped together. But the curtains did not fasten well to the windshield, and I usually ended up soaked. Yet, heaven help me, I actually liked my job—my *volunteer* job—driving round and round the grounds for three and a half hours twice a week. How else would I meet people from every part of the U.S., Canada, and sundry points in Europe? Meeting and greeting, that's what I do now, and quite a change it is from my former occupation.

I waved at Mike, who was behind the Security Desk, pushed open the outside door, quickly closing it behind me to shut out the blast of heat. Slowly, I made my way around the west corner of the museum, crossed behind the courtyard—not failing to examine *David*'s anterior portions as I limped by. But the heat was horrendous, and even *David*'s nether cheeks could not tempt me to linger. I passed the "tram barn," the skimpily roofed area where the trams recharged each night, and made my way to the driveway on the north side of the museum. George, who drove Tram 3—"my" tram—on the morning run, would see me and come to pick me up. The distance, about the length of a football field, was not one any of us cared to walk under the blazing Florida sun.

A golf cart bounced toward me over the broken pavement, skidded to a halt beside me. "Rory, what's up, girl? Been moonin' over that statue again?"

Mooning. An apt description of my appreciative peek at *David*'s cheeks.

"Billie." I returned his grin, although I couldn't help but notice his high-watt personality seemed dimmed this morning, his customary teasing more habit than genuine high spirits. When I first met him, I would swear he said his name was Billie Ball Hamlin, but since that seemed unlikely, perhaps I had misinterpreted his Florida drawl. So I'd settled for first-name only, which was all anyone seemed to use at the Bellman. Billie's about my age and has that Florida-born look—lean and fit, permanent tan, sun-streaked blond hair, blue eyes with crinkles at the corners, and an easygoing attitude that never seems to mind rendering "service" to the rich and powerful. Or even to the senior volunteers, who were mostly has-beens. Like me.

If you're thinking I feel sorry for myself, you're right. I do. If you think I'm suffering from depression, you're right about that, too. Tough to be Miss Merry Sunshine after losing your man and a promising career in less than thirty seconds. So go easy on the judgment. Spare the kicks 'til I'm out of rehab.

I'd assumed Billie was one of the many groundskeepers at the museum complex, but, truthfully, I wasn't sure. He was simply a fixture, part of the sixty-acre landscape. The grounds are huge, you see, and a startling variety of people are scooting about in golf carts at any given time. Nubile young ladies, barely out of the art departments of prestigious universities and thrilled to be on staff at the Bellman. Security guards, mostly stalwart men of middle years, wearing the Bellman's burgundy polo shirts with laminated IDs hanging from a ribbon round their necks (the same uniform worn by tram drivers). The guards tended to return my greetings with solemn nods. The grounds-keepers inevitably smiled, waved, and granted the trams precedence. The nubile maidens (I speak classically only, of course) and the security guards did not.

Billie, I was nearly certain, ranked among Those Who Get Paid. Other than that, his role at the Bellman remained a mystery. Some months ago, I had abruptly ceased to be one of Those Who Asked Questions. Undoubtedly, Billie and I had drifted into occasional conversation due to our shared (and rare) age group. We were, nonetheless, still in the tentative early stages of acquaintance.

"Want a ride?" Billie offered. "Save George a trip?"

"Sure." I climbed into the passenger seat, although I wasn't sure if George, who was closer to eighty than seventy, would appreciate the gesture. I'd probably have to run him back to his car.

Billie sat, staring at the steering wheel, his foot resting, unmoving, above the pedal. "Bad morning," he said at last. "I was in early—been up all night—uh, never mind, forget I said that." He grabbed the steering wheel, pushed back against the uncompromising white vinyl seat. "Anyway . . . I was first out on the grounds, doing a quick check to make sure everything was shipshape before the thundering herds arrived. And down near the House—you know that big old banyan nearest the water?—this kid from the Honors College . . . he'd taken a bed sheet and . . . well, he was just dangling there, turning in the sea breeze, right alongside those damned twisted trunks and hanging roots . . ."

"Oh, Billie, I'm sorry." I laid my hand on his bare arm, hoping to give comfort, even as my heart ached for the student who had been so desperate and confused that he had taken his own life.

The college next door to the Bellman grounds is the Honors College of the State of Florida, often described as providing an Ivy League education for half the price. But even an unusual amount of brain power couldn't protect a person from depression. No one knew that better than I. But now, with the low, wrenching creak of cracking open a long-shut lid on an antique chest, something long dormant stirred inside. "How do you know he was a student?" I asked. Curiosity, thy name is Rory.

"Student ID. And he left a note, carefully typed and placed under a broken branch big enough to keep it from blowing away. Very precise. Just like the computer geek he was."

"You knew him?"

"No, but I hung around long enough to hear what happened when the police came. His name was Tim Mundell. Some cop went over to the campus, and it seemed like half the student body came back with him. It's a small college, y'know. They all know each other."

"Did anybody suggest how he managed it? I mean, was there a ladder or a stool—"

"Rory," Billie interrupted, "you ever take a good look at a banyan? They got trunks going every which way. Any kid that age could climb up high enough to drop a noose off a limb."

He was right. Banyans were definitely the oddest trees I'd ever seen. Even I, in my present debilitated state, could probably climb a banyan, with a bed sheet already knotted around my neck. Tie the other end to a branch and simply jump . . .

"Any motive, or was it simply depression?" I had to ask; couldn't help myself.

"Note was kinda vague . . . sounded like life had overwhelmed him. Seemed a bit odd, though, y'know. Exam week, I could see it, but when the semester is just starting . . . ?"

"Billie"—prickles surged up my spine—"are you saying it might not be suicide?"

"Don't know," he mumbled, putting his foot to the pedal. The electric golf cart moved silently forward. "Just seems a strange time to check out . . . tuition all paid and classes barely begun."

"But he was hanged with his own bed sheet, right?" I asked.

"Doubt anybody's checked on that. Y'know, Rory," Billie added, "you're the only person I know would've said 'hanged' instead of 'hung.' You Yankees are just so perfect when you talk . . . like some damn news anchor on TV."

"Sorry." Only later would I wonder if he'd thrown out a deliberate red herring.

"And you ask a lotta questions. You some kind of cop, Rory?"

"I'm a tram driver," I told him as he pulled up at the Main Tram Stop, where George was patiently waiting with Tram 3, fully loaded with passengers for the Casa Bellissima.

Billie volunteered to take George back to his car, I slipped into George's seat, and we were off. Rory Travis and six passengers on their way to view Richard and Opal Bellman's mansion on Sarasota Bay.

Usually, my volunteer job at the Bellman did exactly what it was supposed to do—keep me from thinking about how badly I had messed up my life. For a few hours I could lose myself in being a tour guide, in driving my specified route, smiling, answering questions—at which I had improved considerably in the last two months—while enjoying the Bellman's precious peace and quiet.

But, today, every time I made the circle in front of the Casa Bellissima, I saw yellow tape circling one of the huge banyan trees. Yet all was quiet, the breeze barely stirring the rope-like roots dangling from a tangled multitude of branches. As the student's body had dangled, only hours earlier. Now there was only a single patrol car, as unobtrusively parked among the other cars nearby as it was possible for a clearly marked police car to be. Keeping watch until the ME's report came back? Very likely.

There was a time when I could not have passed by, could not have ignored the tragedy that happened here this morning. But six months ago I'd taken a fall from a third-floor fire escape, shattering my body and shattering my life. I was grounded, big-time. Fit only to drive round and round and round the grounds of an art museum, a peaceful oasis in a world set to the pace of its senior citizens.

And yet, something inside me had begun to stir, quivering faintly to life. Prickles skittered up my spine. Bitter memories, or premonition of disasters to come? Was I about to lose my refuge? Was this beautiful day—filled with happy visitors, lush greenery, colorful flowers, exotic trees, and sun sparkling off the slight chop in the bay—merely the calm before the storm?

Though I hate to admit it, I sometimes have a feel for these things. As it turned out, this fall—instead of the usual hurricane scare—Chaos, Hell, and the Devil were bearing down on the Richard and Opal Bellman Museum of Art (not necessarily in that order). Our days of paradisiacal serenity were numbered.

CHAPTER 2

As it happened, the Devil came first. Although inactivity had turned my mind so sluggish it took me a while to put a name to the threat. Oh, I knew he was dangerous. How could I not when he appeared in my tram out of nowhere, accompanied by a blaze of lightning, an all-enveloping explosion of thunder, and the acrid smell of air rent asunder by an electrical charge?

But I get ahead of myself.

It was late afternoon. I was returning empty from the Casa Bellissima, after letting off three visitors for the final tour of the day. Although the rainy season was dwindling to a close, I'd been hearing rumbles for the past half hour. As the first drops began to spatter onto the lower half of my semi-open windshield, I pulled up under the multi-trunked shelter of a great banyan and readied my tram for the storm. First, I folded up the top half of my windshield and fastened it in place. I hated to lose the air, but being soaked to the skin is surprisingly chilling, even when the temperature is ninety-five. Then I began to unsnap and roll down the plastic side curtains. If you're having trouble visualizing this process, think of Tram 3 as an elongated golf cart, with three bench seats facing front (including the driver's) and one bench seat facing to the rear. The front three seats have plastic curtains on each side that roll down; the back seat, a curtain that encloses the whole rear end. Then, each panel fastens to the one next to it with a heavy-duty plastic zipper, with pull tabs both inside and out. In the other trams at the

20

museum, the driver and passengers end up as snug as bugs in a rug. In Tram 3—my tram—fastening the front panels to the windshield is iffy. Even my best efforts never stayed in place more than five minutes, allowing the front panels on both sides to flap in the wind like the wings of some gigantic prehistoric bird, beating against the insistent storm. It also meant that, no matter how meticulous my efforts, I usually got soaked. Which is why I carry two terry towels and a roll of paper towels in the trunk of my car.

This time, I had left it too late. The rain increased from infrequent blobs to a downpour so fast that I was at least half soaked before I crawled back behind the wheel and attempted to coax the plastic at my left to adhere to the sticky loops along the edge of the windshield. The thunder changed from rumbles to sharp cracks. Ready at last to offer shelter to our visitors, I scanned the road, the rose garden, and the lawn in front of the Casa. Not a single soul in sight. (I swear it.) But it was definitely time to remember what my mama told me about sheltering under trees in a thunderstorm. My right foot pressed the pedal. Obediently, Tram 3 rolled silently forward.

Lightning struck—not my banyan, thank God, but one close by, or perhaps one of the tall slash pines not far away. The thunder was a physical blow, rolling over me with the inevitability of a freight train on a downhill run. My foot came off the gas, my hair stood on end. Not just my arms. I could feel my scalp prickle. The smell was . . . well, maybe sulphurous isn't the word, but, looking back, it seems appropriate.

A body—lithe and solid—slid onto the seat beside me. "Good timing," said a voice that echoed oddly inside the close confines of my eight-passenger plastic-coated tent. "Thanks."

Unfortunately, at that moment all my horrors came back in a rush of Act First, Ask Questions Later. But the apparition grabbed my arm before my hand could chop him in the throat.

21

Quite calmly, he reattached my hand to the steering wheel, closing my fingers around the black plastic wheel cover. "Sorry I startled you," he apologized. Then, more softly, "Interesting reaction."

He appeared out of thin air and wondered why I was startled! Had I been stunned by the lightning? Suffered a lapse of time? Where had he come from? I'd swear he hadn't even unzipped the curtain.

Okay, so tram drivers don't usually assault their passengers with karate chops.

"I beg your pardon," I mumbled, keeping my eyes straight forward, as if fascinated by the deluge waterfalling down the windshield. "I thought I was alone out here."

"No problem," he rumbled in a baritone so intimate my stomach executed what must have been its tenth somersault in the last sixty seconds. "But you might want to pull out from under this tree."

I hated him. He'd materialized out of nowhere, a lean, dark wraith, with flashing eyes, radiating danger signals from every pore. He'd manhandled me, thrusting me back behind the wheel as easily as if I were a child of nine instead of . . .

Truthfully, a child of nine might have managed the whole thing better.

And now he was telling me how to drive my tram. I put my foot on the pedal and crept forward until we were in a relatively open space. I shifted my right foot over to the parking brake and pushed hard. I could feel his eyes following my foot, noticing I had not used my left. Well, damn him, anyway. Since I already hated him, what was one more sin to chalk up against him?

"Josh Thomas," he said. A hand appeared before me. I glanced down, pointedly ignoring his offering. And then it hit me. I was a tram driver, the front line of the museum's phalanx of meeters and greeters. No matter how odd this man's sudden appearance in the front seat of my tram, he was a *visitor*. My entire job—perhaps even more important than transportation—was being gracious and friendly to visitors.

I unglued my hand from the wheel. His grasp was exactly what I feared. It pulled me in, skin to skin, as if declaring it would never let me go. It insisted I look up. Look *at*. Lose myself in eyes so black and opaque, they were like those black holes astronomers study, places where every bit of matter is swallowed up, and nothing ever comes out.

The face matched. Black hair that might have had a bit of curl but was currently hanging in sodden strands, one or two drooping down far enough to dangle over his well-arched black brows. He could have been any age from thirty to forty. He had an angular face, with a Roman nose, a slash of a mouth, skin as pale as mine. A creature of the night, perhaps? Venturing out only as the museum approached its closing hour?

Perhaps from that place beneath the statue of *David* that Richard Bellman had once intended to be his crypt?

You're past invalid, Rory, my girl. Try breakdown. Two bricks shy of a load. Certifiable.

I retrieved my hand, returned it to the safety of the steering wheel.

"Tram Drivers Anonymous?" he taunted.

"Rory Travis," I muttered. Good manners had been drummed into me since childhood, yet I struggled with a strong desire to say, "Damn the Deluge," and run for my life. I was not so far gone from the world I had once known that I didn't recognize Fatal Attraction when it was sitting next to me, hip to hip. This man, however, was dangerous to more than my fragile heart. I recognized the type. He might be wearing casual clothes—black T-shirt, black jeans, sneakers so white they looked as if they just came out of the box. There wasn't even room for—

Look again, Rory. Those aren't jeans. My eyes strayed where they probably shouldn't have. My mysterious stranger was wearing full-cut trousers, not jeans. Of course. Where else would he put the gun? A .22, maybe even a .32, could hide behind those pleats with no difficulty at all.

Take my word for it. His was a type that never went anywhere without one.

"Well, Rory Travis, how long do these storms usually last?"

I'd nearly killed him, and he was making mundane tourist conversation. The whole scene was surreal.

Not that I would have finished that chop. I wasn't that far gone. But since he'd countered my blow by moving as swiftly as the lightning that brought him, he had no way of knowing I would have pulled that chop before it landed. Yet, here he was, blandly talking about the weather.

"The worst should be over soon," I replied, matching him cool for cool. "Then I'll do a pick-up at the Circus Museum and take everyone to the main tram stop. I'm afraid you'll have to make a run for the parking lot." Casual Visitor Reply Number One Thousand and One.

But casual indifference was all that would save me. I was sitting shoulder to shoulder with the living embodiment of a Black Hole . . . caught in an awareness so strong, it blotted out the world around us, as if we were the last survivors in some primeval jungle . . .

"Do you drive every day?"

What? "Twice a week." My reply was so wooden I might as well have been a robot.

"Volunteer?"

"Yes."

"How often do you get soaked?"

The man was trying, I had to admit. At this moment his manners were considerably better than mine.

"Not too often," I told him. "Usually the storm doesn't come on quite so hard or so fast, but it does rain nearly every afternoon from June through September."

"Maybe I should come back when the weather is better."

"By mid-October it's beautiful," I offered, then winced, certain my words sounded more like an invitation than casual conversation.

"I came late today, not realizing there was so much to see," Josh Thomas admitted, as if he were just another tourist.

Which he wasn't. Josh Thomas was Fate. Like the inexorable statue stalking toward Don Giovanni, sealing his doom.

"So next time I'm in town, I'll be back."

Polite conversation? Incipient flirtation? Threat? My intuition failed me. The deluge had dwindled to a steady rain. Wishing I had the luxury of windshield wipers, I put my foot on the pedal and drove east toward the Circus Museum. Beside me, my mystery man, rebuffed by my lack of response, turned silent.

Betty, the Security Guard, must have been peeking out the door watching for my delayed arrival, for she promptly shooed a full complement of six visitors out the door. There was a great rustling of zippers up, zippers down, and then we were squelching down the bumpy tarmac, turning off onto the crushed shell road that became more pockmarked with each day's rain. Giant stalks of bamboo (no pandas) could be glimpsed through the rain-streaked plastic to our left. Up onto smooth tarmac and a straight run back to the Art Museum.

The rain was still pretty hard. Taking pity on my passengers, I daringly departed from my route, making my way up the sidewalk to the front of the museum. Where I was now faced with the problem of how to turn around without backing onto the grass. Sigh. Not even my mystery man could have done it. Unless, of course, he had Powers. Inwardly, I scoffed, while quivers shot up my spine. Josh Thomas was dark, wet, well spoken, and well mannered. Josh Thomas, I assured myself, was *human*.

Really. Wasn't that a very solid, if wet, thigh tucked up against mine? Obviously, I had been an invalid too long. My brains had gone missing in some Stephen King fantasy.

My passengers, uttering grateful thanks, piled out of the tram and scurried out the front gate toward the parking lot across the street. Josh Thomas remained.

"I'll look for you," he said. "When I come back."

Was there the tiniest gleam of warmth in those unfathomable black eyes?

I actually heard myself say, "I drive Tuesday and Friday afternoons."

"*Arrivederci,*" he murmured. For a moment I actually thought he was going to kiss my hand.

Tram. Turn around. Get the hell off the lawn.

But I sat there and peered through the scratched and dripping plastic, watching him lope toward the gate. In those baggy pants there was no way to tell if his cheeks rivaled *David*'s, but the upper body—his black T-shirt molded to his skin by the rain—might well have given Michelangelo's version of the young Israelite a run for his money. Nice. Very nice. Even if he was nowhere near seventeen feet tall.

Just before turning the corner outside the gate, he paused. Waved. My hand insisted on waving back. Afterwards, I held it up before me and glared. *Traitor!* I scolded my betraying digits. *If there's one thing you don't need, it's another man who carries a gun.*

I shifted into reverse, backed up over the shimmering green lawn and scooted back to the tram stop before I got caught by one of the Art Museum's security guards, who were, fortunately, all sheltering from the storm.

★   ★   ★   ★   ★

I lingered over putting my tram to bed that night. The other two drivers on my shift go home at five, leaving me to finish the last forty-five minutes on my own. The grounds behind the museum were deserted, just a long stretch of well-manicured grass, flanked by trees, with Sarasota Bay once again beginning to glimmer as the sun, low in the west, broke through the rapidly diminishing clouds. At the front of the Art Museum (to the east) I knew people were pouring out, heading for the parking lot. On the south side, most of the security guards would also be heading out, along with the staff, docents, and gift shop attendants. But here all was quiet. Even the yellow crime-scene tape on the banyan near the bay wasn't visible from here.

Yet Billie's words nagged at me. *Tuition all paid and classes barely begun.*

My awakening brain refused to give the problem up, maybe because Tim Mundell's death had not been the only disturbance to the Bellman's customary serenity. The sudden appearance of Josh Thomas at the Bellman was like dropping a tiger shark into a softly bubbling stream full of brook trout.

Tim Mundell . . . Josh Thomas.

No! I refused to listen to the insidious whispers in my head. I was done with all that. Washed up.

I pocketed my tram key, pulled out the long electrical cord, and plugged it into the outlet. Then, instead of heading for my car, I unzipped a corner of the back flap and sat on the rear-facing seat, doing a darn good imitation of Rodin's *The Thinker.*

The whispers had a will of their own, sibilant and insistent. There had been something very odd about Josh Thomas. He would have been perfectly at home in New Haven, melting into the *mafiosi* without a ripple. He would also fit into the complex puzzles of the Middle East, Afghanistan or Chechnya, anywhere men were dark, secretive, and lethally dangerous. Josh Thomas:

international hit man? International spy? Arms dealer? Drug smuggler?

Assassin?

But where was the connection with young Tim Mundell? What possible association could there be between a computer geek from an Honors College and a man of international suavity laced with lethal undertones?

Face it, Travis. If Josh Thomas had had anything to do with Tim Mundell's death, he'd have been long gone by afternoon. Not dodging raindrops, while making eyes at a down-and-out tram driver.

I'll look for you. When I come back.

The man was going to haunt me, and I hated that. Hated being helpless, my body frail, my mind in neutral, stubbornly refusing to get off its duff and create so much as one original thought. *Josh Thomas, Josh Thomas, Josh Thomas.* He'd been determinedly charming. To a rain-bedraggled female who had tried to take him out. My enfeebled brain circled round and round, with nothing happening beyond a vague speculation about how many other names my mystery man might have.

And—finally—if one of them was Lucifer.

At close to six I dragged myself up, re-zipped the plastic curtain and limped to my car. Or, rather, to Aunt Hy's car. The family had breathed a collective sigh of relief when Aunt Hy turned over the keys to her 1993 gold Cadillac Seville (with twelve thousand miles). She'd once gone shopping at the mall and taken a taxi home, her confusion gone unnoticed until her frantic call to the police the next day, reporting her car stolen. The county deputies, long accustomed to the vagaries of seniors, had been very understanding. Or so Mom told me.

It's a short drive from the Bellman to the Ritz-Carlton, situated on the bay in the heart of town. Less than ten minutes, even at rush hour. How to describe the Ritz? Open only a year, it had already been named one of the Top Twenty hotels in the world. It was built on a narrow strip of land between Sarasota Bay and the famed Tamiami Trail (constructed between Tampa and Miami in the twenties at considerable loss of life, particularly as the road slogged its way through the Everglades). The architects of the Ritz-Carlton faced some of the same problems as the builders of the Trail. Dig a hole along Florida's Gulf Coast, and you get a pond, a canal, or a harbor, depending on how far inland you dig. Water lurks just beneath the surface, making basements and underground garages nearly impossible. At the Ritz, the practical, as well as the aesthetic, challenge of constructing an inoffensive parking garage while building on what was basically a small lot had been cleverly solved by putting the garage on the ground floor, then burying it beneath tons of earth, so the hotel appeared to be sitting on a hill. (Even though the West Coast of Florida is flat as the proverbial pancake.)

You get used to driving into a cavernous grass-covered hillside, I supposed. I was still at that stage where I never failed to shake my head as I greeted the attendant, then pulled into Aunt Hy's assigned "underground" parking space.

What can I say to prepare you for Aunt Hy? She and her cook/housekeeper, Marian Edmundson, have been together so long that, in the fashion of many married couples, they have begun to look alike. Put Marian in a flowing gown of the Art Deco period and Aunt Hy into a severe gray cotton-poly uniform, and the switch could almost pass unnoticed. Marian might be younger by five or ten years, but Hyacinth Van Horne had the advantage of a series of face lifts. Neither of them would see seventy-five again.

A year earlier, about the time Aunt Hyacinth gave up her

imposing waterfront mansion and moved into the brand-new Ritz-Carlton, she had, in a flash of inspiration, hired a local girl "to add a bit of life about the place," as she put it. Jody Tyler lived up to expectations. She wore no uniform; her job description would have been tough to summarize. She was the bright smile and strong young legs needed in a household of two elderly women. Gofer, companion, watchdog. Raised in a state dominated by seniors, Jody had been brought up to serve the host of senior invaders from the North. That was, after all, Florida's primary industry. She was, however, one-hundred-percent independent American. Nobody's subservient maid, she worked with amazing forbearance and a nearly constant cheerful grin. Any relation to a proper English, French, or Latina maid was almost nonexistent.

In fact, Jody Tyler was so young and lively, so perky and totally competent, so totally Pollyanna-meets-Barbie, that I sometimes wanted to strangle her. Today, she met me at the door, whisked away my still-dripping raincoat, and, shooing me into the "drawing room," promised, "Glenlivet on the rocks, coming up!" (Okay, so sometimes it's hard to remember why I balked when Mom insisted on sending me to Florida.)

Aunt Hy's drawing room is almost impossible to describe. Perhaps if you've been to Versailles or one of the palaces in Vienna? Except none of those places have the luxury of a corner penthouse view of Sarasota Bay to the west and a sheltered man-made inlet full of luxury yachts on the north. If, however, you can pry your eyes away from the panoramic view, you will see that the condo's stark off-white walls, carpet, sofa, and deep armchairs are a mere backdrop for furnishings of ebony, rosewood, burled walnut, and other one-of-a-kind creations, including exquisitely carved consoles and cabinets, delicately painted in the Oriental style or swimming in oceans of ormolu. The mantel over the pink marble fireplace boasts eighteenth-century ceramic candlesticks by Meissen, a shepherd and shepherdess, complete with dog and sheep and surrounded by a backdrop of ceramic flowers. A small silk Savonnerie carpet shimmers on the wall, much too priceless to be trod upon by twenty-first-century feet.

The remainder of Aunt Hy's eclectic collection of *objets d'art* is tastefully arrayed on a series of impeccably designed matching étagères. To name only a few of my favorites: a Tang horse, a blue and white bottle vase (late Ming), an exquisitely shaped Chrysanthemum dish from Japan, a Dresden clock whose ceramic figures blended well with the Meissen candlesticks across the room. And, more modern but no less beautiful— displayed side by side with Venetian glass—were twentieth-century designs by Steuben and Waterford and Aunt Hy's exquisite collection of intricately woven ceramic baskets by Belleek.

A small sigh escaped. I had not realized I had a taste for the finer things until I had lived a few months with Aunt Hy. Until the sheer beauty got to me, and I woke up and started asking questions. Even then, I thought her treasures reproductions until, after taking over paying Aunt Hy's bills, I saw her insurance premium.

"Here y'are," said Jody, handing me my drink, the ice cubes clinking nicely in their sea of scotch.

Incurably middle-class, I thanked her. Then lowered my voice to a whisper, "What's she up to today?"

"Today was the beach again," Jody hissed, settling onto the overstuffed arm of the chair in which I was stretched out, my feet planted on a matching satin-tasseled ottoman. "Got on her bathing suit, put that funny-looking thing on her head—"

"Bathing cap," I supplied.

"Can you even buy something like that?" Jody demanded. "I mean, I never seen—saw—nothing like that in my whole life.

It's got *flowers* on it, you know. Plastic."

Suddenly, the day seemed brighter. For a moment I could even put the pulsing intensity of Josh Thomas behind me. "They used to make them like that, once upon a time," I confided, straight-faced. "I imagine that cap's about twice as old as you are."

"Really?" Jody's sky blue eyes twinkled at me. Then she nodded. "Guess they must have, or how else would the old girl have got it, right?"

"It's actually rubber," I told her. "I think it may pre-date plastics."

Chortling, Jody elbowed me (gently) in the shoulder to indicate she knew I was exaggerating. I was, but only a little. I suspected my aunt's bathing cap dated from the fifties or early sixties when plastics were a young industry. (I'm sure you recall the famous scene in *The Graduate,* when a wet-behind-the-ears Dustin Hoffman is urged to get into "Plastics.")

"So what did you do?" I asked.

Jody had no difficulty making the adjustment back to our primary topic. "Well . . . I went down in the elevator with her— you know, those funny bathing sandals she has must be as old as the cap." I nodded, and urged her on. "So I walked her to the pool and found her a lounger, but she wouldn't sit down, o'course. Said it wasn't the right place. There was supposed to be sand and boats. It was sad." Jody shook her head. "So I told her what you said. I reminded her she sold her house at the beach, that she was in a hotel now, so there'd be lots of people to look after her day and night. I ordered her a gin and tonic and got her to sit by the pool a while, then we came back upstairs."

"That was good, Jody. Thank you." I closed my eyes a moment, mourning the fragility of our senses, as vulnerable to wear and tear as our bodies. "Do you recall how many times she's done this?" I asked.

"Third time since I've been here. 'Course if she did it on my day off, Mrs. Edmundson'd never tell."

I sighed. Life was a bitch. Aunt Hy's occasional lapses reminded me how small-minded it was to feel sorry for myself just because I had to carry a cane. "Aren't you late for a date or something?" I asked.

Jody grinned. "No problem. Jeff's picking me up at seven."

Jody lived "out." With a boyfriend who worked construction, permanently employed by one of the area's largest development companies. I liked to think the two of them put off their perfect façades at night, gleefully bitching to each other about all those Tall Tales of How Much Better Everything Is Up North. Or perhaps they counted coup on the latest Lost Tourist's attempt to turn left from the farthest right of three lanes.

I savored the last of my Glenlivet single malt, made sure I placed the moisture-beaded glass precisely on the coaster so as not to damage the intricate hand-painted design on the end table. Then I levered myself up and went in search of my Aunt Hyacinth. Aunt Hy had a few other eccentricities that needed careful watching.

CHAPTER 3

According to the newspapers, and confirmed by the Bellman grapevine, Honors College senior Tim Mundell had taken his own life. Case closed. *Leave it, Travis. Not your problem. Curiosity killed the cat. Oh, yeah, I knew all about that.*

A week after I met Josh Thomas, I drove toward the Bellman, uttering dire curses against my physical therapist with whom I had spent ninety minutes that morning. He was a ghoul, a sadist, an unlicensed imposter. He was, in fact, a crew-cropped Adonis, built like a fullback, with the mental attitude of a drill sergeant, incongruously combined with the patronizing cheerfulness of a huckster. My scowl lasted until the first tram passenger stepped aboard . . . and then the magic of the Bellman took over. I smiled. I greeted. My tram full, I drove off into the soothing serenity of the grounds.

I had done my spiel at the gatehouse (*a live-in dollhouse—the gatekeeper must have been single or* very *happily married!*), dropped two passengers at the Circus Museum, pointed out the restaurant and Opal's Rose Garden. As I continued on toward the Casa Bellissima, I explained about the banyan trees, how the general story—however apocryphal it might be—was that Thomas Edison had given the first banyan starts to Richard Bellman. Before that, it was said, Edison and Henry Ford had imported the originals from India in a search for a substitute for rubber. In any event, if you've never seen a banyan, they are amazing trees. As they grow, they drop down rope-like shoots from their branches. These "ropes" root into the soil and form new trunks. With each passing year, the trees look more and more like giant asymmetrical spiders, with gnarled trunks spreading out in a vast circle from the original. Since most of the banyans at the Bellman were now around seventy-five years old, the trees were impressive.

"As we make the turn up ahead," I intoned, "you will have a particularly fine view of the House. And, on your right, you'll see a surprise, a statue *inside* a banyan tree." Directing my passengers' gaze, I glanced toward my second-favorite statue—a full-sized bronze of a man (naked, of course) lying prone, neatly tucked into a narrow opening between the banyan trunks.

My foot came off the pedal. Tram 3 came to an abrupt halt. I gaped. It was gone. The huge bronze, blued with age, was gone. As far as I could tell from my tram seat, the solid mat of brown fibers covering the ground where it had lain had not even been disturbed. I murmured an apology to my passengers and moved on, the words of my familiar spiel rolling off my tongue without conscious thought. I pointed out the arch the banyan had formed over the road . . . the sausage tree with its inedible "fruit" . . . the blue diamond tiles that marked the Bellman's swimming pool. *It was thought to be a hazard, so they filled it in and made a garden.* As usual, whispered sighs of regret echoed from the rear.

"Is that Tampa Bay?" someone asked.

"No, ma'am, that's Sarasota Bay. Tampa Bay is some miles north of here."

"Beautiful!" breathed another female voice.

"After your tour, you can sit out on the terrace, if you'd like," I said. "There's even a café where you can get a drink or a snack." I pulled to a stop in front of what we all referred to as "the House"—the Casa Bellissima, Richard and Opal Bellman's unique contribution to America's castles. I pointed out the greeter standing at the top of the ramp. "The man in the red vest will tell you if you're to go in now or wait in the chairs under the canopy."

With a chorus of "thank-yous," my passengers debarked. (Visitors to the Bellman are *very* polite.) No new passengers piled in. Evidently, all visitors were still viewing the House or waiting for the next tour. I pulled away empty, my mind free to seethe with the shock of the missing statue.

I had taken the elevator up to the museum library one day and spent an hour or so trying to find a name for that statue. As far as I could determine, since the records did not include a photo, it was called *The Sleeping Satyr*. Well, wouldn't you know? I'd thought. Trust me to ignore the Apollo Belvedere out front in favor of a satyr. The problem, you see, wasn't merely that the statue had gone missing. My problem was that that banyan tree was close to the one where I had sheltered while readying my tram for the rain last Tuesday afternoon. Maybe thirty feet from where Josh Thomas had appeared out of nowhere, sliding in next to me in a burst of fire and brimstone. (Okay, so I'm exaggerating . . . but not by much.)

And now *The Sleeping Satyr* had gone missing.

Na-a-w. No way. Obviously, my head needed therapy worse than my leg.

It was more than an hour before I finally spotted Billie charging across the lawn in his golf cart. Even though I had passengers, I flagged him down. "The statue in the banyan down by the house—what happened to it?"

"Went to Tallahassee," he responded cheerfully. "Going to get all clean and beautiful. Like *David.*" He winked.

Relief flooded through me. Not that I'd really believed . . . I murmured my thanks and put my foot to the pedal.

To understand that remark about Tallahassee, you have to

know that Richard Bellman left his sixty-plus acres, his art treasures, his private castle, and other outbuildings to the State of Florida. After many years of barely keeping its head above water (sometimes, literally), the museum had recently become associated with one of Florida's large state universities, thus acquiring an unprecedented inflow of cash for long-neglected maintenance. So *The Sleeping Satyr* had gone off to the capital city to be restored to its original shining bronze.

I was not quite sure, however, that its essence had gone with it.

Ridiculous! Josh Thomas was a visitor, like all the others. Our lives touching for a moment or two, a five-minute ride . . . then gone, never to pass this way again.

But he stuck with me. Unrelentingly. Even rain-soaked, Josh Thomas had burned with an inner fire. With suave charm wrapped round glowing coals of danger. And possibly deceit. Everything I was—everything I had been—told me I was right. Josh Thomas was an enigma. An intriguing one. For six months my heart had been dead, shattered one horrible night as thoroughly as the rest of me. But since the advent of Josh Thomas, both mind and heart were shifting out of neutral, creaking erratically . . . toward what?

Damn the man! I suspected his soul was as dark as his hair.

He haunted me.

That night, as I left the museum, I almost forgot to drop my tram key at the Security Desk.

I should probably explain how museums work. At least, how the Bellman works. As I tell our visitors when they ask: most of the "staff" they see at the museum are volunteers—the people at the information desk, the greeters, docents, and tram drivers. Visitors have only minimal interaction with ticket sellers, groundskeepers, and security guards, and none at all with the

Director, the Deputy Director, the Chief Financial Officer, Conservation, Marketing, Education, and Archives, who are all tucked up in their offices doing what paid Staff does. The volunteers are the ones out on the front lines, meeting and greeting, the true Goodwill Ambassadors of the Richard and Opal Bellman Museum of Art. Most are stationary, seeing only their own tiny portion of the three museums. The tram drivers, however, in their constant circle from Art to Circus to Casa, are the true scouts—the eyes and ears of the museum grounds. And we interact with our visitors on a less formal basis than the other volunteers and have to be ready with answers to an astonishing variety of questions. And, yes, we tend to think we're the hotshots of the volunteers. There are, I have to tell you, certain docents who still believe they are More Equal than others.

That afternoon, for the first time, I met one. She was tall, elegant, perfectly coiffed, and impeccably dressed, and I have to admit she put my black slacks and Bellman burgundy polo shirt with laminated pendant ID ribbon to shame. She came bustling out of the Casa's solarium, ushering a young couple with two children, one a baby fast asleep in one of those imposing strollers about the size of an old-fashioned baby carriage. I knew before she opened her mouth that I was in trouble. Docents did not usually escort visitors on anything but tours. I suspected this particular couple were her friends or relatives. There were several people already waiting on the tram benches. I braced myself.

"Here's the tram now," I heard the docent say from the top of the ramp. "It will take you to the parking lot."

Parking lot. I was in even more trouble than I had thought. The trams did not go to the parking lot across the street from the museum.

Visitors waiting to enter the Casa politely flattened themselves against the railing as the couple pushed their way down the ramp. No one goes down the ramp, I was thinking. The Exit's on the other side of the house. I shrugged. None of my business.

But who rode the tram was.

"You'll have to fold up the stroller and put it on the back," I said. "And hold the baby in your lap."

"But she's sleeping," the young mother protested.

"I'm sorry, but the stroller has to be folded," I said.

"Now, see here—" the young father began, but was cut off from above.

"How dare you?" the docent cried. "Let those people on this instant!"

I leaned over and peered up at her. She was poised, full of sound and fury, partway down the ramp. "They have to fold the stroller," I explained, reining in my temper. "Otherwise, I can't take them. Believe me, there really isn't room. And there are people in line ahead of them."

"What's your name?" the docent demanded. "I'm going to report you. For insolence," she added to make herself perfectly clear.

I told her. Then I turned to the father and raised my brows. I thought I saw his lips twitch. He stood at attention, snapped off a smart salute. "We'll walk," he said.

"You haven't heard the last of this," the docent shrieked as I drove away with the six passengers who had calmly piled aboard while our little altercation raged.

"Good for you," said a white-haired gentleman from the seat behind me. "They're young, they can walk. One can only hope their endurance exceeds their manners."

I tossed him a grin of thanks, although, obviously, I couldn't comment. Truthfully, I felt the young couple understood the problem. They had chosen not to wake the baby. It was the docent who was the Wicked Witch of the West. Ah, well, perhaps one day the Casa Bellissima would fall on her.

It was a thought that would come back to haunt me.

The insidious thought that the sudden disappearance of *The Sleeping Satyr* had left some evil essence behind took root in my mind and wouldn't go away. It was like the proverbial pebble thrown into a pond, a disturbance that rippled out over the grounds, infecting the air, the people, the very quality of life we so treasured at the Bellman. Threatening that certain something that kept all five hundred volunteers coming back time and time again. But at the time I chalked up my unease to outrage. I had heard there were those who believed there were two classes of unpaid employees at the Bellman—Docents and Volunteers. The reality, however, was disturbing. I was still seething when I ran into Billie for the second time that afternoon.

It was five o'clock, the quiet time, a half hour before the last lingering visitors burst out of the three museums, all demanding a tram at the same time. It was also the time the other two drivers went home, leaving me as the last tram running. I was sitting at the main tram stop at the Art Museum, waiting to see if anyone needed transportation to Handicapped Parking down by the Casa when Billie pulled up beside me. For the very first time, I noticed the walkie-talkie on the seat beside him. In spite of heavy-duty training in being observant, I had previously missed this tool of instant communication that distinguished the security guards from the tram drivers. Since my injury, I'd had tunnel vision. I knew that. I had shut the world out, asking no questions, as I had no wish to give answers in return. So I'd gone eight weeks as a tram driver and not realized Billie was Security instead of a groundskeeper or simple gofer.

I leaned on my wheel and smiled at him from under my rolled-up-plastic side curtains. "I've a confession," I told him, "I can't remember your last name."

"Billie Hamlin, but most of my friends call me Billie Ball. Around here, though, just Billie seems safer."

I digested this for a moment, mentally apologizing to my ears for questioning their hearing. "Mind if I ask why?" I said.

He unfolded his lean well-over-six-feet from his golf cart and came over to duck his head below the level of the curtains. Although he set off no romantic pitty-pats in my wounded heart, he was definitely a hunk.

"I work Security, y'know. And I'm at the Bellman School of Art, part-time. Student." He leaned closer. "But it's hard to keep it all together, y'know, so I do a little moonlighting on the side." He paused, far-seeing blue eyes examining me with solemn intensity, deciding if I was trustworthy. "They'd crucify me if they ever found out. I'd be out on my ear so fast—here *and* at school, probably."

"I promise you, Billie, I'm a reliable keeper of secrets." Lots of secrets.

He nodded. "Okay . . . well, there's good money in golf balls, y'see. And there are so many golf courses around here, it's a wonder there's any room left for houses. So I thought to myself, 'You can dive, boy, so why not use it?' "

Billie flashed a mischievous grin, glanced around to make sure no one was close by. At the moment, there wasn't another person in sight from the front corner of the Art Museum to the far edge of the vast lawn where it met Sarasota Bay.

"Most nights I go golf-ball diving," he confided. "You'd be amazed how many balls there are in those ponds. Chock full, most of 'em. I can get a couple o' thousand in two hours. Sell 'em, mostly on the Net, for twenty to fifty cents apiece, depending on condition. Maybe four to eight hundred for a couple hours' work. Keeps me goin' just fine."

I laughed. For the first time in months, I laughed. And then the implications hit me. "Do you have permission?" I asked.

"Well," Billie hedged, "I have an arrangement with one of the courses, but they want their cut, so . . ." He shrugged.

"So it's trespassing and theft," I finished for him.

"Not a real worry," Billie replied calmly. "All the courses know we do it and aren't about to stir up a fuss. They'd soon have big white piles of balls instead of all those pretty ponds if the ball-divers stayed home. 'Course the gators and water moccasins can be a bit of a pain."

I pictured big blond Billie groping about the bottom of a pond in the dark, gathering golf balls, having no idea what might be lurking just out of sight. Night after night after night. Surely his luck had to run out one of these days.

"Billie?" I questioned.

He patted my shoulder. "Not a problem, darlin'. I'm bigger'n most of the gators. And a moccasin'd have to have pretty big teeth to get through my wet suit."

"You're insane," I told him.

"That's what my mom says, but in two hours a day I make five times what she gets in a week from her Zoning job with the county. And her there twenty years now."

"So what are you doing working Security?"

"Part-time," Billie said. "Trying to keep my face before the Museum, so to speak. I'm hopin' for a grant, maybe a chance to work on sculptures to go with all the new buildings they're gettin' now the State's gone and given them all that money."

"You're a *sculptor?*"

He straightened up, struck a pose similar to *David*'s. "Just call me the modern Michelangelo," he declaimed.

Eight weeks, and I'd never really talked to Billie Ball Hamlin. I'd settled for exchanging a few platitudes as we passed each other on the grounds. Was my newfound reality another unsettling ripple from my favorite Satyr? Or was it just a nudge to tell me it was time to get back my life? Or at least salvage what was left of it.

I told Billie I thought he was amazing. But he wasn't listening. He'd straightened up, his attention focused solely on something behind me. I leaned my head out of the tram and took a look. Billie was standing there, his face suffused with that perfectly asinine look some men get when in the throes of unrequited love.

" 'Lo, Lygia," he said, and I realized he wasn't as far gone as I had thought.

Her name was Lydia. One of the nubile young things who worked their tails off for entry-level salaries, she was, at the moment, driving an oversized golf cart with a boxed-in carry-space, similar to those driven by the groundskeepers. Except hers was piled high with rolled-up posters and sundry other replacements she was obviously trundling from storage to the Gift Shop.

"I told you not to call me that!" Her sea-blue eyes regarded Billie with considerable annoyance. Even her long dark waves of hair seemed to quiver with outrage. I suspected Billie's admiration was going to stay unrequited.

In order to understand Lydia's anger, you have to know about the bull sculpture at the entrance to the Art Museum. Back in the early years of the twentieth century, a sculptor named Giuseppe Moretti was given a commission to create a bronze based on the novel, *Quo Vadis.* When complete, it was placed in a Philadelphia park, only to be promptly retired to a warehouse when the good citizens of the city declared themselves scandalized. Naturally, Richard Bellman bought it and placed it at the front of his brand-new Museum of Art.

I had long since decided I liked Richard Bellman.

But I digress. You're wondering about the scandal. Moretti's sculpture is of a beautiful young girl named Lygia, clad only in two ropes skimpily adorned with occasional flowers. She is in the process of being sacrificed to the raging bull, her perfect young body splayed over the beast's horns and back. It's dramatic. It is not a reproduction.

It is, however, a bit awkward if you happen to be an equally lovely, long-haired young woman named Lydia who has to pass by the statue every day under the not-so-subtle salacious glances of the younger groundskeepers and security guards.

"But Lygia's so much more intriguing," Billie cooed. "I was thinking of doing the bull thing in miniature for my next project. Wanna pose?"

Lydia jammed her foot onto the pedal, zooming off up the slight rise to the front of the museum. If any dust had been allowed to gather at the Bellman, she would have left us in it.

"Billie," I chided, "I don't think that's quite the right approach."

"I know," he groaned, "but she's so . . ." He molded a curvaceous figure with his hands, shrugged, looking adorably smitten. "I know I haven't a chance, so I get her attention the only way I can."

As we talked, we'd both been keeping an eye on an elderly couple making their way slowly down the sidewalk toward the tram. Chat time over. It was back to work for both of us. Billie, his Southern manners firmly back in place, folded up the old gentleman's walker and stowed it in the rear of my tram. Then he blew me a kiss, slid back into his cart and was off down the bumpy back road toward the rear of the museum.

I greeted my new passengers and headed for the Handicapped Parking down by the Casa, where I dropped them off a few steps from their car, which was parked in the shade of yet another giant banyan tree. They thanked me profusely, and I drove off.

It had been more than just another day at the Bellman. A seminal moment, if you will. I had looked outside my own misery, made tentative contact with another human being. Billie Ball Hamlin, sharing his secret, had moved closer to being a friend. I had even managed to empathize with poor Lydia's hot embarrassment. (Okay, the statue *was* pretty racy.) I had lifted my head and seen something besides a reflection of myself. For a few moments I'd cracked the wall and actually made a connection with someone in my new world.

I'd done it with Josh Thomas in ten seconds flat. But, then, I still wasn't sure if he truly *was* of this world.

CHAPTER 4

In spite of rush-hour congestion, I floated home that night. I'd done it. I'd reached some sort of psychological milestone. I'd looked up, and out, and actually seen that life still existed around me. There were *people* out there. And they hadn't shut me out. I'd done that to myself. I had only to reach out and touch . . .

When I walked into the condo, Jody informed me that Aunt Hy had been talking to Madame Celestine for the past hour. My buoyant spirits plotzed.

Shortly after arriving in Sarasota—and after a hint from Marian Edmundson who had been writing out her employer's checks for a quarter century or so—I had taken over the payment of Aunt Hy's bills, using the excuse that I needed something to do. That was when I discovered the elegant and sophisticated Hyacinth Van Horne harbored a secret addiction. Aunt Hy was enamored of Madame Celestine. Or, more precisely, of the television guru's psychic predictions. (Although Aunt Hy had never actually met Madame Celestine, she considered the self-proclaimed seer her nearest and dearest friend. At phone rates that seemed to hover around twenty dollars a minute, I am quite sure Madame Celestine considered Aunt Hy *her* best friend as well.)

When one's phone bill begins to resemble the National Debt, even people as sinfully rich as Hyacinth Van Horne need to reassess the situation. I begged, I pleaded, I lost my temper (a

46

surprise, as I had no idea it still lingered beneath my apathy). Aunt Hy had merely looked at me through her eight-hundred-dollar Daniel Swarovski spectacles and breathed, most solemnly, "But she tells me such lovely things, Aurora, my dear. Today, she predicted you will meet a dark, dynamic stranger. Isn't that glorious? A new man in your life."

Her words, spoken two weeks ago, echoed in my mind. *Dark, dynamic stranger.* My steps faltered. Dammit, no way was I catching the Celestine disease. Dark, dynamic strangers were the fortune-teller's stock in trade, assuring that the only fortune making an appearance was what went into their own pockets.

Gently, I removed the phone from my aunt's delicate hand. "Good-bye, Celestine," I murmured and hung the cream and gilt Art Deco dial phone back on its stand.

"Aurora," my aunt chided, loading that single word with the immensity of her disappointment in my behavior, "our whole conversation today was about you. Celestine cares about you, truly she does. She warned me that dark days are coming."

"What happened to the dark, dynamic stranger?" I demanded, attacking when I knew I was teetering on the slippery slope of disrespect. This was Aunt Hy's home, her money to waste as she chose—

"Oh, he's already come," said Aunt Hy. "Merciful heavens, Aurora, didn't you notice?"

I opened my mouth, closed it, took a deep breath. I sat down hard on the edge of Aunt Hy's elaborately draped four-poster, where she was reclining, propped up against a stack of needlepoint pillows. Hyacinth Van Horne, my maternal grandmother's elder sister. Aunt Hy, whose hair was as blond and well coiffed as it had been when she was a newly married matron sixty years ago. Aunt Hy, who encased her still-slim figure in the flowing fashions of the Art Deco era and inevitably made me feel like an underdressed clown about to do a pratfall.

At what I suspected was eighty-odd years (sometimes very odd), her face was beautiful, in that way most women never achieve, even when they're twenty.

I loved her, I truly did, but she was well on her way to making me as dotty as she was.

Ignoring her question about the dynamic stranger, I said, "Tell me about the dark days to come."

The rings on Aunt Hy's fingers winked at me as she plucked at the quilted bedspread. Her multitude of rings—diamonds, sapphires, and rubies in a nicely patriotic display—stopped just short of being gaudy. Unless, of course, you subscribe to that quaint rule about anything over five carats being shockingly *nouveau riche.*

"I fear Celestine was rather vague," Aunt Hy admitted.

Would wonders never cease. "She must have given some indication," I prompted.

Aunt Hy frowned, her parchment-skinned nose wrinkling in concentration. "Dark days at work," she crowed. "That was it. A warning about trouble at work."

I stared at her perfectly innocent face, wreathed in triumph because she had remembered. I fought down a wave of nausea, panic. Despair. "I've already had that, Aunt Hy," I said as gently as I could. "Remember? That's why I'm here. Lots of trouble at work. And I lost Eric as well." But he wasn't dark. Dynamic, yes; dark, no. Eric had been blond. Golden. A being to warm the heart, like my private pipeline to the sun.

I shouldn't have mentioned the past. Why should I inflict my anguish on poor Aunt Hy? Her face crumpled, a tear rolled down her cheek. She patted my hand. "Yes, dear, I know," she murmured, "but Celestine has promised you someone new. Perhaps he will help you through the dark days ahead."

I didn't need any more dark days. Never. Ever. Wasn't that why I had agreed to exile in sunny Florida?

The phone jangled, startling us both. Surely, Celestine didn't make call-backs. She must have enough other gullible clients to keep her occupied. I picked up the phone, not sure what to expect.

It was Burt, the Tram Boss. Could I do a morning shift tomorrow as the regular driver was flying north to see his new grandchild?

Reprieved. It wasn't that I didn't want to face Aunt Hy's problems . . . or my own . . .

Yes, it was. Driving my tram was such an easy escape from reality. I welcomed it, almost as eagerly as the hypochondriac welcomes his next trip to the doctor. I would report for duty in the morning and be too busy to think about Madame Celestine, dark days at work, dark, dynamic strangers, or that insensitive ape, my rehab therapist.

But in the morning, Chaos arrived. Secretly, silently. Unseen until the security guards began unlocking the multitude of doors into the Art Museum's courtyard. And, even then, it seemed an almost welcome glitch in the serenity of the Bellman. If any of us experienced a frisson of warning, we kept it to ourselves. No one stepped forth to prognosticate. No one declaimed in pretentious tones (as academics are wont to do): "Even Chaos begins with a single event."

Face it, we were clueless.

The next morning, with all the cars streaming south toward offices in the center of the city, I made the drive north to the Bellman in eight minutes flat. I stopped by the Security Desk, picked up a tram key, and drove cautiously over the pockmarked shell roads that wound through the museum grounds. After parking next to the tram barn at the back of the Art Museum, I made sure I had my bottle of water, my car keys, my cell phone, and my hand bell (for unwary visitors walking down the middle of the road), then I locked everything else in the trunk of my car. I was backing out my tram when the excitement started. Golf carts erupted over the lawn, all headed toward the Security Entrance. I heard shouts from the courtyard—from behind the wall topped by the bronze figure of *David,* currently glowing in the morning sunlight.

Shouts? At the *Bellman?*

Instinct—and that old bugaboo, curiosity—got the better of my sense of duty. I swung the wheel and headed my tram up the rear sidewalk, squeezed between the hedges, and headed toward Security. I parked my tram and joined the mass of burgundy-shirted guards streaming into the Art Museum. Bypassing the Security Desk without asking questions, I followed the general hubbub down the hall. Obligingly, the elevator full of guards squeezed together and made room for me.

On the second floor we all tromped across the Special Exhibit lobby and down shallow steps to the loggia. I, naturally, fell to the rear as I clutched my cane in one hand and the banister in the other. But, blessedly, the phalanx of guards spread out as they reached the broad expanse of the loggia. Ahead, I could see quite a crowd about halfway up the courtyard. Most were simply standing against the loggia balustrade, where, nicely framed in bougainvillea, they were staring out over the courtyard. I hitched myself along, my cane whapping the tile floor at a brisk pace, and finally caught up. Someone made room for me at the rail.

The courtyard at the Art Museum is so large it is in three tiers, accommodating itself to the natural slope of the land down toward Sarasota Bay. (Which is why it is necessary to take an elevator from Security up to the second floor to reach the loggia.) Richard Bellman's love of art did not stop with paintings. Although most of the sculptures he imported from Europe are described as "modern casts of Roman copies of Greek originals," they were, nonetheless—like *David*—spectacular and ubiquitous. The vast courtyard was, in fact, littered with classical figures and fountains. One of the most innocuous of these was a Biga, a two-horse Roman chariot, so realistic it looked as if it might have raced in the Coliseum.

Today, it was even more realistic, for it had acquired a driver. A figure, perfectly proportioned to the half-size chariot and horses, standing regally tall, reins in his hands, the guy wires holding him in place nearly invisible. He was dressed in the garb of a Roman officer, from plumed helmet to knee-length white tunic and ornate breastplate. All in brilliantly painted *papier mâché*.

It was a marvelous joke. And a stunning puzzle. The Bellman wasn't Fort Knox, but security was tight. The courtyard was enclosed on three sides by the museum itself and, on the west, by the imposing raised walkway, a good twenty feet high, from which *David* surveyed his realm.

The connection came so fast I realized my dormant brain was truly beginning to revive. Or was it what some people insisted on calling my "gift"? My occasional flashes of insight that come out of nowhere? Useless information at odd, unsuitable moments. Or so it had seemed to me ever since I'd led my lover to his death. I hadn't had so much as a twinge of insight since.

Not so. There were those insidious whispers after Tim Mundell's supposed suicide. And my absolute certainty that Josh Thomas's polished exterior harbored deep secrets. Just as, today, I knew the perpetrator of this outrageous prank—which required talent, agility, and daring—was most likely a certain hunky part-time security guard. *Oh, my charming Billie, this isn't the way to get the Museum's attention.*

Billie Ball Hamlin was young enough and quirky enough to think of such a stunt. He was capable of sculpting and painting such a remarkable effigy. He was strong enough to scale a wall, carrying a half-size model of a Roman warrior. (For there was no way he had slipped something this size past the Security Desk or through the Art Museum's locked and barred front doors.)

Not that there weren't a lot of students in the area. Not only was the Honors College next door full of high IQs with creative ideas and rebellious proclivities, but only a mile or so down the road was the Bellman School of Art, also full of budding young geniuses with eccentric tendencies. So why was I so certain it was Billie?

It wasn't much of a leap. Young men who dive into Florida ponds in the secret and dangerous depths of the night would not be fazed by a twenty-foot wall guarded only by a seventeen-foot man of bronze. Billie Ball Hamlin would, in fact, have reveled in the challenge.

I turned away and slunk back to my tram, leaving the crowd of guards, docents, and other volunteers to gape their fill. After all, excitement at the Bellman usually consisted of a rare faint from the heat or someone off a tour bus irate because they had not been allowed time to see "everything." An unauthorized Roman warrior could only make everyone's day. Hopefully, if the culprit was discovered, the Powers That Be would go easy on him.

I arrived at the main tram stop just as hordes of school children came trooping down the hill. Fortunately, each group was required to stay with its teacher and chaperon, so the children—all sixty of middle-school age—walked in well-controlled snake lines past the tram stop, hiking down to the Casa Bellissima, where I figured the docents, well warned, were quaking in their sensible shoes. The Casa's restoration took six years and fifteen million dollars. How would you feel shepherding sixty sixth-graders through such a home?

And then it hit me. In less than a week we'd had a Suspicious Suicide, a Mysterious Stranger, and a Spectacular Prank. Connecting the first two was a stretch. Adding the third was nearly impossible.

And yet . . . my inner alarm was clanging as loudly as my tram bell. Somehow, some way, there was a pattern to these disturbances. That exaggerated intuition of mine insisted on it. Wouldn't take no for an answer.

I looked around for Billie, but I suspected he was lying low, riding his golf cart, engulfed in an aura of innocence. Although snatches of conversation about the morning's aberration in the Bellman's serenity could be heard everywhere, it seemed things were blowing over nicely, shocked ripples calming to amused speculation. Even admiration.

But I had forgotten this was Florida. Most of the Board members of the Richard and Opal Bellman Museum of Art were wealthy retirees from stellar careers in business, the military and/or politics. Now it is not easy to find yourself retired in what seems the prime of life. Therefore, there were a remarkable number of Board members who found the Bellman the only place they could flex their once-powerful muscles. And, evidently, this morning they had leaped at the chance.

A man was waiting at the tram barn. Though maybe an inch shy of six feet, he looked as stalwart as the giant live oak that drooped low over his head. He was wearing a long-sleeved blue-and-white-striped shirt and conservative navy silk tie with a tie clip that proved—as my replacement dropped me off almost at the stranger's feet—to be a tiny gold revolver. When he looked me over from my determinedly waveless brown hair to the tip of my cane, I realized he had been waiting for me. I returned the favor. His face was that of the boy next door. His eyes were not. They were gray and sharp. Very sharp. The rounded features of his Everyman face were set in a scowl. I got the impression he would rather be almost anywhere but at the Bellman, and that, as far as he was concerned, the *papier mâché* Roman Warrior in the Biga was just so much kindling. A great waste of his valuable time.

For some ridiculous reason, I decided to challenge him. Perhaps because I thought the days when a man could openly assess a woman were long gone. (I had, of course, forgotten this was Florida.)

"My mother always told me not to look like that," I said. "My face might freeze that way."

His scowl deepened. He flashed a badge. "Detective Sergeant Ken Parrish. I understand you were here early this morning."

Oh-oh. I felt the weight of a full burden of guilt, even though I was incapable of sculpting so much as the Roman warrior's toenail. All because I was almost certain I knew who did.

"Very much after the fact," I told him. "I just followed the crowd to the action."

"See anyone on the grounds? Anyone who shouldn't have been here?"

"It was so quiet I didn't even see a groundskeeper." Which was true. Only security guards in golf carts rushing to the scene of the crime.

"Any guesses?"

I dug my cane into a crack in the broken pavement. I squirmed. He could see my guilt, I knew it.

"Surely a student prank," I offered, peeking at the bulging muscles under his cotton-poly shirt, the square set of his jaw, the bored, yet steely, glint of his eyes, the slither I could feel ascending my spine as I blithely lied to Sarasota's finest.

"You saw nothing at all?" Detective Parrish persisted.

"Nothing, Detective, really." I prayed he would let it go.

"You've been at the museum how long?"

"Two months. But just on Tuesday and Friday afternoons."

"Long enough," he intoned. "Do you know anyone who might want to play a little joke on the museum?"

I gulped, recalling an oath I had once taken. "Really, Detective," I reiterated, "I believe it's just a lark."

He flashed a look that nearly curled my toes. He knew. I knew he knew. And he knew I knew he knew. Then he surprised me.

"Which is your car?" he asked. I thought I saw his lips twitch when I pointed out Aunt Hy's gold Cadillac. He took me by the arm and steered me carefully over the broken tarmac and gnarled roots of the old oak. "Keys." He held out his hand. Dumbly, I complied.

When the driver door was open, he waved me inside. Some indefinable emotion swept over me. Mortification? Gratitude? Despair? For I realized my interrogation wasn't over. With the quiet manners of the Old South, Detective Sergeant Ken Parrish had decided he had kept the cripple standing long enough.

With one arm draped over the open car door, he leaned down and said in a voice suddenly purring with insinuation. "And now maybe you'll tell me why my briefing said to contact a Rory Travis, tram driver. She might be able to help me out."

I gripped the wheel, closed my eyes, and thought dire thoughts about my Aunt Hyacinth. She had never been discreet, even in her youth (or so my mother and grandmother told me). So how could I have expected her to keep her mouth shut when she had so many dear friends—wealthy and influential friends—on the Board of the Bellman.

I popped the trunk. "Would you mind getting my purse?" I said, with a nod to the rear.

I had to dig for it. Way, way down beneath wallet, checkbook, address book, notebook, a plastic baggie of pills, a card case, and an embarrassingly large array of crumpled tissues, I found the folding black leather wallet with my badge. I held it up for his inspection. "Long, long ago, and far, far away," I told him.

Detective Parrish nodded. His Everyman face was perfectly blank, but I felt he understood my anguish over being a has-been warrior.

"So why," he asked, "won't you tell me what you know? There can't be many around here who could manage a trick like that. Even I know that Roman's a damn fine bit of work."

"I truly don't know," I said. "I might be able to guess, but I'm not slinging names around over a rather clever prank." I looked straight into those questioning pewter eyes and added, "If there's more . . . if things get out of hand . . ."

For a few more moments I got the searching look, then he allowed himself a smile. It was a nice smile. Sternly, I reminded myself of my prior loyalty to Billie Ball Hamlin. I didn't want complications in my life. I had enough troubles—

"Hopefully, this is it," Detective Parrish said. "As you say, just a student prank." He held out his hand. "Nice talking to you, Special Agent Travis."

Automatically, I shook his hand, which felt just as I expected. Warm and solid. Even friendly. Almost, it took the sting out of his use of my title.

He closed the car door, stepped back, waving a casual salute as I negotiated the bumpy circle by the tram barn and headed out.

That night I waked to instant alarm. The bloodred figures on my digital alarm read 1:40. A natural-born night owl, I hadn't been asleep that long. I scanned the dark room, even though I sincerely doubted even the most enterprising burglar could find his way to the penthouse of the Ritz-Carlton. Not a shadow moved. Not a shadow out of place. I listened. Nothing.

I sniffed.

And then I came fully awake to the acrid stench of burning

metal. I raced to the kitchen, spotted the lop-sided tea kettle slowly melting onto the burner, had sense enough to arm myself with potholders before attempting to remove it from the stove.

The kettle was stuck, glued to the electric burner by its melted copper bottom. I switched off the burner (which would have to be replaced), then stood there, glaring at the damaged stove as if it had made the mess all on its own.

Aunt Hy? Even the ever-faithful Marian Edmundson was not above suspicion. This was not, after all, an unusual disaster. Even my mother had once put a tea kettle on without checking to make sure the whistle mechanism was properly in place.

But it was scary. Like my dilemma with Billie Ball Hamlin and Detective Sergeant Ken Parrish—where did my loyalty lie? Did I keep quiet and wait to see what happened next?

And then I thought of Madame Celestine's prediction. Dark Days.

A Roman effigy did not constitute Dark Days. The television psychic was still a con artist, I assured myself. She had told Aunt Hyacinth about Dark Days at work. Nothing about Dark Days at home.

Or had she?

And that was when I realized I was standing in the kitchen with my cane still lying on a chair in my bedroom down the hall. I considered my mad dash. There was, it would seem, life left in the old girl after all.

Twenty minutes later, when I was certain the burner was cooling as expected, I went back to bed, feeling just slightly smug. That misbegotten son of a slave driver at the Rehab Center was going to be proud of me.

CHAPTER 5

When I asked Aunt Hy about putting on the tea kettle at midnight, she looked at me, wide-eyed, and said, "But, my dear, you know I go to bed at ten." Marian and I exchanged a speaking glance. She rolled her eyes toward the kitchen, and I followed.

"Miss Travis," she said quite formally, standing ramrod straight in front of white cupboards that gleamed only slightly brighter than her short cap of hair, "I feel I must tell you I did not do it."

"I know, Marian," I said softly, for I was certain Aunt Hy's faithful housekeeper would not lie. "Do you suppose she walks in her sleep?"

Marian Edmundson's shoulders slumped out of their military stiffness. "I believe she may, on occasion, Miss—though I feel the traitor for saying so."

"It's dangerous," I declared. "Oh, not just the fire hazard, but she has a balcony off her bedroom, and we're eighteen stories up." I paused as a shiver took me, rocking not only my spine and my mind, but my heart as well. The kitchen faded, and I was back atop a roof in Philadelphia, fighting for my life.

"Miss? Ah, come sit over here, Rory dear, and I'll fix you some tea." Mrs. Edmundson pulled out a chair and guided me into it, switching from offended long-time retainer to trusted housekeeper and friend at my first sign of distress.

It was Aunt Hy who was ill, I told myself. Not me. I just

needed more blasted rehab. That was all. Really.

In the end, I dropped my feeble attempt to investigate the Case of the Consumed Tea Kettle. If my mother could burn up a tea kettle at fifty, last night's little lapse didn't seem so serious. I filed Aunt Hy's possible sleepwalking with all the other serious problems I would deal with when living day to day did not seem so much of a challenge.

Oddly enough, for the next week or so, Aunt Hy seemed rejuvenated. I wasn't sure if it was the tea kettle scare or the invitation to the Bellman Gala that had kicked her sharp intelligence back into gear. I suspected the latter.

"Come with me, Rory dear," she trilled two days before the Gala, for which she had had me reserve two shockingly expensive tickets.

Meekly, I followed her into her wardrobe room. (Yes, Aunt Hy has an entire room devoted to the clothing she has collected over a lifetime. Walk-in closets rate no more than a disdainful sniff from Hyacinth Van Horne. For this twenties fund-raising event at the Museum there would be no need to visit a costume shop.)

She led me past shelves stacked high with hats, past row upon row of perfectly arranged shoes, then through a maze of rolling racks groaning under garments of every description. Aunt Hy stopped at last before a rack encased in carefully zippered plastic. For an idiotic moment I was reminded of my tram, cocooned against the rain. "Here we are," she declared. At her nod, I unzipped all the zippers and tucked the plastic up on top of the rack. I then stood back, respectfully, and received a lesson in designers of that last Golden Age, the time between the two great wars when gracious living still struggled to stay alive. The world that was smashed forever by the tramp of Nazi jackboots and, finally, the roar of Allied air power and artillery in reply. And, not incidentally, by women going to work and discovering the power of independence.

"Chanel," Aunt Hy said, touching a knee-length black dress trimmed with a double row of drooping pink chiffon scarves. She moved on down the line: "Vionnet, Molyneux, Worth, Paquin, Patou, Poiret, Schiaparelli." There was even an Erté, a designer, she kindly informed me, more noted for his theatrical costumes than ensembles for socialites.

After numerous sighs and several scurrilous reminiscences associated with her collection of vintage gowns, Aunt Hy finally selected a turquoise silk Vionnet with scarf hemline, topped by a beaded tunic with long sleeves that flared in an almost medieval manner. (Truthfully, she was quite sensitive about her arms that revealed her age far more than her face.)

I was harder to please, for I had grave doubts about displaying myself in a gown of any kind.

"The Schiaparelli," Aunt Hy stated firmly. "It's sleeveless, but that scar on your arm is practically invisible now. And it's full-length, which will cover your legs quite nicely. It's thirties, but no one will know the difference. And the rose will put some color in your cheeks." She held the gown up in front of me, critically assessing the result. It was gorgeous, I had to admit. The slinky rose silk was decorated with three-dimensional flowers, each petal hand-painted and hand-hemmed with the tiniest stitches imaginable. Awed, I nodded my agreement, so dazzled I failed to notice just how low the V-neck was, or that the V was even lower in back than in front, making a bra absolutely impossible.

I was, in fact, so dazzled it was the day of the Gala before I thought about shoes. I burst into Aunt Hy's room. "I can't go," I wailed. "I can't wear a Schiaparelli with sneakers!"

We stared at each other. Clearly, neither of us had remembered my wearing heels was out of the question. "You must have flats somewhere, Rory," said my aunt in the perfectly reasonable tone of an adult dealing with a forgetful five-year-old.

I hadn't worn flats since my first date, an interminable evening with the height-challenged son of one of my parents' good friends. "Loafers," I offered, "but they're not much of an improvement on sneakers." I pictured arriving at the Museum in my rose silk Schiaparelli and black suede loafers. I cringed. "It's a good thing Martin is escorting you," I told Aunt Hy. "You don't need me at all."

"Aurora," she declared, "I would not be going to this affair if it were not for you. You have hidden yourself away too long. I am dragging my old bones to this event so you may meet some of Sarasota's finest. It is *important.*"

Obviously, compliance was the only response. But how would we manage?

My aunt picked up the phone. "This is Hyacinth Van Horne," she announced as she requested a connection to Guest Services. Far below, the perfectly ordered service mechanisms of the Ritz-Carlton hummed into action. By the time Aunt Hy's old friend (and Bellman Board member) Martin Longstreet picked us up in a chauffeur-driven white limo, a pair of shiny white satin slippers (a perfect fit, of course) had arrived at our door. And, eschewing my Florida routine of once-over-lightly with pressed powder, I had dug out the works—foundation, loose powder, rouge, eye shadows, eyeliner, mascara. The effect was startling. I remembered this woman, I thought as I looked in the mirror. Someone I used to know up North.

But when I added the necklace Aunt Hy insisted I borrow—a choker of pink diamonds which, instead of providing cover, would draw every eye to my startling décolletage—I realized I could have skipped the rouge, for my cheeks now matched my rose-colored gown. *Well, hell!* Going for broke, I squirted on some of Aunt Hy's three-hundred-an-ounce perfume from her antique millefiore perfume bottle and declared myself ready for the Gala.

And, yes, thoughts of Cinderella kept flitting through my twenty-first-century head. Driving a tram had not prepared me for the rarified world I now was entering. Almost, I left my spanking-new cane at home. But common sense prevailed. Imagine the damage to the Schiaparelli if I measured my length on the Bellman sidewalk or fell into the soup at supper on the loggia.

No trams tonight. For tonight, the Bellman had hired six trolley cars. Delightfully vintage, even if they ran on wheels instead of rails. Our limo driver maneuvered so skillfully we found ourselves with only a few feet to walk between limo and trolley. Martin—darling Martin—provided a firm hand to help Aunt Hy, and then myself, aboard.

Martin Longstreet, like Hyacinth Van Horne, was one of those whose age was impossible to estimate. More than seventy, probably less than ninety, although Florida boasted a surprising number of spry nonagenarians. He was slimly elegant, a man who had probably lost breadth, rather than gained it, through the years. He was still good-looking. Women must have panted after him in his younger days. From his general aura of *savoir faire* to his cultured voice and impeccable manners, he gave every indication of being born into old money. Exactly the escort I would expect Aunt Hy to choose. Martin's costume for the evening was a tux, with tails and white tie. As classic and timeless now as it was in the twenties or when Beau Brummel revolutionized men's wear more than a hundred years before that.

I pressed my nose to the trolley's glass and gaped. I had driven these same roads over ten weeks now, and it was as if I had never seen them before. Great banks of spotlights on rolling wheels, hired for the occasion, lit the shell and cement driveway down which Richard and Opal Bellman's guests had once been driven to the Casa Bellissima. On our right, lights from neighboring houses and the Honors College peeked through a heavy growth of greenery. To the left were the deeply shadowed Bellman grounds, with only a faint glow rising from the courtyard where we would enjoy supper after our tour of the Casa, for the Art Museum's original windows had been stuccoed over many years since. Not a smidgen of light leaked from the galleries.

Nonetheless, I spotted a raccoon and thought I caught a glimpse of the Museum Cat as he did his duty, prowling the grounds for rodents less armored than the armadillos who were seldom seen, but left deep holes in the ground as their sharp noses dug for food. (I had been assured that the rattlesnakes that once plagued the grounds were long gone.) The armadillos, by the way, seemed particularly fond of the grass around *Lygia and the Bull*. Perhaps the tramp of so many visitors' feet around the scandalous sculpture softened the ground and made for easy access to the grubs and worms below.

As we approached the bay, darkness vanished. The Casa Bellissima had been transformed into a fairyland of lights and beautiful people. A veritable rainbow prism of color shimmered through each tall multicolored window. Across the water, lights from the houses and condos on Pelican Key penetrated the faint mist rising from the cooling bay and added to the breathtaking loveliness of the setting, which managed to be both sylvan and aquatic. If Aunt Hy had tolerated my excuses . . . if she had allowed me to stay home . . .

What if I had missed all this?

I'd been in The House before, of course. Twice as a child visiting Aunt Hy and once shortly after joining the tram service. Richard Bellman had included an elevator in his original plans, so I had not had to entrust myself to the narrow winding marble staircase, more attractive than functional. But seeing the Casa Bellissima in daylight with a group of tourists and seeing its treasures shimmering at night in company with people dressed in the clothing of the Casa's heyday were two entirely different things. It was a land of enchantment.

Since even two-hundred-dollar-a-plate guests were not allowed to wander alone through the Casa's treasures, we were promptly herded into a carefully counted group of twenty, and then we were off, viewing the home of Richard and Opal Bellman as guests might have seen it seventy-five years earlier.

I hesitate to admit it, but I'd made a surreptitious shopping excursion the day before. If my sneakers didn't fit the Schiaparelli, neither did my ineffably common aluminum cane. I now possessed a folding cane, decorated with painted flowers, mostly lavender, and topped by a vaguely Egyptian cat of carved ivory. (I had also indulged in a walking stick of curled sassafras, a luxury to which I intended to graduate as soon as possible.) For tonight, the flowers would do quite well. They blended rather nicely with my gown's hand-painted petals.

I leaned hard on the cane, as I stared up at the twenty-two coffered ceiling panels in the Bellman ballroom. Each octagonal gilded frame featured a colorful painting by Willy Pogany, depicting dancers from around the world in native costume. When I lowered my head, taking a moment to rest my neck, I glanced casually about the room. Martin, I noticed, was not gazing at the gilded coffers. He was smiling down at Aunt Hy as if he could think of no place he would rather be.

Abruptly, I studied the toes of my white satin flats. Calling on all the Travis pride, I repelled a rush of tears. We hadn't even been engaged, Eric and I, just beginning—perhaps too coldbloodedly—to discuss what marriage would do to our professional partnership.

That was, of course, before I'd managed to get him killed.

Somehow I was swept along with the group as it moved into the Bellman's primary public room—a central Great Room whose ceiling towered thirty or forty feet above, with a second-floor gallery on three sides. Its exquisite furnishings were too much to take in all at once. To name the most obvious: outlined against the background of a seventeenth-century tapestry was a crystal chandelier from the old Waldorf-Astoria (purchased by Richard Bellman when the famed hotel was replaced by the Empire State building). The pecky cypress beams and ceiling (forty feet up and illuminated by a skylight), were hand-painted by Robert Webb (every inch recently cleaned by a judicious application of bread dough).

There was one item in the Casa still awaiting renovation. On the far end of the "courtyard" room was an Aeolian organ console. Though now resting in air-conditioned storage, more than two thousand pipes had once been hidden inside the Casa's walls, providing Richard Bellman with a twenties' version of Surround Sound. It's said that in the organ's heyday its music traveled all the way across the bay to Pelican Key. (Alas, the Museum was going to have to dig up some more millions before it could be repaired.) One of the docents emphasized this problem on each of her tours by telling her groups that the Bellman was in need of "organ donors."

"Look at those chairs," I whispered to Aunt Hy. "Did you ever see such exquisite needlepoint?"

"Well, of course, my dear. Two of those seats are mine."

Aunt Hy did needlepoint? I thought of the needlework pillows adorning her condo and was once again struck dumb by my tunnel vision, my inability to see what was right under my nose. Aunt Hy had been one of the devoted women who had reproduced the needlework for Casa chairs too far gone to be repaired. And yet, I had never seen her at work. Were her eyes failing, along with her sharp and sophisticated wit?

Aunt Hy poked me in the ribs. I turned my attention back to our tour guide, who was frowning at me. "If you will come along into the Breakfast Room," she said. "Right this way." Our group began to snake forward. I was passing the organ console, almost out of the Great Room, when the second round of Chaos struck.

A scream. A tremendous cracking sound echoed through the house. More screams. All from behind me. A wail. A sob. Shouts. The pounding of heavy male feet.

I ducked behind the organ console, bypassing the red plush ropes that kept visitors out of the Great Room, and kept right on going, the fire horse racing toward the smell of smoke. I skidded through a sea of plaster chips littering the floor's black-and-white marble diamonds and dropped to my knees beside a torso—no arms, no legs, no head—bulging beneath a crumpled layer of white satin.

For a few moments I was all cop. Cool and analytical. Although the torso was artfully arrayed in a full-length evening gown, there was no mistaking it for human. Real bodies didn't separate into sections—a leg coming to rest in front of the fireplace fender, an arm draped, rather gracefully, against a tall electric torchère of white ceramic. Another leg had skidded beneath a marquetry card table; the second arm—in multiple pieces—was crushed beneath the torso.

The mannequin's gown had once been beautiful, possibly even vintage, but it was now marred by great splashes of red. I estimated three or four bottles of nail polish had been needed to create these shiny splashes of brighter-than-blood red. The supposed wound? I looked around, spotted the head where it had come to rest against the back of a burgundy velvet sofa, lolling drunkenly against the passementerie. A gaping wound had been painted, rather carelessly, against the pale skin tones of the mannequin's neck. The idiotic thought ran through my mind that it was fortunate all that brilliant red polish was dry before our plaster lady took her plunge. Otherwise, the clean-up job would have been a bitch.

I looked up, up, up, to the tiny, black wrought-iron balcony two stories above. Although that floor was not currently on display to the public, I had been up there many years ago with Aunt Hy. It was a huge game room, with fast access to the Casa's tower. From the tower, sixty feet high, an intrepid miscreant might, with the right equipment, be able to make a fast getaway—

And then it hit me. Female—fallen from a great height. Shattered. Destroyed. *All the king's horses and all the king's men*—

Nausea rose in my throat. Eyes closed, I slumped into a sitting position. I shook.

I knew excitement swirled around me, never quite touching as a pair of black satin-striped trousers stood next to me, protecting me, the authoritative voice above the legs snapping out orders. Martin. Dear old Martin. The crowd was quiet now, perhaps indicative of our modern age which has become all-too-immured to violence. Even the people who had broken off their tour of the second-floor bedrooms, charging onto the gallery or down the precipitous pink marble stairs, were once again turning toward their guides, moving along, doing as they were told.

"Get this mess cleaned up. Fast." Martin's orders to the phalanx of security guards who now surrounded the "body" left no room for argument.

It also brought me out of my blue funk with a snap. "But shouldn't we—"

"No," Martin barked. "If we move fast, only the few people here now will know it happened. That leaves six hundred or so who can enjoy their evening in peace." In spite of his pragmatism, Martin Longstreet's faded blue eyes held a glitter I had never seen before. Evidently, as a Bellman Board member, he considered this vulgar disruption of the festivities a personal affront.

I suggested a call to Detective Parrish. Martin didn't bother to reply. The guards were already moving off down the hall to the kitchen with various body parts tucked under their arms.

"Excuse me, Miss," said a younger man I didn't recognize as he bent to pick up the torso, still clad in the limp red-spattered white satin gown. With surprising delicacy, he carried out the remains, held in his arms, almost as if she were a real person, felled by a sudden bout of faintness.

We were so civilized at the Bellman. Why, then, were such bad things happening?

Martin signaled two guards who had just come bursting through the door, evidently summoned by walkie-talkie. With stalwart hands on each side, I was soon back on my feet, if not without some embarrassment. The guards' ears were pink. They must have had a good look, back and front, as they bent over to help me to my feet.

As Martin and I went in search of Aunt Hy, we passed some of the on-site security guards returning with push broom, dust pan, and brushes. A few more moments, and the Casa would be Bellissima once again. I could only hope the mannequin's remains were not going to end up in the nearest Dumpster. I suspected Detective Ken Parrish was going to have a fit. Though not on a par with the student's death, the shattered mannequin was far worse than the effigy of a jaunty Roman soldier driving a Biga.

And had to be unrelated. No way would Billie ever play such a sick joke. Nor did this crudely painted mannequin bear any resemblance to the finely sculpted Roman warrior.

So . . .

My eyes widened as I glanced down. I tweaked the silk framing my cleavage. Each side of the deep V promptly slithered back into place, leaving me as shamelessly exposed as before. A last ferocious scowl straight down to where Aunt Hy's pink diamonds pointed the way, and I reverted to the cop who insisted, in spite of debilitating weakness in body and soul, that she wasn't quite down for the count.

Since the day Tim Mundell allegedly hanged himself . . . since the day Josh Thomas slid into my tram in the midst of a towering thunderstorm, a pall had shadowed the Bellman. Disturbing the serenity. Sending out growing ripples of unease that had now spread to the world of the Bellman's primary supporters, the ones with the money to attend events like tonight's Gala.

Not good.

And not Billie. Who just wanted the museum to recognize his talent.

Yet a student was found hanging from a Bellman banyan, a bloody "body" tossed at the feet of Sarasota's wealthiest patrons of the arts . . .

I could almost hear Richard Bellman's roar of anger. See the defiant shake of his fist. *"Not at my Museum!"*

I was angry, too. I made a promise to Bellman's remains, buried only a stone's throw from the Casa Bellissima. A vow from a cripple, maybe, but I was coming alive, catching a whiff of the good old days when I thought myself infallible. Discovering some of what I was still lingered.

Darkness had descended on the land I'd learned to love. And I was going to do my best to scatter the ghosts, and maybe a few of my own along with them.

CHAPTER 6

Martin and I found Aunt Hy in the Gift Shop (once the Bellman kitchen), listening raptly to the words of a lady of uncertain years and considerable girth who, beneath her shaggy salt-and-pepper hair and moon-round face, had somehow managed to pour herself into a royal purple twenties chemise with a double layer of foot-long black fringe. It would seem, however, that her powers of observation were superior to her taste in clothes.

"I saw him, I tell you," she declared. "No one will listen to me. The guide hissed at me to be still. Can you imagine anything so rude? I saw him do it, and nobody wants to hear about it."

"My niece will," Aunt Hy promptly assured her. "Ah, here you are, child! Come, Rory, I have been keeping this dear lady here just for you. I was sure you would wish to speak with her."

I did. But how Aunt Hy could possibly know my analytical instincts, dormant now for so long, had suddenly been aroused I could not guess.

Purple Chemise, her grievance bottled up for too long, burst into a spate of words. "We had just come into the living room. I've been through the house twice before, you see, so I wasn't listening to the guide, just looking around at the things I'd missed. Something moved, way up high, above the second-floor gallery. There was this . . . creature." Her voice dropped to a whisper; she glanced around the kitchen, as if suddenly fearful the creature might pop out of one of the massive cupboards. "He was like the Phantom of the Opera," she confided. "Or maybe Zorro. Big black cape, the kind that swirls."

Purple Chemise had a lively imagination. "Top hat?" I inquired faintly, struggling to hide my incredulity.

"Oh, no, dear. One of those flat things—like Mexicans in an old movie."

"Zorro," Martin murmured in my ear. I couldn't look at him. I was afraid we might set each other off into whoops. "Mask?" he inquired with perfect poker face.

"Oh, my, yes," said Purple Chemise. "The kind that covers just the eyes."

"Zorro," said Aunt Hy, nodding in satisfaction, evidently pleased that the description was dovetailing so nicely into place.

"And then?" Martin prodded, while I took a deep breath and thought dire thoughts about little old ladies whose lives were too dull. Dear God, Zorro even fit the arcane time period of the Bellman's much-vaunted authentic ambiance. The tiny balcony where he'd been seen opened off the Casa's game room, and I was itching to get up there and look around, and here we were allowing ourselves to be led astray by a dotty old lady.

"It was *so* dramatic," Purple Chemise sighed. "He had this woman in a long white gown in his arms—just like King Kong, you know—and then he raised her up and tossed her over the rail, like so much garbage. A hard toss, you know, to clear the second-floor gallery." Our tale-bearer clutched her heaving bosom somewhere in the vicinity of her heart and declared, "I nearly fainted, truly I did. It was quite horrible. And then that awful splat, and she—the woman in the white gown, I thought she was real, you see—flew in every direction. My dears, I cannot describe how shocking it was."

Martin and Aunt Hy made soothing noises, murmuring their appreciation of her courage in being able to tell us of her perfectly awful ordeal. I wondered how I could sneak back to the elevator and get up to the third floor.

"I suppose he was wearing gloves," I offered. My moments of incredulity were fading fast. Purple Chemise's details held the ring of truth.

"Naturally, dear. Long ones, with a flared cuff. Like the old movies. The only skin I saw was his chin."

Solemnly, Martin thanked her and offered to escort our informant on the remainder of our tour of the Casa. In the background I could see Aunt Hy shaking her head.

"Don't you want to see the second floor before we go?" I asked.

"I saw it in the spring before the House opened," Aunt Hy declared firmly. "At the moment I've had quite enough excitement. I believe we should find our seats for supper."

"Perhaps a drink on the terrace?" Martin suggested. (I'd almost swear the old boy was conniving at giving me time to slip away.)

"I'll join you in a moment," I said. "I'd like to take a look at the second floor." Sure enough, as Martin escorted the two older ladies out the door, he turned and winked at me.

The advantage of having a cane is that I was qualified to ride the elevator. Instead of "2," however, I pushed "3."

I moved slowly down the short hallway to the game room, looking in vain for any sign someone had passed this way. It was completely empty, the tap of my cane sounding hollow and forlorn. On my right, the removable wall panel that hid the door to the walk-in vault was firmly in place, looking as fixed and innocent as it was supposed to. I stepped into the game room, a huge L-shaped chamber, lit only by light drifting up the convoluted staircase from the well-lit second story and in through the tiny balcony far above the Great Room's floor. An electric charge shot through me. I could see him standing there on the balcony, in swirling cape, Zorro mask, and gloves with flared cuffs, holding the satin-clad mannequin high above his head, hurtling her over the edge . . .

Head whirling, I leaned back hard against the door frame. I clutched my cane so tightly my knuckles cracked. Conquering my personal phantoms was hard enough, but I'd let Purple Chemise fill my head with nonsense. Yes, someone had been here, but it sure as hell wasn't Zorro. I snapped my eyes open, poked my head around to the right and checked out the small bathroom. Empty, of course. Undoubtedly, Security had already come and gone, finding the game room as deserted and unproductive as I was. There was, after all, no place to hide. Just a great expanse, minimally furnished with a poker table, an ancient gramophone, a few chairs.

What made the game room special were Willy Pogany's brilliantly colored whimsical paintings on the walls and ceiling. Although subdued by shadows, they seemed to dance along above me, urging me on. Cautiously, I turned the corner of the L. Nothing but the green baize expanse of a billiard table. Frankly, there wasn't even a place for a mouse to hide.

If there's a clue, you know where to look.

Sure I did. But nothing was going to get me out on that balcony. The balcony I'd bypassed by ten feet on my passage across the game room. When I'd fallen from the very same height, my head hadn't come off, my arms and legs hadn't separated from my body, but my bones had broken into nearly as many pieces as that poor mannequin. My leg was only the last of many disarranged parts to heal.

No, not quite the last. My head was going to be last. If ever. When I had forced myself to lie in the sun on Aunt Hy's balcony far above Sarasota Bay, I had been challenging myself. Sweating it out. Telling myself it was doing me good.

Believe me, I seized, on a vast rush of relief, the opportunity to get my fresh air via tram-driving.

Face it, Travis. There's nothing here except your own phantoms.

73

Catalysts to nightmare.

What did I expect to find? A golden hair from the mannequin? Useless. A muddy boot print when we'd had nothing but sunny days? Zorro's calling card?

But if I didn't look, I was the worst kind of a wimp. Keeping a firm grip on the game room wall with my right hand, I edged out onto the tiny balcony. Its bowed black wrought-iron railing seemed to be wavering, moving in and out, in and out. My stomach churned. I transferred my grip to one of the balcony's upright iron bars and knelt. Teeth clenched, I checked every inch of the balcony floor. Nothing. The mannequin had materialized out of thin air and thrown itself off the balcony.

Which brought me to how anyone could get into the Casa carrying a . . .

I scrambled back into the game room on hands and knees, all the way to one of the hand-painted support columns, which I used to drag myself to my feet. I stood with my back to the colorful geometric shapes until my breathing was close to normal. How long, how long, how long must I suffer for my sins?

Okay, how *could* someone get into the Casa Bellissima carrying a full-size female mannequin? From the basement, up the servants' stairs? But the basement, a Florida phenomenon, was locked up tight. Compartmented into maze-like sections to deter flooding. The Casa had vast attics and the dark hidden recesses that had once held organ pipes. Easy enough to hide a mannequin. But only with inside help. The security system at the House since its renovation was state-of-the-art.

Or had Zorro climbed the sixty-foot tower, with the mannequin on his back, lain in wait . . . and entered from the outside staircase through a door that was as securely locked as the cellar?

Obviously, my analytical talents were as rusty as my intuitive ones. Time to move on.

I climbed one more flight and peeked into the bedroom Will Rogers once enjoyed. I didn't dare announce my presence by turning on a light, and I was well aware ten Zorros could have hidden themselves in the gloom of the private bathroom, not to mention the recessed nook in the far corner, or even under the bed. I finally had sense enough to recall that I was *hors de combat,* far from able to take on a Bad Guy armed only with my flowered cane. Reluctantly, I headed back to the elevator.

In front of me, a door heaved open on a rush of sea breeze and cool night air. The security guard and I stared at each other, each too stunned to speak. He was, thank God, someone I knew by sight.

"Hi," I managed, leaning heavily on my cane. "I punched the wrong button. Sorry about that."

If he wondered why I'd gotten out of the elevator instead of simply correcting my error, he was too polite to say so. Or perhaps he was so excited by his find that his mind was preoccupied by the very human desire to share. In spite of my Schiaparelli, he recognized me as one of the privileged who had security clearance. Proudly, he displayed the items he was carrying. "Found 'em in the Tower," he told me. "Guy must have run out of the game room and straight upstairs."

"But how would he get down?" I'd seen those stairs. Treacherous, outside stairs curving up and around to a tower with a sixty-foot drop on the east side straight down to the driveway. On the bay side, the tower rose twenty or more feet above the uneven expanses of the Casa's slanted and slippery red-tile roof.

"Rope," the guard told me. "He must've rappelled all the way down. I left it up there. Thought the police might like to see it." He looked down, rather guiltily, at the items in his arms. "Maybe I should have left these, too, but I was afraid the wind might blow 'em away. Evidence, y'know."

He whipped a flat-brimmed sombrero out from under his arm, waving it triumphantly. A strip of black cloth dangled from the chin strap. With eye holes. Then the guard shook out what had been draped over his arm. A long black cape unfolded straight in front of my nose, its sides swirling to encompass the corridor.

Shit. It was Zorro.

The courtyard of the Art Museum glowed with enough ambiance to warm the cockles of the most gimlet-eyed fund-raiser's heart. Seventy-five round tables, seating eight each, twinkled down the two long sides of the loggia, white tablecloths vying for sparkling honors with the silver tableware, all lit by candles in protective glass tubes. The white-jacketed cooks stood at their food stations, bartenders at attention in front of their glassware and high-end labels. Waiters hovered discreetly. Beautiful people wafted by, found their tables, and sat, to the accompaniment of bright chatter, a few leaning forward to impart the breaking news of tonight's events at the Casa Bellissima.

In the center of the grassy courtyard rose a spectral contraption of poles, wires, and double bars, swaying in the light sea breeze, quietly waiting for what was supposed to have been the highlight of the evening's entertainment. A performance by one of the Bellman Circus's finest artists, a strong supple lady just coming to the close of a year's maternity leave. When the Circus returned to winter quarters in a few weeks, she would be plunging into rehearsals for next year's season. Tonight was to be her return to the world of performance. Although I had never met the high-flying lady, I felt for her. I feared she had already been badly upstaged. Voices around the courtyard were growing louder. News of the latest incident at the Bellman was spreading fast.

Poor Martin. He should have known he couldn't keep it quiet.

It occurs to me you may not have made the connection. Yes, Richard is *that* Bellman. The most famous of the brothers who tore their way out of poverty by establishing a circus. *The* circus. The most famous circus on earth. The brother who raised his eyes from the sawdust long enough to discover real estate, railroads, oil wells, and—finally—art. The brother who bought paintings enthusiastically, then gave them away when he became knowledgeable enough to recognize his early mistakes. The brother who made few mistakes after that, eventually acquiring one of the greatest collections of Baroque art in the world.

Richard Bellman's business practices, however, tended to be highly creative and secretive, to say the least. It is, most experts agree, a miracle the bay-front property with Richard and Opal's house and the Art Museum, survived to become the property of the State of Florida, as Bellman specified in his will. And now, in the new millennium, the property was rising from seventy-five years of strict, often painful, economy to float, blissfully, into a new roof (no more buckets strategically placed in the Rubens' galleries), a new learning center, a welcome center, library, more galleries, and sundry other long-needed repairs and expansions.

No wonder the Director and Deputy Director were customarily seen with smiles on their faces. Or was that all part of the PR skills needed to rise to such exalted heights?

Martin escorted us to our seats with such aplomb, I swear he'd had a look at a master seating chart beforehand. He was that kind of man. No wandering around the loggias, peering at table numbers, for Martin Longstreet.

Others soon joined us, filling the table. Except, of course, for the seat next to me. Not that I wanted to be obligated to shallow social conversation with some stranger, but, still, that empty seat beside me loomed. I told myself it didn't matter. I tried not to think of better times when I would have had a date. I tried, very hard, not to feel shunned. But recognizing I was suffering from depression and shaking off my exaggerated feelings were two separate paths. I took the low road, unfortunately, succumbing to an antisocial display of stoic face and monosyllabic replies to all attempts at conversation.

I was deliberately not looking, therefore, when something solid, but lithe enough to squeeze into the last seat at a table for eight, inserted itself beside me. The something leaned close, whispering intimately in my ear. "Very nice, Ms. Travis. Perhaps you should consider braless on a daily basis."

The voice was forever embedded in my brain. I closed my eyes. Introductions flew over my head. I heard the scrape of Josh Thomas's chair as he half rose to shake hands with Martin and brush a kiss over Aunt Hy's limp fingers. (Yes, I peeked, damn him!) Aunt Hy, ignoring Martin's attempts to shush her, immediately launched into a description of the events at the Casa. All other conversation at our table ceased, seven fascinated faces—including Josh Thomas's and even mine—focused on Hyacinth Van Horne in her turquoise silk Vionnet.

When all the *ohs, ahs,* and gasps had finally subsided, Josh once again bent his dark head to mine. "Sounds like you were right in the middle of it," he said, the black pools of his eyes quite unfathomable.

I opened my mouth for a deliberately bland reply when I realized the significance of his remark. The person for whom that dirty trick had the most significance had been right there in the room, trailing her tour guide. An arctic breeze rippled over my soul. What was happening at the Bellman couldn't possibly be personal. *No way.*

"Rory, dear, did you learn anything upstairs?" Aunt Hy called from across the expanse of Martin's conservatively ruffled white shirt.

"I was doing the standard tour," I declared, loud enough for the whole table to hear. Not difficult, as their ears were *en pointe.* "I saw Richard's bed, Opal's bed, the marble bathtub, the barber chair, and Napoleon's sister, hanging on the wall, *au naturel.*"

"Of course, dear," Aunt Hy murmured, with a look so arch a child of five would have suspected a conspiracy was afoot. Our four tablemates—and Josh—eyed me with considerable interest.

I dropped my eyes and lowered my voice to hiss for Josh's ears alone, "And where were *you?*"

"Europe, actually," he replied, deliberately misinterpreting my question. "I do work occasionally."

"Tonight," I ground out. "When the mannequin bit the dust."

"Moi?" He did a nice imitation of wounded ego. "But I've just this minute arrived. Straight from the airport."

I didn't believe him. Unfair, unjustified . . . my intuition coming back with a vengeance? Perhaps I associated Josh with bad things because I'd met him on the day Tim Mundell died. Or maybe my skepticism was as simple as the black shirt he was wearing under his tux. Worn with white bow tie pierced on one side by a diamond stud. Truthfully, when I got up the courage to examine him, the impact was worse than anticipated—and I'd anticipated something pretty dire. Hair—blue black, dark and shiny as an indigo snake. The eyes of a cobra. A Wellington nose (or was it *David*'s?). Cheekbones as sharp as the sharks' teeth that wash up on Gulf Coast beaches. A mouth so grim I couldn't imagine him ever kissing a woman. Attacking her maybe; kissing, no-o-o. He was scary. Yet like a flame to a suicidal moth, he beckoned. He sat there, politely applying himself to the salad of baby greens just delivered by the waiter, and I could feel him burrowing in. Oozing through my pores, into my flesh. Into my cracked but mending bones.

Our connection had been born on an electrical charge, baptized by thunder, and nurtured by an awareness so strong, so frightening, I could actually taste it. Somehow this table pairing had been arranged. How? A couple of octogenarians sprang to mind, though how they knew Josh Thomas I couldn't begin to imagine. And, yet, I doubted Josh knew anything about our Roman warrior. And only pure contrariness on my part associated him with Zorro and a shattered mannequin. For why on earth would any man, even one so smugly comfortable with his wicked image, bother tossing a mannequin into a crowd of Gala attendees? It was a nasty, motiveless crime. Surely beneath his touch.

Yet it nagged at me. Was I sitting next to a man who had played such an ugly prank for the hell of it? A man so motivated by an unknown something that, after tossing that miserable mannequin practically at my feet, he had climbed to the tower, shed his hat, mask, and cape, rappelled sixty feet to the ground, then calmly walked back to the Art Museum through the rose garden?

He would have been seen coming off the tower. Had to have been seen by Gala patrons, trolley drivers, security guards.

As I had seen him before he slid onto the tram seat next to me to the accompaniment of fire and brimstone?

Josh Thomas: invisible man. Yet as we sat, squeezed elbow-to-elbow and hip-to-hip, I could feel his presence solid as a rock. The most dynamic and least invisible man I'd ever met. And I heard every word of his conversation with Martin Longstreet, passed so casually across me. All that was said, and all that wasn't. Old friendships and old wars. Unspoken knowledge hovering, elusive. Words coded for public consumption . . . the significant pauses. Martin and Josh were tightly connected, and I was beginning to gain an inkling of how.

Because of Aunt Hy, for whom *secret* was not part of the

English language, I knew a good deal more about Martin Longstreet than I should. Martin had been CIA, upper echelon. Josh Thomas's father, I now gathered, had been part of that world. I reminded myself that CIA agents were bound to be acquainted with a lot of strange people. Including dangerous young men they were willing to invite to a Bellman fund-raising event? No matter what I thought about Josh's black shirt and mysterious motivations, his character was validated by his presence at our table. Martin Longstreet vouched for Josh Thomas. That ought to have been enough, but of course it wasn't.

Later, as Josh passed the dessert tray of petit fours, mini key lime pies and cream puffs, he leaned in close, his breath scalding my ear. "Do you trust me enough to let me drive you home? If not, may I meet you in the Ritz bar? I'd like to talk to you."

And which of my elderly companions had blabbed about where I lived?

My fingers betrayed me, rustling the pleated paper cupping the pie I had selected. "Did Aunt Hy put you up to this?" I demanded, hoping a blandly pleasant expression was firmly fixed on my face for the benefit of the rest of the table.

"Your aunt is charming, but a stranger before tonight."

"Martin?"

Sinfully long lashes opened to wide-eyed innocence. "Martin and my father knew each other in 'Nam. One of those amazing coincidences, I assure you. Well?" he challenged.

I clutched my lavender-flowered cane, folded in three pieces, that I was balancing in my lap, tucked beneath the drop of the tablecloth.

"I'm fond of women with canes," Josh purred, as if he could read my mind or see beneath the white cloth. When I stared, he added, "Perhaps I fancy females who can't run so fast. I'm told I can be terrifying."

"Tell me," I countered, leaning in as if bent on seduction. I fluttered my nicely mascaraed lashes. "Where do you carry your gun?"

"Which one?" He didn't even blink.

Since I wasn't sure if we were playing with the same nuances, I decided to forget about guns for the moment.

He had, of course, seen my cane that first day in the tram. There could be no other explanation for his clairvoyance. Nonetheless, I recalled that I hated him. He was worse than my physical therapist. But I took up the challenge. I said he could drive me home.

Aunt Hy was ecstatic.

CHAPTER 7

It's difficult to choke on something so innocuous as a mini key lime pie, with flaky crust and pale green custard, topped with some twenty-first-century version of whipped cream. But I came close to managing it. As I joined the general shuffle to turn our chairs for a better view of the performance in the center courtyard, I saw a young woman of about my own age and build—wearing a spangled minimum of clothing—climbing up, up, up into the rigging. Intellectually, I had thought myself prepared for the performance. Evidently not. My last bite of pie turned to concrete in my throat, bile rising beneath it. My fingers white-knuckled around my cane. The woman was going to perform thirty feet up with no safety net. *Thirty feet. Three stories* . . .

A hand, firm and surprisingly warm, dropped over mine, lending strength like a transfusion of good red blood. I kept my eyes on my lap, where the long pale fingers of Josh's left hand rested over mine.

A strange man, Josh Thomas. Was there a heart beneath that suave, sophisticated surface? In spite of his compassionate gesture, I suspected his motives. Whatever pumped blood through his veins was as hard as *David*'s bronze. He was all but unreadable, a misty sorcerer's mirror that reflected only what he wished you to see. Or—if a girl was stupid enough to be gullible—only what she *wished* to see.

To others, Josh might look innocuous, fitting right in with the

Bellman crowd, but when I looked at him, I saw a sign in flashing red neon: WARNING—DANGER.

Only when applause broke out did I allow myself to look up. The talented young woman was back on the ground, making her bows to the crowd, graciously acknowledging her assistants. "Do you know the origin of the expression 'Break a Leg'?" Josh asked. I shook my head. "In the early days of theater," he told me, "everyone bowed ballerina style—knee bent, one leg back. None of this bowing from the waist." He nodded toward the trapeze artist, who was now bowing to the opposite loggia.

"It's a killer position," Josh continued. "Do it enough times, with one knee pumping up and down, and you'll probably wish the audience had sat on its hands. So wishing a performer 'Break a leg' meant you hoped he got enough curtain calls that his leg broke from the strain of taking his bows."

I took a deep breath. I could feel color coming back into my cheeks. I peered at my mystery man. His face was a mask of bland civility. "Thanks," I said. And meant it.

He patted my hand, then rose to his feet. "I wouldn't mind beating the crowd out of here," he said. "Shall we?" When I managed a tentative smile of agreement, he reached for my cane, flipped it into its upright position and handed it back to me with a gesture as courtly as Sir Walter Raleigh spreading his cloak for the queen. Perhaps I didn't hate him, after all. We made our farewells to Aunt Hy, Martin, and the rest of our tablemates, then followed the trickle of wealthy patrons getting a head start toward the parking lot.

By the time we negotiated the length of the table-filled loggia and passed through the marbled lobby, the trickle had swelled to a moving, but gracious, stream, carrying us along in its midst. Ignoring the wheelchair ramp out front, Josh put one arm around my waist and swept me down the front steps as if I were no more than a ten-pound sack of sugar. While I was busy further readjusting my attitude, the crowd deviated from the front gate, veering left across the grass on a swell as inexorable as the tide. Voices rose. Politely. This time, no screams or pounding feet.

We were moving faster now, Josh pushing his way to the front, still holding me tight, my feet touching the ground only every other step. His apologies were polite but firm; no one questioned his note of authority. And then we were at the front of the crowd, standing there gaping like all the rest. At *Lygia and the Bull*. Except now there were two Lygias. One, a superbly crafted effigy spread-eagled over the bronze original, and far more startling in her painted nudity than Moretti's Lygia that had once scandalized Philadelphia.

Mimicking the original, the Lygia of *papier mâché* was tied to the bull's horns and body by two ropes. In this case, genuine sisal. Her sea-blue eyes were open, wide with terror, her long dark hair (a wig?) tumbling down over the Lygia of bronze. The roses scattered over the effigy and onto the ground around the life-size sculpture were real. (There were going to be some furious gardeners at Opal's Rose Garden in the morning.) One large pink bloom was tastefully placed in the spot where it would most protect her modesty. A nice touch, I thought.

Like the Roman warrior, this effigy was the work of a very fine sculptor. I would have bet a goodly sum that whoever created this scene had no idea what had happened at the Casa earlier this evening. The sculptor had simply planned his prank for the Gala, then planted his Lygia while everyone was inside eating. Unfortunately, he had decided to up the stakes this time around. For, unlike the original—who was merely stretched out over the bull's back—this new Lygia was in the next stage of the unequal contest. The effigy's pale peach shoulder was impaled on the bull's bronze horn. Bloodred paint spilled from the supposed wound, dripping down the Lygia of *papier mâché* to fall over the bronze flank of the bull as well. (The outrage of the curator and conservators would surely eclipse that of the gardeners.)

Unlike the crude mannequin, this sculpture was magnificently executed. Beautifully life-like, the face of Lydia Hewitt was unmistakable. *Oh, Billie, you idiot!*

For about thirty seconds Josh simply stared at the great bull with its double burden of Lygias—memorizing the scene, no doubt. Then, without a word, he turned me around and slipped us sideways out of the crowd, moving along the front fence toward the gate. "Stay put," he growled after we passed through the black wrought-iron gate, then sprinted off to retrieve his car from the parking lot across the road. Gratefully, I leaned back against a pink stucco wall and reviewed the evening's events. *Curiouser and curiouser.*

There was no reason to blame Josh Thomas for any of this mess. Yet after he had made his mysterious appearance out of thin air a few weeks back, things had gone steadily downhill at the Bellman. Associating him with disaster was irrational. Absurd. Yet I couldn't get away from the uncomfortable suspicion that somehow he was mixed up in all this. He had to be. Why else was he here?

Josh Thomas, patron of the arts? Not likely. Josh Thomas, businessman spending a few off hours at the Bellman? Possible . . . still unlikely. Josh Thomas, gone to ground? What better place could a man with multiple guns find to hide in plain sight—taking a breather, as it were—than at the Richard and Opal Bellman Museum of Art? Screening for weapons was not part of the Bellman's routine.

And yet, both times Josh Thomas had come to the museum, he'd ended up sitting next to Rory Travis. An unacceptable co-incidence.

Josh pulled up in front, ushering me into his rented car as

solicitously as if we were on an actual date. Perhaps we were. As we turned onto the drive leading to the Tamiami Trail, I looked back in time to see Detective Sergeant Ken Parrish stepping down from a silver gray SUV. *Oh-oh.* My next interrogation was going to be unpleasant. *Damn it, Billie, what have you done? I don't want to be mixed up in this.*

Yet something was going on besides the plea of a young and unwise sculptor for recognition. The trouble was, I had no idea what. A mannequin tossed from a third-floor balcony made no sense at all. Unless . . . prickles started in my toes and swept all the way to my head. Unless . . . it had been personal. Aimed at me.

Na-a-w. Couldn't be. No motive. No one had anything to gain from my reliving my life's worst moment.

As it turned out, I was wrong.

"A copycat?" I said to Josh as we sipped our drinks at the Ritz-Carlton's dark and atmospheric Cà d'Zan bar. We'd been examining the evening's events for half an hour and were back to Square One, up against an impenetrable wall. "Someone heard about the Roman warrior and decided to use a mannequin to disrupt the Gala?"

"The problem remains the same," Josh countered. "No motive. What can anyone gain from causing trouble at the Bellman?"

"Someone out of the past, fighting old battles? Someone who doesn't want the museum to survive?" I warmed to my topic. "Someone furious because the millions from the state take away the museum's autonomy?"

When Josh nodded, I suspected he was humoring me. "Possible," he agreed. "Sick, but possible." For a fraction of a second, his cobra eyes flickered, offering the tiniest hint of emotion. "There's something you're not saying," he told me. "We agree the mannequin doesn't fit with the other two effigies, but there's more. You're hedging on the sculptor. You know him, don't you? You can tell me, you know. I'm safe. I'm off to Lima tomorrow."

I knew he didn't mean Lima, Ohio.

"Perhaps," I conceded. "Perhaps not." I cupped my hands around my snifter of brandy, warming my favorite B&B. And deliberately changed the subject. "Tell me about yourself," I said. "Who is Josh Thomas?"

The silence lengthened, as I knew it would.

"An international traveler," he said at last.

"Making occasional stops in Sarasota." He nodded. "And whose father knows Martin Longstreet."

"Knew. A long time ago."

"When Martin was CIA."

"That's a leap."

"So is the coincidence of you turning up here just as all hell breaks loose at the museum."

His eyes flicked over the room, checking it out. It was late, the customers few. We were totally isolated at our window table overlooking the terraces and the marina outside—the wood, fiberglass and chrome of the expensive craft gleaming under a barrage of security lights.

"Okay, my turning up here is not a coincidence. And, yes, I'll tell you about it some day." He leaned forward. As if I had no control over my body, I leaned in as well. Our noses were inches apart. Our eyes met. "One day, when you're ready, I'm going to offer you a job," Josh Thomas said. "I hope to hell you'll take it."

"On which side of the law?"

"That," he returned steadily, "is occasionally in doubt."

He paid the bill, throwing down bills as carelessly as Aunt Hy. Arms dealer? Trust fund baby? Maybe both.

Correction . . . Lima. Peru. Lots and lots of coca leaves. Not a pleasant thought.

Josh walked me to the elevator (under the sharp eye of the Ritz-Carlton security guard who also knew dangerous when he saw it) and there, in the tastefully lit, plush-carpeted corridor, he leaned close and whispered: *"Arrivederci, cara mia. Sta' bene."* And then his lips—those two thin uncompromising lines of flesh—touched my cheek. *"Corragio,"* he added as the elevator doors slid open.

When you grow up on the Connecticut south coast, you inevitably acquire a few words of Italian, *omerta* being high on the list. With words of love, whispered by dark-eyed Lotharios, close behind. Take my word for it, *cara mia* was basic minimum in the love department. Nor did I need to be wished well. I was doing just fine, thank you, before and after the fleeting appearances of Josh Thomas. *Corragio,* however, I considered an insult. I did not need to be wished *courage,* particularly by a dark-eyed satyr who carried more than one gun. And maybe had a penchant for swirling black capes and rappelling off sixty-foot towers.

And then the elevator doors closed, obscuring the face that somehow managed to look saturnine and smug at the same time. When I got to my room, I scrubbed my cheek until it was as pink as the rose over Lygia's privates. But the kiss didn't come off. I was branded. Seared to the soul.

And tomorrow I had to face Billie Ball Hamlin. And Detective Sergeant Ken Parrish.

The next morning, after a snarling good-bye to my physical therapist, I set out to find Billie. After the Roman warrior incident, I had cornered him in the staff snack bar in the farthest southwest corner of the Art Museum basement. Although the snack bar's five miniature tables, tucked amidst shockingly modern vending machines, had been empty except for us, I'd not been able to get any satisfactory answers from him. Yet I was certain his eyes were dancing with delight over the sensation created by the Roman charioteer. And he had looked positively smug when I praised the workmanship. But, other than that, Billie "Golf Ball" Hamlin was accustomed to keeping secrets. He did it with as much style and panache as he put into his sculptures of *papier mâché.*

Alleged sculptures.

But today I wasn't going to accept evasion. Billie seemed to have a surprising amount of talent, yet he was burning whatever bridge he hoped to have to the museum. (I had overheard Martin Longstreet expound on the Bellman Board's opinion of the Roman warrior prank, and learned a few sophisticated substitutes for the "F" word that I had memorized for future reference.)

Today, I didn't dare ask where Billie might be on the vast grounds, for I had no doubt Detective Parrish would hear about it if I did. I settled for eating my bag lunch at the picnic tables behind the restaurant and keeping an eagle eye on every golf cart that passed by. Each driver nodded or waved, but none of them was Billie. The seventh, one of the slightly less nubile young things en route from the Education Department to the Circus Museum, stopped to talk. We had a nodding acquaintance from the docent training classes, which I had audited so I could answer all those questions visitors ask their tram drivers. Patricia Arkwright was tall and severely slim, with blond hair cut short below her ears. She had the authoritarian personality of a nineteenth-century schoolmarm—learn or get your knuckles rapped—although I judged she was not more than a year or so older than I. And she tended to treat the roomful of gracious, well-educated, and well-dressed volunteers training to be docents as if they were on the same intellectual and social level as a busload of fifth graders.

Today, it seemed Patricia had heard that I was present when the mannequin splintered on the Casa's black-and-white marble diamonds. "Is it true the man was dressed as Zorro?" she demanded.

"There was a witness who says so," I replied, blithely ignoring any claim she might have to a need to know.

Her blue-gray eyes regarded me with only minimal suspicion. I was, after all, merely a tram driver. A volunteer. Not a docent. Not even a tour guide. She was wasting her time. What could I possibly know?

" 'Lo, ladies," said Billie as he pulled up beside us. "Lookin' good, Pat," he added with a glance that didn't miss an inch of the blond from Education.

Patricia Arkwright blushing? I'd expected her to give Billie the cold shoulder, no matter how good looking, how macho, or how talented an art student. So . . . under that brittle exterior Pat liked men. Had I ever heard her put down one of the male trainees? A definite *no*. I tucked that seemingly irrelevant fact into my slowly awakening brain.

"Oh!" Pat exclaimed, "I'm late for a class." After a final brilliant smile aimed at Billie, she put the pedal to the metal and scurried off toward the classroom at the Circus. (She was, of course, teaching, not taking, the class.)

Billie offered me a vacuous grin, peeping at me through half-closed lashes, undoubtedly lowered to mask his guilt. Blast it, I didn't even know where to begin!

Billie did, seizing on the obviously handy diversion. "Pat's not so bad when you get to know her."

I raised my brows. "What about Lydia?"

Billie shrugged. "Pat and me were a long time back. We're— uh—sort of kissin' cuzzins now." He grinned. "She's moved way, way up since then. Got something going with upper management, I hear, maybe even a Board member. I'm surprised she even remembers my name."

My mind seethed with so many questions, I only nodded before reaching for my own momentary diversion. "How's the golf ball business?"

"Great! Got some beauties this week. So high end I can put 'em on the Net for twenty dollars a dozen." He lowered his voice. "Big fancy new course where memberships cost a mint. Play with nothing but the best. Really gives a boost to my business."

I struggled against my months of apathy, against the Bellman's smothering bonds of serenity. Here we were, chitchatting about golf balls when last night . . .

Once again, the shock and anguish of the shattered mannequin washed over me. But this time, instead of turning me weak-kneed, the powerful emotions kicked the Travis temper into action. Billie Ball Hamlin—even more surely than Josh Thomas—was part of whatever anomaly was shaking the Bellman.

"Listen to me, Billie," I demanded. "Did you have anything to do with that mannequin at the Casa?"

"Rory!" he wailed, obviously severely wounded. "You can't think I'd be part of anything so crude."

"Actually . . . no," I agreed. "But the Roman charioteer was a high-class work of art and the Lygia effigy looked remarkably like your darling Lydia," I said. "You even got her hair and eye color right."

Billie looked down at his steering wheel. A squirrel zipped by, setting off a fit of barking from the restaurant dog that, as usual, had been sleeping in the middle of the tramway. "Have you ever seen twenty hundred-dollar bills, Rory?" he asked softly. "There they were, all those Ben Franklins in an envelope slipped under my door. All I had to do was make two effigies, create two harmless incidents, no questions asked." He looked up, anguished but defensive. "Two K, Rory, what was I to do?"

"Four nights on the golf course?" I suggested, none too gently.

"But, Rory girl, you got to understand—the bodies were so much more fun!"

Of course they were. I thought of a few of Martin's astonishingly creative expletives.

"Was it really necessary to impale her?" I demanded. "There were a lot of elderly people there last night. The blood was a bit over the top."

"But it's only three days to Halloween," Billie said, as if that were all the explanation needed. "Be a sport, Rory. Don't let living with seniors make you forget you're still young."

I sighed. "Billie, didn't it occur to you there might be something sinister about all this? What did you do with the note?"

"Burned it. It said I should." Billie raised his eyes to the rose garden behind me, figuratively whistling Dixie. After a seething pause, he added, "When that City Cop comes sniffing around, you're going to tell him, aren't you?"

"Billie, are you absolutely certain you don't know what's behind this? You really, truly, have no idea why you were asked to make those effigies?"

Billie held up his hand. "On my honor as a Bucs fan," he intoned. "Two effigies, delivered in obvious places for maximum effect. Two thousand bucks. Believe me, there was no return address."

"And I'm right about the mannequin? You had nothing to do with that?"

"Not a clue. Strike that," he revised with a bare hint of his customary grin. "I hear it was Zorro."

"Right." I admitted my own skepticism—until I had seen the telltale hat, mask, and cape.

93

"*Rappelled* off the tower? Way to go!" Billie exclaimed, then added plaintively, "But why?"

"Why throw two *papier mâché* effigies into the museum mix?" I countered. "None of it makes sense."

"So?" Billie challenged, giving me his best portrayal of Little Boy Lost in a Sea of Misunderstanding.

"I'll do what I can to evade the issue," I said, "but Detective Parrish doesn't give the impression of being the careless type. He may not let me wiggle out of it."

Billie slumped in his seat, nodded his understanding.

"I hope all those golf balls add up to a good lawyer," I said. "You may need one."

"Sorry," he mumbled, and slunk off in his golf cart across the grass towards the Casa driveway and the maintenance trailers beyond.

And wasn't that just like Billie and his Southern gentleman manners—apologizing for the hot seat he had put me in.

I limped back to my car, climbed behind the wheel, then sat, staring blindly at the pink stucco of the Circus Museum. Thinking.

For as long as I can remember I've had my odd gift. The ability to add two and two and get five. Or maybe seven or even nineteen. Most people think it's bunk until they've seen it work. Also, I'll be the first to admit my gift works at odd moments, seldom when I want it to, and it frequently comes up short when it's needed most. Inconvenient and annoying. But perhaps you begin to see there might be a reason, beyond charity, for Josh Thomas to offer me a job.

Sometimes my moments of insight are so strong I double over in agony from a combination of nausea and the painful confusion of not being certain what I'm "seeing." But, far more frequently, my insights are quiet leaps that could almost pass for the mental agility of an expert analyst. Which I am. Was. But last night, as I'd heard Josh and Martin talk, I began to wonder just how far the old-boy connection ran. Had it survived Martin's retirement? And where was Josh's father now? Was *he* the one pulling the strings of whatever was happening at the Bellman? Possibly for a private, more sinister, organization of spooks? Or was my Aunt Hy's friend, dear old Martin, the Boss? Master of Daddy Spook and Son of Spook?

Until that night at the Casa, with Martin standing over me like a sentinel, directing the swirl of events around me, I had not thought of him as anything more than an elegant old gentleman, his days of derring-do long gone. But that might not be true. Once a manipulator, always a manipulator. Martin was a man who made things happen. Like getting Ken Parrish assigned to the problems at the Bellman. Age might have slowed Martin down, but his brain was as razor-sharp as ever.

The trouble was, I couldn't figure out the name of the game. Two effigies and a mannequin? Two effigies, a mannequin, and a hanged computer geek, whose body was discovered by Billie Ball Hamlin.

Strange. Very strange.

CHAPTER 8

"The Gatehouse is designed in a similar style to The House," I pointed out, caught up in my customary tour-guide routine. "It's an actual live-in residence, with rooms on each side of the gate. You notice the screen porch—"

A voice bellowed from the rear of the tram—female and belligerent: "Stop talking and take us to The House. We're going to miss our Tour!"

I told myself sternly that, while driving, I represented the Bellman. And since I had already explained to this particular visitor that when we were busy—as we were today—tours began every seven and a half minutes, I was forced to accept that reasoning with her was hopeless. So I clamped my teeth over my tongue and drove. I did not point out the Circus Museum, the restaurant, Opal's rose garden, the banyan trees, the sausage tree, the swimming pool, or the quiet, well-hedged spot where Richard and Opal were buried. I did not point out Sarasota Bay or Pelican Key beyond.

Okay, so I did a slow burn all afternoon. I kept telling myself that one nasty visitor in three months was not enough to precipitate my resignation from the tram service. And, finally, I cooled off enough to remember all the wonderful people I'd met while sitting in the driver's seat of Tram 3.

Nonetheless, I was still simmering when I pulled up at the Art Museum in the relative quiet of the five o'clock lull. Detective Parrish unfolded from one of the wooden benches and

96

wandered over to speak to me. After the usual chorus of "thank yous" from my passengers faded, he leaned in and said, "Can you meet me on the Casa terrace after your shift?"

There was, of course, only one response. If I'd had plans—which I didn't—I would have had to cancel them.

Yet there was something comfortable about Detective Sergeant Ken Parrish. Although he was younger, taller, and better looking than Columbo, he had that same deceptive laid-back feel. He was the type, I speculated, who had married his high school or college sweetheart and already had two kids with another on the way. He was also the type criminals would scoff at, right up to the moment the handcuffs clamped tight.

I found I was looking forward to my interview. To hell with the wife and two-point-five kids.

At five forty-five, after coaxing Aunt Hy's gold Caddy along the now-deserted drive from the tram barn down to the bay, I parked under a banyan canopy next to a silver gray SUV. The driver door opened, and Ken Parrish leapt nimbly down onto the cracked and humpbacked tarmac. He was carrying, I noted with some interest, a backpack in his left hand. Evidence? I rather hoped it wasn't the mannequin head complete with sloppy fingernail polish slash across its throat. It was too lovely an afternoon for reality.

We walked, side by side, past the closed outdoor Café, past the locked Gift Shop, and up the ramp to the terrace. The sun was low enough to give promise of another of the Gulf Coast's glorious sunsets. The warmth of the day clung to the air, lingered in the twenty-seven kinds of marble in the terrace beneath our feet. The small tables scattered here and there were circles of wicker that matched the neutral beige of the classic wicker armchairs. Josh Thomas, in a burst of thunder, had cracked the glacier I had erected around myself. But now, at this moment with Detective Sergeant Ken Parrish, I could actually feel the ice melting. Because he was familiar territory—a cop? Because his boy-next-door face and general attitude were about as nonthreatening as a cop gets? Because we were in an absolutely gorgeous private setting, and he was male and I was female?

It doesn't get any more basic than that.

Brakes: Emergency. *Now.* I turned and gazed out over the sun-kissed water, beginning to take on reflections of gold. Cool, sophisticated, indifferent, I inspected the panorama of Sarasota Bay, Pelican Key, and the incipient sunset while the City Cop rummaged in his backpack.

"Jaeger?" he inquired.

My ears came close to flapping. I turned to discover two small glasses sitting on the table, each brimming with what did indeed appear to be Jaegermeister. There was also a bag of high-quality potato chips. Obviously, Ken Parrish had depths as yet unexplored. What were the odds, I speculated, of coming across two intriguing, fathomless men within days of each other? It was rather like being caught between the Devil and the Deep Blue Sea. Though there was little doubt about which was the Devil.

"Off the clock and off the record," Detective Parrish drawled, with only a hint of wry humor, "I thought you might be more willing to talk to me."

I helped myself to a crunchy sour cream and onion chip, then picked up my Jaeger and held the dark liquid up to the sun's reddening light. "Your instruments of torture are formidable," I admitted. I took a sip, savored . . . and sighed.

Yes, he was pleased that I approved of his offerings. His poker face slipped a little. I was beginning to suspect Detective Parrish's interest wasn't all professional. Fleetingly, I wondered what had happened to the wife and two and a half kiddies. I dropped my eyes to his left hand. No ring. Not that that meant much.

"There's a security guard, named Billie Hamlin," he said. "You know him?"

"I see him around occasionally."

"I'm told he's an art student, a sculptor."

"So he's told me. I'm not familiar with his work." Which was not quite the same thing as saying I'd never seen it.

"Supposedly, he's good enough to have done the guy in the chariot and the girl on the bull."

"I'm sure there are a lot of students around here who might have done it. There's nothing unusual about a Halloween prank."

"Throwing a mannequin into a crowd of partygoers is just a prank?" The brown bristles on Ken Parrish's head seemed to rise in tandem with his eyebrows.

"The mannequin is another matter entirely," I pronounced, rather severely.

He leaned back in his wicker armchair, the corners of his mouth downturned. "No kidding?" he drawled.

"Sorry," I muttered, quickly stuffing my big mouth with a couple of chips.

"I realize we hick cops don't rate highly with the Feebs, but it's amazing what we can do when we try real hard. It has actually occurred to me that a mannequin painted by what looks like a four-year-old and a nude woman who almost qualifies as a work of art might not be the work of the same person. Particularly when they appear on the same night and—"

Just to be difficult (and because I was more than a wee bit embarrassed), I burbled, "All three were motiveless."

"As far as we can tell," he amended. "Nonetheless, the mannequin has to be a copycat." Slowly, I nodded. "You're a fed," Ken Parrish reminded me sternly. "I need to know what you know about Billie Hamlin."

"I'm a Feeb," I grumbled.

"You're Aurora Travis, and I like you."

Oh, damn! I struggled to remember there still might be a wife and kiddies . . . and failed.

I finished my Jaeger. In silence, as the sky turned to pink and gold, lavender and rose, and the underside of a thin row of cirrus clouds began to glow like a spaceship in a Sci-Fi film, beaming its rays toward the defenseless earth, Ken Parrish picked up his backpack from the marble floor and poured refills for both of us.

"He was paid," I said. "Two thousand dollars. Two effigies, placed to create a sensation. He burned the envelope and the note that went with it. Please don't arrest him," I burst out as Ken's mouth opened on the inevitable scold for withholding information. "He's been wanting to show the museum how good he was. The temptation was just too much for him."

"He *burned* the note?" Detective Parrish choked.

"He thought it was a prank."

"For two thousand dollars?" he scoffed.

"To some people that's pocket change," I pointed out.

Ken Parrish dropped his head into his hands, swearing softly. "I can't let him walk," he groaned.

"You said, 'Off the record.' "

"So I did." He appeared ready to hurl his backpack (or maybe me) into the bay, perhaps even take a chomp out of the wicker tabletop.

"Okay, so *why?*" he demanded at last.

"Haven't a clue. Neither does Billie. Unless . . ." I stopped. Why bring up almost senseless speculation?

"Well?" Ken demanded.

I told him my theories about old feuds, old debts, a possible desire to cause trouble for the museum just as it had been granted much-needed millions from the state. "Of course, it's more than fifty years since the estate was finally settled," I sighed. "That's a long time for animosities to last."

"You have an 'in' with some of the old-timers?" Ken asked.

"My aunt does."

"Then I wouldn't mind if you'd check it out. See if there are any rumblings among the families who thought they didn't get a fair share of the Bellman settlement." Detective Parrish's gray eyes were limpid, as if he weren't challenging me to get off my duff and do his job for him. A big payoff for a couple of glasses of Jaeger and a bag of chips.

Finally, I nodded.

"So what's your theory on the mannequin?" he inquired, but I caught the twinkle in his eyes. He was pushing it, and letting me know he was well aware of it.

"A second kook," I snapped. "Art-challenged. Perhaps from the Honors College, which is crawling with nerds with strange senses of humor. Or so I'm told."

"More Halloween?"

I shrugged. "What else? All three incidents are senseless."

"Yet someone paid two thousand dollars for two of them."

Right. Of course they had. "Can't you talk to Billie without having to arrest him?" I pleaded.

"I'll try. If worse comes to worst, you might use some of those old-timers your aunt knows to get the museum to go easy on him."

Gratefully, I nodded. "Detective . . . Ken?" He regarded me steadily, with a respect I very much appreciated when I had only the barest thread of confidence left in myself. "There was one other thing—probably totally crazy, a sign of supreme egotism—but it occurred to me the mannequin might have been personal. Aimed at me. I didn't actually see it come down, but I was in the room. The coincidence seems almost too much . . ."

"Tell me." No exclamation, no surprise, no sharp questions. Just a simple request for information from a fellow officer. Could I do it? Break the silence? Without staggering to the Mediterranean-style railing and heaving my Jaeger and chips into the bay?

Make it simple. No long explanations needed. Another cop would understand.

"I went off a fire escape in Philly. From three flights up. My partner and I had tracked a child molester to the apartment. The freak wouldn't give it up. And Rory Travis, with an ego big as a barn, got to the window first. The guy was Mr. Ordinary, you know. It never occurred to me I couldn't handle him. And Eric, my partner, was right behind. My gun was out, I gave the perp a warning. He kept right on going. I know I should have shot him, but I'd never killed anybody . . . I jumped him instead. Really stupid, I know, but I thought I was such a hotshot . . .

"Maybe the guy worked out, maybe he was high on something, but it was like tackling an octopus. There was no way Eric could get off a shot, so he piled on. I've tried to remember, but it's just one big blur, with the three of us bouncing from one side of the fire escape to the other. And then Eric and the perp went over the edge. Eric was hanging by one hand. I grabbed for him, thought I had a good grip. But the perp, who still had one leg hooked around a post, climbed back in. Instead of taking off, he heaved us both over. I'd be dead except for Eric, who took the brunt of the fall. The bastard got away."

"Your partner?"

"He didn't make it."

"You two were tight?"

I nodded.

"Oh, hell, Travis, I'm sorry." Ken Parrish ran his hands

through his buzz cut. He frowned. "But why would anyone want to be so fucking cruel as to remind you of it?"

"I told you, I'm letting ego rule my world. It couldn't possibly have anything to do with me personally. It just seemed that way because that fall looms in my mind night and day."

Ken sat there a moment, glaring at the brilliant beauty of the sunset as if it were a personal affront. "Do you want to bow out of the museum mess altogether?"

"No," I whispered. "I can handle dead mannequins better than dead people."

I was halfway home when I remembered my tram key. At the next break in the median, I did a U-turn and slunk back to the Bellman. Fortunately, the guard at the Security Desk had his back to me, doing something at his computer. I slid the key onto the counter and sneaked back out the door before he could look up. Perhaps he'd think he'd overlooked it earlier.

Brisk, efficient, oh-so-clever Rory Travis, gone all to pieces over bitter memories and a few moments' attention from a City Cop with a kind heart and a crooked smile.

CHAPTER 9

Two days later I was forced to make another raid on Aunt Hy's vintage clothing. Martin Longstreet, that true gentleman of the old school, invited Aunt Hy and myself to the Ritz-Carlton's famous Tea. "In reparation for our appallingly disturbed evening at the Gala," he said. As far as I was concerned, any excuse would do. Aunt Hy had taken me to tea shortly after my arrival last July, and I promise you "Tea" at the Ritz-Carlton is an epic experience.

Today, I chose a slinky thirties dress with scattered pastel flowers that looked as if they had dropped off an Impressionist canvas. It was calf-length, with lots of gores . . . and I found myself wishing Ken Parrish could see me. After all, Josh Thomas already knew what I looked like when I made an effort. And, besides—most annoyingly—Aunt Hy never stopped singing Josh's praises. "An excellent young man," she purred. "So hard to find a real one these days. I just knew I could count on Madame Celestine."

I didn't disillusion her. I didn't tell her that for a girl who wasn't looking—thank you very much—Ken Parrish was a much safer fantasy.

Aunt Hy gilded the lily by selecting a picture hat for me. Its circumference was wider than one of my tram wheels. The hat was navy blue straw and had a matching velvet ribbon trailing down the back. (Shoes, fortunately, were no longer a problem. I had gone shopping and purchased flats in nearly every color of the rainbow.) I stared into the room's full-length mirror (with ornate gilded frame) and saw a slim, almost elegant creature, whose straight brown hair gleamed softly just shy of her shoulders. The green in her eyes seemed to dominate the blue today, providing an extra sparkle of interest. Skin glowed healthily over rather fine cheekbones, and the lips looked positively . . . inviting. I tried to make the corners of my mouth turn down. They refused to move. Let's face it, I looked great. Truthfully, it would have been nice if Ken or Josh—or maybe both—were waiting in the lobby below.

Aunt Hy was still babbling on about Madame Celestine and Josh Thomas as I followed her into the elevator. As we swept into the Tea Room, following the hostess, who was also gowned in a flowered print à la the thirties, I recalled the first time I had been to Tea, when I had hunched my shoulders and made a spectacle of myself, staggering across the bright, sunny room, wearing black slacks, a white shirt, and loafers, and leaning heavily on my aluminum quad cane.

Yes, baby, I'd come a long way. Until this moment, I hadn't appreciated how far.

As we crossed the room, the harpist was playing, a marvelous cascade of sound that made me feel all that music was just for us. Martin rose to greet us, his spare figure emphasized by his height, gray-blue eyes sparkling behind his bifocals and capped by a thick crown of white hair. At his insistence, we ordered the champagne tea, which included a tulip glass of bubbly to add that little something extra. Our choice of teas, however, was as varied as our personalities. Aunt Hy, a creature of habit, chose her perennial favorite, Earl Grey. I, perhaps dazzled by the advent of two men into my life, experimented with something called China Rose Petal. Martin, ever an intriguing man, ordered Lapsang Souchong. Pungent and smoky. It occurred to me that Josh Thomas—if tea ever touched those thin lips—

might also drink Lapsang Souchong. Ken Parrish, I decided, was more of an English Breakfast Tea man.

Three flowered china pots arrived, each carefully set on its own warmer. The hostess poured. Our flutes of champagne appeared next to our bone china tea cups. We sipped, we savored. Then, ignoring good manners, I pounced on Martin. (Fortunately, the harpist had just gone on break, so I didn't feel I was stepping on her exquisite notes.)

November is not yet full Season in Florida, so we had the room almost entirely to ourselves. There was no danger of being overheard. "Martin," I said, leaping straight in, "is there anything going on with the hierarchy at the Bellman that would provide a motive for the effigies?"

His reaction was not at all what I expected. Martin Longstreet was as much the master of the poker face as Josh Thomas and Ken Parrish. But I saw a flicker of something—guilt?— quite clearly. I'd hit a nerve.

"I'm sure you are aware that we seem to have two different factions causing trouble," Martin replied, recovering his smooth façade and neatly deflecting my question.

"Yes." I waited, looking hopeful.

"You do not accept the theory of student pranks?" Martin Longstreet at his most bland. Sunlight, filtering in from the terrace, glinted off his glasses.

"One maybe, even two, but not all three." Not to mention an alleged suicide.

Aunt Hy was watching us, eyes shifting back and forth like a spectator at a tennis match. With precise skill, Martin poured himself another cup of Lapsang Souchong. "Martin," I said, striving for a patience I didn't feel, "have you heard so much as a rumor of anything odd? Anything at all?"

Ignoring his freshly poured tea, he took a healthy swallow of champagne. "There's a bit of a flap with one of the Board members," he conceded. "Nothing that could possibly have anything to do with *papier mâché* or mannequins."

And that, I realized, was all I'd get out of him on the subject. "What about the Bellman family?"

"Richard and Opal had no children," he pronounced. Repressively. Almost as if he were working at giving me a hard time.

"Richard had siblings and associates."

"Rory, my dear, it was a very long time ago. I can't see how any repercussions could have lasted this long."

I opened my mouth and caught a glimpse of the hostess returning with a large three-tiered server. Okay, I can't resist the temptation to make your mouth water. Picture Smoked Salmon on Baby Brioche, Grilled Zucchini and Peppers on Olive Bread, Benne Seed Crusted Chicken Salad on Sourdough Bread, Lemon and Jonah Crab Salad on Pain au Lait, Cinnamon and Ginger Shortbreads, Raspberry Almond Cake, Freshly Baked Scones with Devonshire Cream. And for "dessert," Coffee Opera, Key Lime Pie, Mini Fruit Tarts, Macaroon of the Day, and Jellied Fruit.

The harpist came back, and we floated through the food and lashings of tea to enchanting ripples of music. And then I saw Martin's face go blank, followed by a smile so polished and professional you would have had to know him well to realize he had just spotted someone he disliked. Intensely. Martin excused himself and crossed the room to a couple who had just arrived. Both were early retirement age; the man at least six-three, perhaps mid-fifties; his wife, a forever forty-nine. They were plucked and polished and toned, broadcasting on all frequencies that they belonged only to the most exclusive golf, tennis and country clubs, with the yacht club thrown in for good measure. Motor, not sail, I thought. Sailing might disturb the manicures and the coiffeurs (his as well as hers).

I'd never seen him before, but I recognized *her*. It was the docent who had lodged a complaint over the stroller incident. (I'd received a pat on the back, instead, from the Chief of Security.) At the moment she was so delighted with playing the gracious lady in the Ritz-Carlton Tea Room that she didn't see me for dust. And if she had, I doubted she would have recognized me. She was the type who noticed lesser mortals only when they caused her trouble. Fortunately, her disdain did not extend to Martin Longstreet, a senior member of the Bellman Board of Directors. She was, in fact, practically simpering.

Aunt Hy leaned close. "An awful creature," she sniffed. "Money, but no background, my dear. None at all. I can't imagine what Parker sees in her."

"You know him?"

"Oh, my yes. I've known him since he was born. Good family. Upper East Side, summers on the Cape, winters in Sarasota. Princeton, Wall Street. I believe I heard he started his own company sometime back—perhaps ten or fifteen years ago. And why shouldn't he? He was born with the silver spoon and everything he touched turned to gold. She, however," my aunt declared with asperity, "is a bitch. I'm certain she must mangle her Casa tours quite dreadfully. Her family may be rolling in wealth, but her accent reeks of Brooklyn . . . or perhaps it's the Midwest . . . or Texas." Aunt Hy waved a dismissive hand. "Oil, cattle, cornflakes, something of that kind. Totally declassé, my dear."

Sometimes one forgot Aunt Hy had been a very astute lady for more than a quarter century before I was born. And she was so much a product of another age that she wouldn't even recognize PC as Personal Computer, let alone the more current Politically Correct. I opened my mouth to beg for more dirt, but Martin was coming back, bringing guests. Parker and Melinda St. Clair graciously allowed themselves to be introduced. I enjoyed the brief moment of confusion when she tried to place why I looked vaguely familiar. It didn't last long. Obviously, I was not worth the effort.

We exchanged the customary platitudes and, then, succumbing to an urge to mischief, I announced I drove a tram two days a week at the Bellman. Parker St. Clair displayed the full wattage of his perfectly capped teeth. "Splendid," he boomed. "If only we had more volunteers your age." I had to give him points. There wasn't a hint he considered tram drivers second-class citizens. But then my aunt was Hyacinth Van Horne, which definitely counted for something. And Parker St. Clair was the type who was already speculating on the odds of my inheriting her fortune.

Melinda St. Clair, however, had gone pale. She actually placed her hand on her husband's arm, as if to steer him back to their table. An excessive reaction, I thought, to her belated recollection of the day we had butted heads over a stroller. What had Martin told them? *Come meet Mrs. Van Horne's niece, the FBI agent?* Even so, Melinda St. Clair didn't impress me as a woman who would give two shakes about anything less than an introduction to the President, the First Lady, the British Royal Family, and maybe a duke or two.

Odd. I filed it away, along with the few strange expressions I'd caught from Martin. Josh Thomas was, at that moment, in the same deep, murky place in my mind. Along with worry over Billie and my vague sense of impending doom. For Ken Parrish was right. Two thousand dollars was excessive for a prank, even in the realm of the seriously wealthy.

"He's one of our newer Board members," Martin said as the St. Clairs returned to their Tea. Martin's face was completely unreadable. Which meant there was a great deal he wasn't saying.

I let Aunt Hy and Martin chat over the last fruit tarts while I did some quick free associations. Had Martin produced Josh

Thomas from the old-boy network like a genie out of a bottle—a favor for a friend? (Poor Rory . . . let's see if we can find her a job.) But what kind of a job would it be, if created by the machinations of an octogenarian spook, a Vietnam-era spook . . . and Josh Thomas, the enigma?

Legality, Josh had said, *was occasionally in doubt.*

"Aurora? Aurora, my dear?"

Blindly, my purple-flowered cane sinking into the plush carpet, I got up and followed Aunt Hy and Martin out of the room, nodding politely to the St. Clairs as I limped by. I hated every moment of that walk. I could feel my cool slipping, my face turning red. Melinda, blast her, must be consumed with satisfaction. She was the type to enjoy the imperfection of others.

I'd gotten far less from Martin than I'd hoped. Perhaps if the St. Clairs hadn't come in . . . I made a note to try him again when I could arrange more privacy. Aunt Hy, however, turned out to be a fount of information. I hadn't known her husband's family had wintered in Sarasota since the days when Richard Bellman was one of its most prominent developers. Not only did Hyacinth Van Horne know all the old socialite families, she had a surprising knowledge of that other side of the coin, the circus. *The* Circus. The origin of the Bellman wealth. The tiger tamers and elephant trainers, trapeze artists and daredevils, the horses, poodles, and monkeys. The clowns and skimpily clad girls in a circus version of the Ziegfeld Follies. The managers, vendors, and roustabouts. They'd all wintered in Sarasota and Venice for more than sixty years—until stymied at last by deteriorating rail lines no one could afford to fix. Since the early nineties the Circus Train could get no farther south than Tampa, but Sarasota County clung jealously to its museum, its memories, and something far more tangible—its long roster of circus families.

It was quite possible, Aunt Hy told me, that the county had more circus people per square mile than any other place in the nation. In fact, there was so much talent floating about, one of the local high schools was noted for putting on an amazingly professional circus show each year. So even though the Bellman Circus had moved out of the city of Sarasota to the wide-open spaces of Venice in 1960 and was forced north to Tampa thirty years later, it was Sarasota that claimed it, still benefiting from a Bellman advertising blitz seventy-five years in the past.

If any of the current odd events at the Bellman were rooted in Richard Bellman's past, the circus—which created the basis of his fortune—was the place to look. With Aunt Hy's connections, she was able to arrange an interview with the doyenne of local circus folk, a woman of great age and greater inner strength, who had endured tragedy as well as triumph. A woman whose name was synonymous with Circus. To my surprise, I found her living alone in a modest Florida ranch-style home. Maria Joffa was petite, with intelligent dark eyes snapping under hair of the same color. Only a network of not-so-deeply-etched lines gave away her age. I noted with resignation that her birch cane with lion handle in brass was considerably classier than either of my canes.

Yes, she told me, she'd read about the effigies in the newspaper. No, she could not imagine why anyone would do such a thing. All that risk of being caught . . . and for what? "A high-wire walker knows he is there to entertain," she informed me with some asperity. "The trapeze artists, the clowns, even the elephants understand. It is what we do. It is our life. But to make people of *papier mâché?* To toss a mannequin into a crowd? A *paying* crowd?" She threw up her hands, rippling the long fringe of her cut silk velvet shawl. "This is a risk that makes no sense."

Solemnly, I agreed. This was all I would learn, I knew it, yet I lingered, lapping up the tales elicited by a few simple questions. I heard about marriages between dynastic circus families. Births and deaths, scandals and tragedies, the many attempts to start new circuses—the failures, the occasional struggling successes. But nowhere could I find a single slim thread to tie any aspect of the circus or circus families in Sarasota County to two effigies and a mannequin.

Ninety minutes and three glasses of iced tea later, I thanked Maria Joffa and sloshed back to the Caddy, full of wonder, admiration, and guilt. There was nothing like a peek at other people's sorrows to offer a salutary lesson in objectivity. A kick in the pants, to be perfectly honest. It was almost as if Maria had taken a crowbar in her frail liver-spotted hands and pried open that crack in my icy armor another inch or two. Although circus people were devoted to their art, it was seldom fun and games. It was agonizing practice, cutthroat competition, brilliant moments of triumph punctuated by terror and tragedy. With what arrogance had I let my tunnel vision convince me I was the only person who had ever suffered?

On the drive home I contemplated, glumly, just how little I had accomplished in my efforts to help Billie. I'd struck out with the circus connection, and Ken Parrish had come close to laughing in my face when I'd asked about the ME's report on Tim Mundell's suicide, particularly when I'd brought up the fact that Billie had been the one to hint at murder.

"Tell your rent-a-cop pal to stick to sculpting," Ken scoffed. "Mundell was full of scotch and Prozac—for which he had a legitimate prescription."

"But could he climb a tree in that condition?"

"Kids that age can do darn near anything, given the right incentive."

So I'd shoved the suicide of a twenty-year-old computer nerd from Tempe, Arizona, to the back of my mind. I had enough problems, didn't I? But I have to tell you, that boy's corpse wouldn't lie easy. It dangled in my mind, next to the long brown roots of the banyan, swaying in the breeze off Sarasota Bay. There was something . . . something that wasn't right.

After that flash of conviction that Martin and Josh were up to something more than arranging a job for a cripple, my infamous intuition had gone back into hibernation. So I forged ahead, relying on the tried and true—asking questions.

A few days after my interview with Maria Joffa, I found my way to a very different circus-oriented location. A frame house in one of the oldest parts of town, it was tucked back under a canopy of palms, pines, and a massive jacaranda tree. It appeared to have been built in the heyday of local development in the mid-twenties, and it was a wonder Florida's voracious termites hadn't demolished it long since.

The house was charming. And so was its owner. Daniel Miller was old enough to remember the Circus as it was just after World War II. But his knowledge extended farther back, for his father had been part of the old Circus hierarchy, one of those who knew where all the old bones were buried. Or so Aunt Hy told me.

Smaller and younger than Martin Longstreet, Daniel Miller was, I guessed, in his late sixties or early seventies. His gray hair was balding on top, but his general enthusiasm and attitude would have shamed many thirty-year-olds. I had come to hear about his beloved Circus, and he could hardly wait to show me. Everywhere I looked, the walls were covered by photos, the black-and-whites of every aspect of circus life, interspersed with colorful posters from a bygone age. In the living room, even the ceiling was postered over. I leaned on my cane and gaped.

Daniel Miller was pointing, rattling off names completely unknown to me. I smiled, I nodded. Undoubtedly, I looked as stunned as I was, for he stopped in mid-sentence and said,

"Forgive me, my dear. I should have realized it means nothing to you. You're far too young."

He offered me a seat in an upholstered chair so deep and comfortable I feared I might not be able to get out. He disappeared, returning with a tray of crust-cropped tea sandwiches and tall glasses of iced tea.

"Did you make these yourself?" I asked as I helped myself to what might have been tuna or chicken salad.

"I've done just about everything in my life," he said, with a gentle smile, "including playing at chef. I like to keep my hand in, you know."

I complimented him on both taste and presentation. A beaming smile reflected his pleasure.

Like Maria Joffa, he had heard no rumors, could not even begin to imagine who was playing games with the Bellman. He also agreed that Circus people would never be so petty. Well . . . even Circus people went round the bend occasionally, but the community was tight-knit. If someone was having that kind of problem, he'd have heard. And so would Maria Joffa, he added. If she hadn't known of anyone—

"Would she be covering?" I asked.

Daniel thought about it, shook his head. "I think she would have given you a hint that the problem was being solved. And, believe me, it would have been."

And then he, too, began to tell me stories, his enthusiasm spilling out in a tide of nostalgia spiked by frustration, for Daniel Miller was not only a Circus buff, he was actively trying to raise money for a pet project: the renovation of the railroad car that had been Richard and Opal Bellman's home when they traveled with the Circus. "Do you know where they kept the money?" he asked, eyes gleaming. "In a safe under the bed. Richard slept on it!" Daniel chortled. "Everything was cash then, you know. All that money, and he slept on it." He shook his head. "They spent fifteen million on the Casa Bellissima, and no one is willing to renovate the Bellman rail car. It's sad, it really is."

I agreed, sincerely and wholeheartedly. But that, of course, wasn't why I was here. "You must have heard some of the old scandals of that day," I said. "Could any of them have simmered all these years, then sprouted into the troubles the museum's had these past few weeks?"

He took his time, clearly considering the matter seriously. "Near the end," he said at last, "Bellman made a lot of enemies. The circus was mad at him because all he seemed to think about was the darn museum. The Great Depression was on, and he was cash poor. He owned land and investments everywhere, not just here in Florida, but he owed everybody, including his second wife."

"Second wife?" I burbled, thoroughly shocked. In nearly four months at the museum—not even while auditing the weekly docent classes—had I ever heard a word about Richard Bellman's married life other than raptures about his perfect marriage to Opal.

"Opal's health was poor, she died young. No children. Guess Richard didn't like living alone. He up and married Melba in no time at all. A mistake for both of them. He loved Art, the Circus, and was caught up in developing huge tracts of real estate. She had no interest in any of it. He filed for divorce. Very publicly, I'm told, with no attempt at finesse. Pretty it wasn't."

"Did Melba have descendants?"

Daniel shrugged. "Not by Bellman. As for any other relatives, I just don't know. As I said, if Melba's any indication, Sarasota isn't a place they'd ever want to be."

At last I'd found a scandal large enough to linger, festering, for seventy-five years. I forced myself to sit still and ask more questions, the upshot of which was that Richard Bellman had died owing a lot of money, but many of his investments were sound, and the debts had finally been settled. Some local families might have legends in which Richard Bellman was not a hero, but it was doubtful any of them had reason for such petty revenge against the museum as two effigies and a mannequin disfigured by red nail polish.

I thanked Daniel Miller, and paid my debt for his information. He was abjectly grateful when I promised to speak to Martin Longstreet about the Bellman rail car.

For a moment there, I'd been excited. Then reality set in. A failed, childless marriage three generations in the past and debts that had been settled nearly sixty years ago were poor fodder for motive. And Maria Joffa and Daniel Miller had me almost convinced that the pride and honor of the Circus community would never stoop so low. Harass the Bellman Museum, the Shining Dream of the founder of the Bellman Circus? Never! That left Richard's conflict with his second wife hanging out there on a limb all by itself.

I was still stewing over what I'd learned at nine-thirty that night when the phone rang.

"I'm in line for a rental car," said a voice I recognized instantly. "Will you meet me out front in half an hour? Drive out to the beach?"

The beach. In November. At ten o'clock at night.

I agreed, hung up the phone. Then I went to my closet, lifted down a locked case from the top shelf. I took out my Glock .40, shoved in a clip, and slipped it into the deep pocket of my blue denim jacket.

I was ready for my late-night rendezvous with Josh Thomas.

CHAPTER 10

Josh's car was just another rental, a modest four-door, dark green and inconspicuous. The night doorman, whom I scarcely knew—a sad reflection on my social life—opened the passenger door and flashed a sedate smile as he patiently waited for me to insert my bad leg, my cane, and myself inside. Josh sat there, doing his best human imitation—benign, concerned. Not a trace of bronze satyr, as the doorman wished us a good evening before carefully closing the car door.

We wended our way down the artificial hill, negotiated the new Ringling Bridge construction, crossed a small, mostly manmade island—around here, called a key—and five minutes later we were on the large barrier island that featured one of Sarasota County's primary beaches. Unfortunately, there was a problem. Visions of sitting in the car and gazing soulfully at the Gulf of Mexico disappeared as soon as we pulled into the parking lot.

Since sand and canes do not mix, I had avoided the beach and was unaware it had been reconfigured from the days of my previous visits to Aunt Hy. The picturesque view we anticipated had been transformed into a solid berm of sand, anchored by sea oats, with wooden walkways at intervals, stretching up and over to the Gulf.

"Sorry," Josh said, "I didn't realize—"

"Keep going," I told him, pointing south along the barrier island. "There's a place . . . if they haven't messed with that, too," I ended on a grumble.

At the southern tip of the key we found what vague memory had recalled. A secluded park set down in the midst of a shaggy canopy of Australian pines. Across a narrow strip of water, lights shone from houses on the northern tip of the next barrier island to the south. To our left, far across the bay, the city of Sarasota glowed in a balmy haze of tropical splendor. I pictured the Gulf, dark and menacing all the way to Mexico, and was grateful the city hadn't changed *this* park. Somehow it was the shelter needed at the moment. A place with a soft glimmer of light to offset the darkness. Evidently, Josh felt the same way. I could almost hear his tension draining away.

As we made our way across the crushed-shell parking lot and the heavy carpet of long pine needles, Josh held my free arm firmly. Oddly, I didn't mind. Not only did I need support over the dark, treacherous ground, full of undulating pine roots, but Josh's touch felt right. Which made no sense, because he was a very scary person.

We sat on a wooden picnic bench with our backs to the table, so close to the water we could hear the rush of the current. It was beautiful. Peaceful. I forgot the gun weighing down the right side of my jacket.

"Anybody ever try to swim that?" Josh asked, nodding at the pass between the two islands.

"Only if they're suicidal. There are No Swimming signs posted all over."

"Ah."

For one horrified moment I felt as if I'd waved a red flag in front of a bull. Issued a challenge. I could almost hear the clicks inside his head as the enigmatic Josh Thomas wondered if he should strip and give it a try.

"Guess not," he said. "I'd probably make it."

"That bad?"

"Oh, yeah."

"It must have gone bad fast."

"It went sour before I left. I was just picking up the pieces. Trouble was," he added softly, "there wasn't much left to pick up."

"Can you talk about it?"

Josh's arm, in a classic maneuver, stretched out along the back of the table behind me. Was I being played? I didn't think so. Josh's anguish was all too real.

"I was on the far side of the mountains, somewhere around where the Urubamba drains into the Ucayali—"

The Urubamba ran past Machu Picchu. That much I remembered from one all-too-quick trip to Peru. But I'd heard Aunt Hy talk about the good old days when visitors could attend the Quechua village markets where the only money used was coca leaves piled high in a sack beside each vendor, as they sat on colorful woven blankets laid on hard mountain ground.

"You don't want to hear it," Josh said. "People died who shouldn't have. Sometimes . . . things just happen." His arm closed around my shoulders. "But I don't have to tell you that."

He was good. Very, very good. Was he sincere, or playing me for all he was worth? But a breeze had come up—the tide must have changed—and his arm felt good where it was. It had been a long time . . .

"I'm staying for a while," he said. "I'm overdue for a vacation. I'd already rented a condo when I had to make the trip to the jungle. Hopefully, no more emergencies for a while." The park's tall spotlights, filtered through a web of pine needles, illuminated his pale face, black hair, and onyx eyes. He leaned in, distinctly haunting—and terrifyingly appealing.

"You're staying," I echoed faintly, wondering how it was possible to feel this much physical attraction while the Voice of Doom whispered in my other ear.

"Martin found a villa not far from his," Josh said. "On a

canal. I was hoping"—he broke off, gazing for a moment at the swirling white-capped race between the barrier islands—"I was hoping you might be willing to show me around while I'm here."

"The blind leading the blind?"

"You're four or five months up on me. You must have learned something about the area?"

"You need a girl you can take to the beach. Canes and sand don't mix."

He removed his arm. I was suddenly cold.

"Any more trouble at the museum?" he asked, as if none of our previous conversation had existed.

He was Martin's friend, and I'd been rude. Tonight he had shown me something secret and private. A vulnerability I could not reconcile with the ruthlessness I sensed in him. Yet I feared his power. Not over life and death, but over my own vulnerable self. Josh Thomas could matter to me. Very much. And I wasn't ready for that yet.

So I reminded myself that Martin Longstreet and Aunt Hy sanctioned my acquaintance with this man of mystery. Correction. Were actively promoting a relationship. If I used Josh as a sounding board, what could it hurt? If he was involved in what was happening at the Bellman, the worst he could do was inwardly curl his lip and laugh at me. At best, he might actually be of help. So I told him everything, including the gist of my meetings with the old-timers from the circus. When I was done, Josh Thomas knew as much as I had told Ken Parrish.

"You know it doesn't make sense?" he pointed out after several moments of silence.

"Of course it doesn't make sense," I snapped. "That's why it's so damned aggravating."

"Don't like to be stymied, do you?" he said with what sounded all too close to the smug amusement of a professional hotshot to the poor female cripple.

Blast him! If only I weren't so stiff-necked, so scared of what he could make me feel. And then there was the problem of trust. Was he merely enjoying my frustration or was he gloating because *he* knew exactly what was going on. Certainly, Josh Thomas would not hesitate to hire a sculptor to create effigies. And he was born to play Zorro, wallowing in the thrill of tossing a bloody mannequin into a crowd of Beautiful People. Dashing over rooftops, rappelling sixty feet down into the dark shadows of an octopus-like banyan tree.

The image was so vivid, I sucked in a ragged breath. An intuitive flash? Or was it just my imagination roaring into overdrive?

The beam of a powerful flashlight caught us from behind. "Sorry, folks," boomed a voice out of the darkness, "but this place closes at midnight. Time to get going."

I flushed, swept by all the guilt of a teenager caught parking. Thank God Josh had removed his arm. Thank God we weren't sitting in the car.

"You can open your eyes, Rory," Josh said an instant later. "He's gone."

That wasn't quite true. The park ranger had returned to his car and was waiting patiently for us to leave so he could close and lock the gates.

As we made our way back to the car, Josh leaned in close and hissed, "I just hope he doesn't notice that sag in your jacket pocket."

I ignored him. If I'd done what I would have liked to do to him at that point, we'd have been arrested on the spot.

Josh waved, politely, to the ranger as we drove by. "Armed and dangerous," he murmured provocatively as he continued on down the deserted road, with high-rise condominiums and resort hotels looming along the waterfront to our left. "Just my luck to choose a tour guide who carries concealed."

"And you don't," I taunted.

"But I'm a *boy*," he pronounced, with deliberate exaggeration. "A lean, mean secret agent. You're just a girl with a cane."

I gasped and swung at him. He braked, stopping in the middle of the road. Grabbing both wrists, he held me as immobile as he had that first day in my tram. He leaned in until our noses were nearly touching. "Listen to me, Rory Travis. Stop blaming yourself. Stop feeling sorry for yourself. To tell the truth, I'm glad you broke out the gun. I bet it's been locked up tight for months. Right?" He pressed my arms down on either side of me. "Right?"

"Yes." Grudgingly.

Lights flashed behind us. The park ranger going home.

Josh let go of me, drove sedately down the road as if nothing had happened. "Like it or not," he said, "you're going to be seeing a lot of me in the next few weeks. I was serious about the job offer. But I need the *real* Rory Travis, not her gimpy ghost."

"I'm trying," I wailed, "really I am. Do you think I *want* to be like this?"

"I think you're resisting your physical therapist every step of the way."

Damn and blast. Martin, of course. It had to be Martin, who'd heard it from Aunt Hy, who could never keep her mouth shut about anything.

"You're so guilt-ridden you're entirely useless."

"I am not!"

"Prove it."

"How?"

"Figure out what's happening at the museum."

"You set it up, didn't you? You and Martin? *Give the poor girl something to do, get her hand back in the business.*"

"Actually . . . no," Josh said in a tone that almost had me believing him. "But I'm not above taking advantage of the situation. Go, girl, take it on. I'll even help you if I can."

I thought of Ken Parrish. We'd talked on the phone after my visit to Maria Joffa, met over coffee after my visit to Daniel Miller. Compared to Josh Thomas, he was so *comfortable*. And, truth was, he and Billie Hamlin had beat Josh to it. I was already in this up to my neck.

As we pulled into the *porte cochère* at the Ritz, Josh turned his fathomless black eyes full in my direction. "I suppose you'd bite if I kissed you?" he said.

My stomach flip-flopped. God bless all doormen. The door beside me opened. "Welcome back, Miss." Shiny black shoes, a snappy uniform, and a strong impersonal arm to lean on. I limped with dignity into the brilliantly lit lobby. I did not look back.

Josh disappeared again. Had I hurt his feelings? Impossible. He didn't have any. *You're just a girl with a cane. I need the real Rory Travis, not her gimpy ghost.* I hoped Josh Thomas would crawl back under his rock and stay there. What did I care that he'd been back in town three days now and I hadn't heard a word from him. Not so much as a whisper of his presence, not even from Aunt Hy. Evidently, Madame Celestine was taking a Sabbatical.

Surprisingly, Billie was still patrolling the Bellman grounds in his golf cart. It seems, he told me, that the Museum was more interested in knowing who had hired him than in prosecuting him for the end result. Detective Parrish and the Museum hierarchy were hanging tight, waiting for the other shoe to drop. Since nothing further had happened since the night of the Gala, now almost two weeks in the past, there was hope Billie might find another envelope under his door. Hope, however, was waning. Billie was glum, anticipating the snap of handcuffs. If only he could have made a real contribution, he told me. Just let the bastard send him one more letter and the man was toast.

"Maybe it's a girl," I said, just to be contrary.

Billie perked up, eyes alight. "Her highness, Patricia the Professor," he chortled. "Sly and snotty. Just her kind of gig."

"Motive?" I sighed.

"Maybe her lover split on her. I told you he was something big around here. And there's no spite like a woman scorned, y'know."

I thought about it. Somehow it was too subtle, even for Patricia Arkwright, the sly educator. A scorned woman didn't hire a sculptor to embarrass the museum. She'd be more direct. She'd go after the man himself. And, besides, in spite of her prickly personality, I'd gotten the impression she enjoyed her job. Patricia Arkwright biting the hand that fed her didn't rate high on my list of theories.

When I told Billie as much, he shrugged and said, "Hey, I'm desperate here. I wake up at night to the clang of bars slamming shut."

"I take it no one's told Security," I said.

Billie placed his palms together, raised his eyes heavenward. "God and Detective Parrish are merciful," he declared. "Just the cop, the Director, the Deputy Director, and the Chairman of the Board know. If I'm lucky and we get this mess cleared up, I may even get to keep my job, as well as stay out of jail."

"Good luck," I said. He waved and zoomed off toward the rose garden. I continued my long walk from the tram barn to the primary tram stop. Now that the weather topped out at around seventy-five degrees each day, there was no excuse to cadge a ride. My rotten miserable SOB therapist said I should walk. So I walked.

It was not one of my favorite days. Two tour buses arrived together, at least half their passengers convinced a seven-passenger tram could carry ten—and not hesitant about saying so. There was something about tour groups, I decided, that prompted inimical thoughts of a mob psychology course I had once taken.

By five-thirty I was frazzled and thinking of Jody and the glass of Glenlivet on ice that would miraculously appear as soon as I walked in the door.

God bless Aunt Hy.

I am not, I have to admit, a morning person. Yes, my job had required early hours when in the office, but I had reverted quite nicely to my inclination toward being a night owl. Sleeping in, I'd discovered, was one of the few advantages to being an invalid. So I wasn't thrilled, when I picked up the shrilling phone the following Sunday morning, to see my digital clock proclaiming the hour as 7:00 a.m. Burt, the tram boss, was apologetic when he heard my sleepy mumble, but one of the drivers had called in sick. Could I be there by nine-thirty?

Now that I was up, I could have been there by seven-thirty I told him, possibly a bit tartly. He promised, gently, not to call me again before eight.

Needless to say, I arrived at the Bellman well before the appointed hour. Betty, one of the Circus Museum's security guards was just unlocking the door as I drove past. Instead of continuing on to the tram barn, I slammed on my brakes and zipped into the small staff parking lot next door to the Circus. Why stop that particular morning? I would always wonder. But it was only nine o'clock, and I'd been through the Circus Museum only twice before. It seemed a perfect opportunity to take another look.

Yet my sudden urge to visit the Circus might have been more than that. My odd, erratic gift—call it intuition, empathy, whatever—seemed to be making a comeback. *By the pricking of my thumbs . . .*

125

Betty and I chatted for a moment, then I headed straight for the main room, the one with all the old circus wagons, once drawn by teams of horses as the Bellman Circus announced its presence by a parade through countless heartland towns. To me, these were the embodiment of the circus, of the wonder and grace that could never quite be the same after the advent of the combustion engine.

Wrapped in my customary early-morning funk, still vaguely resentful of lost sleep, I charged past the miniature circus, whose animation and sound system had not yet been activated for the day, slowing only when I reached the brilliantly colored wagons. It struck me, for the first time, that they were arranged in a nearly closed circle reminiscent of old movies with the Conestogas circled against imminent attack, as if protecting the miniature circus in their center.

I wandered past a fourteen-foot cage on wheels, painted bright green with ornate gilded trim, its four battered rubber wheels revealing its many miles across America. I wondered what animals had once paced within. Lions, tigers, bears, monkeys? Next was the red calliope cart, with jesters dancing on its sides, an open window offering the public a glimpse of its mechanized innards. There were enclosed wagons that must have carried equipment, one guarded by gilded griffins, in high relief. Its iron-rimmed wheels were painted to resemble a sunset. The huge band wagon, decorated with five classically clad ladies, one in danger of losing the top of her gown—I wondered how that had played in the heartland—, was topped by scrolled bench seats for the musicians. The bass drum was still in place at the rear.

I stood, gazing up at those seats high above my head and pictured the circus parading down the main street of some fair-to-middling town in the Midwest. It had to have been the single most exciting thing that happened in a farming community dogged by hard work from dawn to sunset. The boom of the drum, the blare of the brass, echoed by trumpets from the elephants, the roar of a lion, the cries of the barkers.

Was it a simpler time, a time to be envied? Or should we think of all the progress we'd made? Of diseases wiped out, distances conquered? While so many things—war, poverty, tragedy—remained the same.

Mentally, I snapped my shell back around me, struggled to zip it tight, like the plastic rain curtains on my tram. Philosophy and introspection I didn't need. Like those twelve-step programs, I needed to live one day at a time. Slogging on and letting the world take care of itself. Analysis by Rory Travis was not needed.

I should have seen it, smelled it, of course, the minute I came through the door. But it was only now, as I moved on around the circle of wagons that I saw the blood. Pooling on the cement floor that had once held Richard Bellman's Pierce Arrows and a Rolls Royce. Anger flared. *Billie, you wouldn't!*

No, he wouldn't. And, besides, this didn't look or smell like paint. Or fingernail polish.

Perhaps three seconds for the above thoughts to chase through my mind. I raised my eyes. And knew immediately what I was seeing wasn't an effigy or a mannequin. On the floor of a large white cage a woman was sprawled, facedown, wearing nothing but blood. A knife with carved ivory handle was sticking out of her back. From a pool of red beneath her body a slow-moving rivulet of blood dripped off the edge of the cage floor onto the broad nose of a gilded griffin flaring out from the side of the cage below, some splashing into its open mouth, staining the sharp white teeth, before falling to the floor.

It should have been Patricia, I thought. She was the only young woman who worked in this building. But this woman wasn't blond. Her long dark hair, like the effigy of Lygia, was sprawled across the cage floor. Although her face was turned toward the rear, I found an angle along the bars and used my cane as a prop so I could rise on the tip of my one good foot. Ungainly but efficient.

Oh, dear God! It was Lydia. Dear sweet Lydia, who could not possibly have had an enemy in the world. Lydia, whom Billie adored. Or said he did.

Billie Ball Hamlin . . . who had just gone from the frying pan into the fire.

I knew death when I saw it, but I stretched my hand through the bars and checked her pulse anyway. Not so much as a flicker of life. Then I walked back out to the lobby and told Betty. As she rushed by me on her way to the wagons, a victim of stunned disbelief, I grabbed her walkie-talkie and called the Security Desk.

After the golf carts began piling up outside, I told the Chief of Security where he could find me and went off to do my job. It was nine-fifty, and visitors were already coming down the incline toward the tram stop. I told the other two tram drivers what was going on. Hastily, we revised our route and our speeches.

We're so sorry, but the Circus Museum will be closed today.

And then I remembered that Josh Thomas was back in town.

CHAPTER 11

I kept expecting my cell phone to ring. Twice, while waiting for passengers to load, I checked to make sure the battery was still strong. It was. Evidently, I was last on Detective Parrish's list.

Each time I took the back road that bypassed the Circus Museum, I got a full panoramic view—across a hundred feet of green lawn—of the lineup of police cars and unmarked law enforcement vehicles filling the narrow concrete ribbon of my usual route. And, as if that weren't enough, I had to field the inevitable questions from my passengers. While my head seethed with questions and my mouth spouted platitudes ("an accident of some kind," I kept repeating, "just an accident"), I was certain of only one thing—the serenity of The Richard and Opal Bellman Museum of Art had been brutally shattered. Tim Mundell's suicide had been only a nagging blip on my early-warning radar. The effigies, the mannequin, *nothing* had prepared us— prepared even me, who was accustomed to violence—for Lydia's murder.

So what now? I could pop back into my shell and lock the lid down tight. Or I could punch my way through the breach that was already there.

Panic dictated I wasn't ready, wasn't strong enough. In mind or in body.

Reality dictated I didn't have a choice.

Fortunately, there isn't much time for reflection when you're driving—wasn't that why I liked this job? Yet I had no trouble picturing Billie in an interview room at police headquarters with Ken Parrish and another hotshot or two trying to tear him to pieces. No wonder Ken hadn't yet gotten around to me.

Less fortunately, I happened to be driving by when the body bag came out. There was a massive pregnant silence from my passengers. "Heart attack," I lied, hoping none of them had been aboard earlier when I'd mentioned the word "accident."

Shortly after, I turned over my tram to my replacement, who had already heard the news. When I got to my car, Ken Parrish was not waiting for me. Odd. I had been almost certain he would be. After all, I'd found the body, hadn't I? I recalled my vision of Billie in an interrogation room. Not so odd. It wasn't too soon for Ken and Company to be pinning Billie's hide to the wall.

When I drove off the museum grounds, I turned directly south along the shore road, cruising through one of Sarasota's finest neighborhoods, a mix of mansions built in Richard and Opal Bellman's time, of more modest homes erected in the fifties and sixties, and imposing Mediterranean Revival edifices built in the past ten years, after homes from earlier times had been bulldozed to the ground. For a while, the soothing blanket of beauty worked; but, in the end—just like life—reality triumphed. I was dumped back on the ugliness of the Tamiami Trail and fought rush-hour traffic all the way out to Pelican Key. Eventually, however, I found myself sitting at the picnic table I'd shared with Josh Thomas. Today, the sun was overhead, sparkling off the slight chop in the pass between the keys. The temperature was in the mid-seventies, and I had to remind myself it was almost Thanksgiving. There was a scattering of cars at the west end, near the wooden walk-over to the Gulf, but the area where I was sitting boasted one lone fisherman and a mother watching a toddler play in the sand.

A good place to think. So, since I wasn't ready to think about me, I thought about Lydia Hewitt instead.

On the day after the Roman charioteer first shook the Bellman's serenity, I had tried to talk to Billie. All I'd gotten from him were the glow of dancing blue eyes and a self-satisfied smirk. So I'd made a few inquiries and discovered where in the museum Lydia usually could be found. Unfortunately, it was in the offices high above the Art Museum entrance. I'd opened the door to the narrow staircase and groaned. Did I really want to do this?

I'd grabbed both handrail and cane in a death grip and started up.

The second flight of stairs was reached only by crossing a small room and attacking steps leading in a totally different direction. Sighing heavily, I slogged on. (I swear the place was designed by Escher.) I was eyeing a third flight of steps with considerable anguish when I spotted Lydia on the far side of the large open room on the third floor. The ambiance of the room itself was an anomaly. Nearly every worker I encountered at the Bellman was mid-fifties and up. This entire expanse was filled with a bevy of young ladies, all seemingly thin, lovely, and impeccably groomed. Well, of course. This was Marketing. What better bait to use when attempting to extract money from wealthy patrons, so many of whom were male?

I took a moment to admire the other view. Since I was at least ten feet from the nearest window, I could do so without my heart doing anything worse than continuing to pound from my first stair climbing in seven months. The view was spectacular. The entire central courtyard of the museum, with its terraces, statues and fountains, spread out before me. At the far end, *David* stood sentinel, with a broad sweep of green lawn and the turquoise blue of Sarasota Bay behind him. Pelican Key was a low-lying ribbon in the distance, its skyline pushing up at irregular intervals into high-rise condos. Let's face it, I thought. If a girl had to spend her time on the telephone, asking people for money, this was surely the most inspiring place to do it from.

"Rory!" Lydia stood beside me, looking anxious. "What are you doing here? You shouldn't have climbed all those stairs."

I was inclined to agree with her, but concern for Billie had forced me to it. "What's up there?" I asked, nodding toward the next flight of stairs.

"The *aerie*," she whispered with a grin. "If you think our view's good . . ." She rolled her eyes.

I knew a bit of spicy gossip when I heard it. "Do tell," I hissed, with a matching wicked grin. Lydia beckoned me to follow her to her desk in a rear corner.

"Well," she said when we were both seated, "rumor has it one of the curators had an apartment up there *way back when*. It even had a kitchen and, of course, a bathroom. It's a VIP office now, only we almost never see anyone go up there." Her color high, Lydia played with a pencil on her desk, peeked at me from beneath her long lashes. "Naturally, we've all been up there a time or two."

Sure she had. And she quickly confirmed the visions of my all-too-lively imagination.

"There's a living room overlooking the courtyard, a bedroom that's mostly all bed," Lydia said with a suggestive waggle of her eyebrows. "A bathroom and an alcove kitchen with a little sink and a microwave. 'Course anybody'd have to tromp straight through Marketing to get up there, so I guess it doesn't really get used. At least not during office hours." She shrugged, then spoiled her wide-eyed innocence with a naughty wink.

I laughed, as I was supposed to. Somehow I hadn't realized Lydia had both spunk and humor. I liked her and was beginning to understand why Billie liked her, too.

But I'd climbed those blasted stairs for a reason. One Roman warrior didn't seem like such a heinous crime, but I didn't want to see Billie mess up his life over a prank.

"Lydia, I know you and Billie set sparks off each other," I said, "but how well do you really know him? Do you think he could have made that Roman charioteer?"

Just that fast, her eyes turned cold. "Of course not," she retorted. "Why ever would he?"

"Hey, I'm on his side," I said. "I want to help, but I need to know if he's good enough to have made that effigy. I mean, it's very well done. Somehow it doesn't seem like a guy who dives for golf balls would be good eno—"

She took the bait. "He is, too, good enough!" Lydia declared. "Billie has real potential, that's what the instructor says."

"You're a student, too?" I asked.

Lydia laughed. "I model," she told me. "For both art and sculpture. Just part-time, of course. That's why I work here as well."

Hm-m-m. Maybe Billie hadn't been as out of line as I'd thought when he'd asked her to model for him.

"So Billie could have made the Roman warrior?" I asked.

"Could have. I didn't say he did."

"You haven't heard him bragging about it?"

"Not a word." She looked me straight in the eye.

Now—too late—it began to make sense. Billie had been well paid to keep silent. With ordinary student pranks, the truth always leaks out, as what's the fun if no one else knows you did it? It takes serious money to buy silence.

Billie had been paid to create two incidents. Incidents that somehow had to be related to Lydia's death. Pure coincidence between the effigies and Lydia's death would be way over the top.

So now we had a motive for the effigies. Billie Ball Hamlin had been set up as a fall guy, a patsy, or any other name you want to use for an idiot neatly framed, wrapped, packaged, and tied in a bow for the Sarasota police. Billie who had also had the misfortune to find a young suicide hanging from a tree.

And Lydia—bright, bubbly Lydia—was gone. With absolutely no hint of any personal reason. As long, that is, as I clung to the notion that continued rejection had not snapped Billie's artistic temperament.

The mannequin incident, however, remained a mystery. As well as why anyone would want to harm Lydia Hewitt. What had she known that could have gotten her killed? Certainly, nothing as innocuous as knowledge of Billie sculpting two effigies in *papier mâché*. Had she seen something? Heard something up in that fourth-floor aerie, perhaps?

Or had she been in the wrong place at the wrong time? Encountered a madman, a random act of violence? Making her death coincidental to Billie Ball Hamlin receiving payment in advance of two thousand dollars?

Not likely.

A robbery attempt gone wrong? The Art Museum and the Casa Bellissima were packed full of priceless objects.

Again, professionals who tossed out twenty Ben Franklins to set the stage for a robbery didn't do something stupid like carving up an innocent young woman with a hunting knife.

My cell phone rang. I swallowed hard, dragged myself back to Pelican Pass. By now I recognized the number on the screen. "Good afternoon, Detective," I said in my best, crisp Special Agent–voice.

"Can you meet me at Mike's Place at seven?" It was as close to a bark as I'd ever heard from Ken Parrish. "I'll buy you dinner," he added, just as ungraciously.

In spite of the tone, it was the best offer I'd had in a long time, but at the moment Detective Sergeant Kenneth Parrish was the Enemy. I had no choice, however. Dinner at Mike's Place, which was far more elegant than it sounded, was a vast improvement over being interrogated in some windowless room at the local Police Central. I agreed to meet him. Truth to tell, I was rather looking forward to it.

When I got home, Aunt Hy was all excited. Martin Longstreet had invited us to a concert at the Bellman. I opened my mouth to tell her about my day and realized, in the nick of time, it would be cruel and inhuman punishment. She would find out, of course. She read the newspapers faithfully each morning. And Martin would tell her. But where, I wondered, during a day in which Bellman Board members' lives must have been seriously disturbed, had Martin found time to issue a concert invitation? I found out on Aunt Hy's next breath.

"Martin didn't call himself, dear. It was that nice young man we met at the Gala." She smiled, conspiratorially. "Tall, dark, handsome. The one Madame Celestine told me about. You should wear something sexy, child. He's a hunk."

I closed my eyes and attempted to control my breathing. I was trying to put my life back together, and the very sky seemed to be raining problems. Billie Ball Hamlin, Ken Parrish, even murder I might be able to handle—Josh Thomas was another story altogether.

"A Celtic harpist," Aunt Hy gushed. "You know how you love Celtic music, Aurora. It will be a lovely evening."

"Yardarm time," Jody Tyler announced, thrusting a scotch into my hand.

"You are a treasure," I hissed out of the corner of my mouth as she zipped back toward the kitchen.

"Tomorrow night," Aunt Hy said as she drifted off toward her bedroom. "Choose something lovely to wear. Martin thinks highly of the dear boy, and Martin is an excellent judge of character."

Dear boy. I choked on my Glenlivet, so much so I had to grope my way to the couch and sit down, still coughing. Jody came running from the kitchen, with good old Marian right behind. Lord, how I hated people hovering, still thinking of me as an invalid! After one last hacking cough, I wiped my eyes and told Marian, with as much dignity as I could muster, that I would not be home for supper.

"Mr. Thomas is it?" she asked, eyes alight with romance. (There were no secrets around Aunt Hy.) Jody, still clutching a dish towel, looked just as eager.

"No," I growled. "I'm being interrogated by the Sarasota Police Department."

Only after I said it did I realize I had unnecessarily hurt two people's feelings. For some reason Marian Edmundson and Jody Tyler cared about me. They wanted me to have a date. Be like other women my age. I muttered an apology and fled to my room.

So what does a has-been Feeb wear for a purely professional meeting with a Sarasota City Cop? Detective Parrish had never seen me in anything but my tram garb. Maybe it was a good thing my parents had gone to Philly and packed up nearly every stitch I owned. Hangers whizzed along the rod as I sought one particular little black dress. Jody had unpacked the boxes Mom sent; I hadn't really looked at any of my dresses since . . .

My fingers paused on the shoulder of the little black dress. I backed away, staggering like a drunk at closing time, my mind filled with kaleidoscope visions of other times and places. I'd never wear that dress again. Maybe I should Goodwill the lot of them. No wonder I'd been letting Aunt Hy doll me up in vintage gowns.

I settled for black slacks and a teal silk sweater. At least it wasn't as drab as my tram garb. I'd just learned a bitter lesson. It was going to be a long time before any man could find so much as a sliver of space in my damaged heart.

Mike's Place is a waterfront snack shack that grew with the times. Downstairs is a bar with a large outdoor dining terrace. The second floor and its spectacular view is reserved for more elegant dining. Ken Parrish was waiting and ushered me onto the sidewalk the moment the valet attendant slipped behind the Caddy's wheel. "Out or in?" he asked.

I paused, testing the nip in the evening sea breeze. I'd now been in Florida long enough to adapt my notions of chilly. "In," I told him. Ken promptly turned us toward the elevator to the second floor. The appreciative once-over he gave me just before we turned was not the attitude of a detective to a witness. Nor was it the conscious look of a married man taking another woman out to supper. I was still indulging in a secret little smile when the elevator opened onto the second-floor dining room.

On three sides, behind the expanse of white tablecloths, gleaming silverware, and glimmering candles, was a breathtaking view of Sarasota Bay. Lights shone from many of the boats anchored just off shore, as if they'd been placed there solely to provide us with a picturesque view. Beyond them, also on three sides, were a myriad lights from houses, condos, hotels, and the arch of the bridge out to Pelican Key. I had not been to Mike's Place since a visit to Florida many years ago. It was hard to tear my eyes from the view long enough to read the menu. When I did, I blinked. Obviously, Mike's Place had increased its prices along with its size and the quality of its chef.

"We'll go Dutch," I said.

"Expense account," he drawled.

Sure it was. Sarasota City Cop with an expense account. Ha! We ordered drinks. "Tell me about Billie," I said, forgetting who was supposed to be asking the questions.

"We twisted his thumbs, sent him home. He knows he's not to make any sudden trips."

"He adored that girl."

"Love. Hate." Ken shrugged. "A girl like that. Taking it all off every day for a bunch of student artists. That's a lot of temptation."

"But she wasn't like that!" I hissed, wishing we were having this conversation in private where I could have the satisfaction of shouting at him.

"She was an artists' model."

"So her greatest talent," I mocked, "was being able to sit still for long periods of time. Since when is that a crime?"

"She's dead," Ken said, as if poor Lydia's demise proved his point.

"And I thought you were different—" I snapped my mouth shut as our Guinness arrived, suitably "built" with only a narrow layer of foam on top. I took a swallow, then wondered, idiotically, if I had a foamstash on my upper lip. A patently ridiculous position from which to scold a cop—City, County, State, or Fed.

Ken's face seemed to have permanently disappeared behind his mug. I wiped my napkin over my mouth, tried again. "She was an artists' model, so she deserved what she got," I sneered.

But the City Cop wouldn't fight. "Would you have any idea why Billie is so determined not to say where he was last night?"

"Some people actually stay home, sleep in their own beds."

"We found someone who called Billie at eleven and got no answer. His voice mail recorded the time."

I squirmed, finally deciding an illegal alibi was better than no alibi at all. "He was probably communing with an alligator," I mumbled.

"Say again?"

So I told Ken about Billie's alternate source of income. "He told me he goes out almost every night. The money's surprisingly good. He didn't really need the two thousand he got paid for the effigies."

Ken plunked his mug onto the table and glared at me. "You're slipping, Travis. Hasn't it occurred to you maybe no one paid him at all? Hamlin was just setting a scenario for paying the girl back?"

"He wouldn't! Never." I stopped, thought about it. "All right," I said, "I concede almost anyone can snap if the conditions are right, but premeditated murder? Billie? No way!"

Time out as our salads arrived. It occurred to me I really didn't want to fight while dining out on baked stuffed shrimp. I took a deep breath. "Tell me," I said, "are you getting extra traffic in the Evidence Room since the effigies were added?"

Light warmed Detective Parrish's gray eyes. Humor? Relief? Probably both.

"Lots of traffic," he assured me, straight-faced. "But it's all right. We've got the Roman guy standing guard over the naked girl."

I tried to picture the two nearly life-size effigies in the property room, alongside the array of weapons, drugs, and sundry other evidence. A startlingly real girl, in full color, wearing nothing but rope and an occasional flower . . . yes, I bet both cops and staff were wearing a path to that part of Cop Central.

In unspoken agreement Ken and I finished our meal to the accompaniment of small talk. But, unfortunately, the harmony didn't last long. We got into it again over coffee.

As we settled down to talking about Lydia's murder, things went well enough at first. I went, step-by-step, through my discovery of the body, recalling things that surprised me. Like the padlock on the cage door. The strength that would have been needed to boost the body into the cage four feet above the floor. The lack of a blood trail. "She was killed there," I said, "but I'm willing to bet you'll find she was drugged. No way could anyone have gotten her into that cage alive any other way."

Ken nodded. "Almost surely a man. With access to keys. Like a security guard," he added.

And we were off again, acrimony flying. No way had Billie killed Lydia Hewitt.

My initial impression, the day I met Detective Sergeant Ken Parrish, had been right. Behind his Everyman face was a very hard head. As he handed me into the Caddy, I very much doubted I had convinced him Billie Ball Hamlin was being framed.

CHAPTER 12

Surprisingly, after my posh but rocky interrogation by Ken Parrish at Mike's Place, Josh Thomas was a welcome relief. On the night of the Celtic harp concert at the Bellman, his charcoal pinstripe suit might have looked more at home in New York or Chicago and his sculpted saturnine features might have stepped out of a vampire movie, but he wasn't glaring at me or asking questions I didn't want to answer. He was, in fact, cool, contained, and only as polite as good manners dictated. In an all-too-feminine reaction I despised, I found myself itching to prod him into something more. Maybe even something like the open interest displayed when he'd peered down my décolletage that night at the Gala.

But I didn't, of course. We both had our pride. We sat stiffly, side by side on folding chairs, while the harpist filled the hall with glorious music and wall-sized paintings by Rubens looked down on the crowd of beautiful people, almost as if gleaming with approval. As if to say, this was the way art should be displayed, not just as an object hanging on a wall while people walked by and gawked, but as part of a living environment, where sometimes great art is merely a backdrop for other aspects of fine living.

I have a weakness for Celtic music, so my mood was mellow when we arrived back at the Ritz-Carlton. I didn't even consider protesting when Josh winkled me away from Martin and Aunt Hy, shepherding me straight into the Cà d'Zan lounge. This time we sat on a cozy couch set at a right angle to the terrace and marina outside. In the dim light Josh's hair still managed to gleam blue-black, a darker hue than the oxidized surface of *The Sleeping Satyr*, supposedly transported to Tallahassee for cleaning. His eyes, however, were as blank. But not sightless. Oh, no, never that. Josh Thomas missed nothing.

"Your friend's gotten himself in major trouble," he said. "Any chance he did it?"

"No." I scowled.

For the first time that evening Josh unbent a little. His dark eyes projected a slight warmth, instead of swallowing every sign of emotion whole. "Loyalty," he mused. "I like that in a woman."

I ignored the remark. "If Billie were going to kill someone, he wouldn't have called attention to himself by creating those effigies."

"Crime of passion," Josh countered. "He was trying to impress her. It backfired."

"No way."

Josh leaned back against the end of the Persian-patterned sofa and threw down the gauntlet. "All right, Ms. Travis, what's your theory?"

"Billie was set up. Very neatly. Why, I don't know. But I have a horrible feeling Lydia's death may be part of something more. I'm waiting for the other shoe to drop."

For a moment Josh stared down at his perfectly manicured fingernails. "Interesting," he murmured. "On our way over here tonight Martin said almost exactly the same thing."

I pounced on his admission. "I think Martin knows more than he's telling. Has he said anything?"

"Not a word."

"You're the secret agent man," I said. "Are you sure this has nothing to do with something you're working on?"

Secret agent man. And he didn't even blink.

"I'm between jobs. On vacation. Remember?" he added on a taunting note. *Remember I asked you to show me around. And you turned me down. Remember that's why I'm being so damn cool tonight. I got dragged on this date kicking and hollering.*

Well, so had I!

Not quite. Hell, I *love* Celtic harpists.

"You could help," I said, leaning in, my elbows on the table. "I'm theorizing on instinct, but I think Martin knows something. And you'd probably have better luck finding out what it is." I proffered a slow smile. "Busman's holiday," I said.

"That would make two of us," Josh pointed out.

A neat reminder neither one of us had any legal right to be investigating a murder at the Bellman.

"She was a nice girl," I said. "Yesterday's newspapers called her an 'experienced artists' model.' They made her sound like a whore when she was just a sweet-faced kid, not a day over twenty-three. And Billie being brought in for questioning came out sounding like he was an art student transformed into Jack the Ripper by the sight of all that naked flesh."

"Bible Belt," Josh intoned. "I imagine a lot of people around here have trouble dealing with the concept of naked models."

"This is the cultural capital of Florida," I snapped. "A sophisticated city."

"Scratch the surface," Josh said, and shrugged. "Think positive. It's unlikely your friend will get to meet Old Sparky. The jury will recognize the Temptation of Jezebel and only give him Life."

"That's horrible," I breathed. "Both Lydia and Billie deserve better than that. She was a darling, he's being framed, and I'm going to find out why."

Josh actually smiled. Lightly, he applauded. "*Bravissima,* Rory. I actually see a spark of life in you." He held up his hand to stop my sputtering retort. "Truthfully, I'm finding vacationing without the charming guide I'd thought to have a bit of a bore. So—on the condition you come clean with me, share everything you know, think you know, or even suspect might possibly be true—I'll help. I'll work on Martin, snoop around, do what I can."

I must have looked highly skeptical for he added, "I'm on *your* side. The whole thing's too pat. There's a puppet master somewhere, pulling strings in a very complex performance. I agree that what we've seen so far is maybe only the Prologue."

Let's face it. I was drawn to the man. Wary, but fascinated. There were depths in him I couldn't understand, places I feared to go. Josh was Life . . . and Death. I should be terrified, but . . .

I'd sensed the inevitability of this moment from that first zap of lightning.

I took a chance.

So we settled in and put our heads together. Me and my Awakened Satyr. Only when I woke in the wee hours to my familiar nightmare of falling, falling, falling, did I think to wonder if I'd spent the evening with the very clever Puppet Master himself.

Effigies, mannequins, and murder aside, each day since mid-October, activity at the Bellman Museum of Art had increased as the Snowbirds returned from Up North. As visitors, eager to see the newly renovated Casa Bellissima, increased, so did the tram traffic. In addition, Thanksgiving and Christmas would bring an explosion of visiting family members, to be followed by the height of the Winter Season in January, February, and March. Not surprisingly, a fourth driver—newly retired—had just been assigned to my Friday afternoon shift. His name was Rob Varney, and I met him two days after the concert in the Rubens' galleries.

Rob was early retirement age, still on the sunny side of sixty.

A good-looking man with a tan that suggested golf courses, sailing, or fishing, but, somehow, he was as far from a Parker St. Clair as a man could get. There was nothing false about Rob. He had a firm handshake, and his eyes smiled as well as his mouth. He even had the grace to flirt just a little, enough to show he was aware I wasn't just another one of the guys. I liked him immediately. There was no doubt he'd make an expert meeter and greeter for the Bellman.

Rob Varney did have one startling attribute. He looked remarkably like a twenty-first-century version of Richard Bellman, as compared to Bellman's full-length portrait at a similar age, which now hung in the Casa Bellissima. Both were tall, sturdy men with round faces and dark wavy hair, only slightly shot with gray. When I remarked on the resemblance, Rob looked genuinely surprised. Later, after he'd seen the portrait, he'd admitted to the resemblance, but swore it was coincidental. I, of course, continued to wonder.

Late in the afternoon, when it seemed our visitors had all gotten where they wanted to go, I pulled up behind Rob's tram at the Art Museum stop. He unfolded from his tram and came back to talk to me. He'd heard I'd been present at a number of crucial moments in the past few weeks, and would I tell him about it? His curiosity was natural, I thought, so I went through the whole thing, sticking, like *Dragnet,* to just the facts and leaving out my speculations. Rob nodded, seeming to absorb the complex tale with ease.

"Were you a cop?" I asked.

A slow smile spread across his broad face. "No—just insatiably curious. I'm here because four months of retirement had me climbing the walls. Though I have to admit when I trained to drive a tram, I didn't expect to have to keep an eye out for dead bodies."

He had a point.

"It's a bit odd, isn't it?" he added. "The mannequin and a naked effigy on the same night?"

"Definitely. The mannequin may have been a genuine prank," I offered, once again feeling nausea rise at the recollection of all those shattered pieces.

Rob Varney was quick. "And you think the effigies weren't?" he challenged.

I shrugged. I had not, of course, told him about the two thousand dollars. I had not mentioned Billie at all.

He straightened up, slowly scanned the grounds, which looked as perfectly quiet and peaceful as they always did. "Murder at the Bellman," he murmured. "It seems so very out of place. Makes me wonder what could possibly be so important that a young woman had to die for it."

"Crime of passion?" I found myself parroting Ken Parrish. "There doesn't seem to be much else for a motive."

"Maybe there's a nut running around out there staging murder as a work of art."

"The Roman warrior doesn't fit."

"Trial run? Just to see how easy it was to get past Security?"

The mannequin had had her throat slit. The Lygia effigy had been gored—totally against the story. In *Quo Vadis* Lygia is saved by a Christian bull-thrower who rescues the maiden from Nero's wrath and gains the sympathy of the volatile Roman crowd in the Coliseum. Billie's only excuse for this striking rearrangement of Sienkiewicz's plot? Halloween. Most likely, he'd never heard of *Quo Vadis*.

And then Billie's model—however *in absentia* she might have been when the effigy was created—Lydia, bright, bubbly Lydia, who only wanted a good time—had been gouged with a knife and arranged, not without artistry, behind the bars of a lion's cage.

"The art of murder?" I muttered. Surely not. But it was an

idea that grabbed the imagination. Were we dealing with a plot that made no sense because we were dealing with insanity?

Rob looked up to discover three passengers patiently waiting in his tram. "Later," he called, and galloped off, his broad back a bit hunched, revealing his embarrassment at his lapse his first day on the job. *His* lapse? While Rob and I had schmoozed, four passengers had climbed aboard mine. "Everybody in?" I put my foot down, and off we went.

Nice may be considered an inadequate word, a cop-out, but it described Rob Varney very well. He was definitely going to enliven Friday afternoons. And after the stress engendered by the three younger men who had so recently entered my life, Rob was a relief. Since I'd just taken Ken Parrish off the Safe list and I had quite a few doubts about Martin Longstreet's oh-so-smooth grandfatherly façade, Rob was a welcome acquaintance. As for Billie Ball Hamlin and Josh Thomas, on a Stress Level scale of one to ten, they each rated an eleven.

The next day I called Ken and asked him to meet me on the terrace at the Casa Bellissima. "Could it be a nutcase?" I asked, when I'd finished relating my conversation with Rob Varney. "I mean murder as art is sick enough to make some kind of weirdo sense."

Ken eyed me with what I can only describe as extreme tolerance. "Travis," he said, "I'm willing to grant that no truly sane person creates a Roman warrior, a naked woman dripping blood, then carves up his would-be girlfriend and locks her in a lion cage. But we know Hamlin made the effigies, we know he had his eye on Lydia, we know she rejected him. Just what part of these *facts* does not add up to Hamlin as the killer?"

"He didn't do it."

Ken caught his fist just before it slammed into the tabletop. Sheepishly, he eyed his hand as if chiding it for betraying a temper he seldom revealed. "With all due respect, Travis," he said, "that fall scrambled your wits. Hamlin had motive and opportunity. The girl wouldn't give him the time of day. He had easy access to the grounds. He can't account for his whereabouts the night she was killed. Rejection is a classic motive for murder, you know that. You're clinging to straws, Travis. Give it up."

Ken leaned back in the big wicker chair, looking glum. He heaved a sigh. "I guess this is a bad time to ask you to dinner and a movie?"

"Yes," I snapped. "But not because we don't agree," I added hastily. "I'm . . . I'm just not ready for any sort of personal relationship." *So he really wasn't married.*

"The harp concert wasn't a date?"

Damn! Was he having me watched?

As if he could hear what I was thinking, Ken added, "The City provided extra security Wednesday night. I caught your name on a list. Who's Josh Thomas?"

As if he had any right to ask! "He's on vacation," I supplied. "His father knew Martin Longstreet, Aunt Hy's escort. Martin's a Board—"

"Yeah, I know."

Of course he knew. Martin was probably the person who arranged for Ken Parrish to handle—

Oh, dear God, surely not! Had Martin and Aunt Hy conspired to provide me with *both* of them? And perhaps a mystery, a professional challenge, as well?

Two effigies and a mannequin, maybe. But murder? No way. Not that Martin hadn't once been capable of murder. As, I suspected, was my not-so-Sleeping Satyr, Josh Thomas.

But they wouldn't go that far. Of course they wouldn't. Unless they had some very good reason that had nothing to do with me.

Ridiculous. Martin Longstreet was a member of the Bellman

Board of Directors, Aunt Hy's closest friend. And Josh Thomas was . . . what?

Ken Parrish's sharp gray eyes were so focused on my face I was sure he had read my every thought. I gulped, regrouped, tried to remember what we were talking about.

Dinner and a movie.

"I like you," I told him. "Even when I think you've got your head stuck in the sand. So when I'm ready to date, I promise you'll be first on the list."

"List, huh?"

"Very short." Two names only. *Na-aw. No way.* Martin and Aunt Hy couldn't have arranged—

Damn, but if they did . . . what a pair of winners they'd picked.

Aunt Hy likes to quote that old expression about cutting off your nose to spite your face. It occurred to me—reluctantly, as I hate to admit to being wrong—that playing tour guide for Josh Thomas really wasn't a hideous chore. A modicum of semi-social life was not going to tilt the balance of my world.

Therefore, on Sunday afternoon I guided Josh to a State Park about twenty miles from the city, where we soaked up the atmosphere of old Florida and even boarded a boat for a good look at alligators in the wild. It was a sunny day, and they were everywhere. Basking on sand banks and poking their snouts up out of the murky waters, no matter which direction we looked. This lake might be Alligator Central, but I'd been in Florida long enough to know that if it's fresh water, there's likely to be an alligator lurking. I thought of Billie night-diving into ponds on golf courses and a shiver raised the hairs on my arms.

Josh noticed, his arm casually moving around my shoulders. He had actually dressed down today. Chinos and a navy polo shirt. Among a boatload of tourists, he still looked like a barracuda in a sea of guppies.

He was not, repeat not, a date. I was merely showing him around. In response to respect for my aunt, I was being gracious to one of Martin's acquaintances. Certainly, Martin Longstreet continually smoothed the rough edges of Aunt Hy's life. It was the least I could do in return.

That night Josh and I had dinner together. What else could a girl do when her companion tells her how depressing it is to eat alone?

Afterwards—having talked ourselves to a standstill about Lydia's murder—we went to a movie.

It was not a date. I maintained this firmly to myself right up until the time Josh leaned forward and, under the bright lights and close scrutiny of the hotel's security guard, kissed me on the lips. Gently, but thoroughly. And then came back for more.

He had to put me in the elevator and push the button.

Obviously, Josh Thomas was even more dangerous than I had thought.

On Monday morning I climbed all three flights of the stairs by Escher to what Lydia had called the "aerie." Though I'd never admit it to that masochist, my physical therapist, it was easier this time. Not easy. Just better than last time.

On the way, I paused to talk to the young lovelies in Marketing, each pale, solemn-faced, and unable to hide her fear. There was an empty desk in the corner. One of their own had died under grisly circumstances. The only suspect was still riding around the Bellman grounds under protection of a Security ID.

I told them flat out that I didn't believe Billie was guilty and that I was trying to help him. "Did she have a boyfriend?" I asked.

There was a general shuffling as each of the girls studied her immaculately shod toes. "Actually, I think she really liked Billie," one of the girls offered. Dark-haired, her figure was so svelte she looked as if she never ate anything more substantial than air.

"She just liked money more," another girl, a blonde, sighed. "You know—the best clubs, best food. And even if Billie had that kind of money, she'd never be seen with a security guard."

"Someone who sells used golf balls," added a third girl, more sharp-faced than the others.

Surprised, I asked, "Who told you about the golf balls?"

"Lydia," said the Dark Thin One. "Guess Billie was trying to impress her. And it nearly worked. She kept saying how brave he was to take on snakes and alligators. And how would he sculpt if he lost an arm."

"But you don't know who she was seeing at the moment?" The girls looked at each other, shook their heads. I nodded my head toward the stairs to the fourth floor. "Could she have been seeing anybody after work up in the aerie?"

"Oh, no, that's—" The Blonde took an elbow in the ribs from Sharp Face.

So someone—or should I say, some *two*—were using the aerie for something other than museum business. Which probably had nothing to do with Lydia's murder.

Unless she had seen them . . . But what affair was so desperately secret that a possible whistle-blower must be murdered? Murders were committed over Money. Over Passions gone amuck. Self-preservation. Revenge. Not—in the rarified atmosphere of the Bellman—over who was sleeping with whom.

Blackmail? Had Lydia liked money enough to try that particularly nasty trick?

I hadn't known her well, but, somehow, she didn't seem the type. Art students tended to believe in "Live and Let Live." If Lydia had seen two people sneaking up to the aerie, she probably would have tossed off a salacious grin and proceeded to go about her business.

I thanked the girls and tackled the last flight of steps. At the top was a padlocked door that obviously led out onto the balcony four stories above the museum entrance. To my right was a hallway, lit by a solid phalanx of windows revealing the narrow walkway outside. At the end of the hall was the suite of rooms Lydia had called the aerie. Small, intimate, the view from the eastern balcony was totally eclipsed by the spectacular vista on the west. From here, even my seventeen-foot *David* tended to look small. Lydia had been right when she said the aerie's view was even better than the one on the floor below.

I searched every inch of that suite, including the bathroom and under the modest double bed in the room to the east. In the living room I even took the cushions off the sofa, feeling in all the crevices. I found sixty-four cents in change and a ticket stub. In a bottom drawer of a utilitarian-type desk I found correspondence old enough to have been relegated to Archives long since. But nothing else of interest to the case. It was as if this set of rooms had not been inhabited since the fifties.

In desperation, I checked the bed sheets. They were Ralph Lauren, a new pattern. The glassware, carefully stored in a small cabinet, was cut crystal. There was a can of cashew nuts—the kind you can get at any grocery store—its half-eaten contents protected by a yellow plastic lid. There was, however, a cut crystal bowl to put them in. The liquor in the cabinet was the best. Even the mineral water was the most expensive money could buy.

At least one of the clandestine pair using this room had Money.

There were, I supposed, fingerprints all over the place. But connecting the aerie to Lydia's murder seemed pretty farfetched. All the theories that had flitted through my mind while I was talking to the girls downstairs now seemed feeble. I would, of course, tell Ken Parrish that I had been up here, as I would tell him about my conversation with the girls from Marketing. But my instincts said I'd struck out. If the aerie had any connection to Lydia Hewitt's murder, it was peripheral.

On my way down, I once again thanked the girls for their help. When I finally opened the door onto a tide of visitors, ticket sellers, and security guards filling the museum's main lobby, I was dragged back to the reality of the moment with a visceral shock. Someone had been murdered. And the museum was getting more visitors than it had ever had before. A madman was loose. Didn't they have sense enough to stay home?

And there it was, springing full-blown into a mind weary of going round in circles. I *couldn't* believe Billie killed Lydia. I *wouldn't* believe it was a senseless random act of violence. Yet, even if we could find a concrete motive for what had happened, at the heart of this horror I had come to believe there truly was a madman. A cold, calculating son of a bitch who was getting his jollies out of making fools of us all.

CHAPTER 13

The police tape was gone. The Circus Museum open to visitors. The white lion cage with its gilded griffin and telltale blood stains had been hauled, with considerable effort, into a back room, out of sight of gawking eyes. Which didn't keep me from standing there in the semi-dark room, staring at the place where Lydia's body had been, willing some semblance of a theory into my mind.

There had been no fingerprints, of course. Not on the effigies. Not on the mannequin. Not on the lion cage. With packages of latex gloves available at every corner drugstore and discount retailer, why should there be? Only people whose wits were scrambled—by drugs, by passion, by momentary insanity—failed to think about fingerprints in this day and age.

Passion. Or, in this case, the lack of it. I could hardly wait to point out this little anomaly to Ken Parrish. Lydia had been killed with premeditation and great care. I had been right about her being drugged. The autopsy had found traces of Rohypnol, a drug that would have made her pliant. Able to walk, to climb into the cage on her own, if steered in the right direction. The killer had come prepared with knife and gloves. Lydia had not been strangled or beaten in a lover's quarrel. There was nothing passionate about her death. It was cold and calculated.

Someone, for some reason, had wanted her dead.

In a lion cage at the Circus Museum?

Rob Varney's words echoed through my mind. *Murder as a*

154

work of art. I pictured Lydia's fresh, young beauty bleeding out on the floor of an antique lion cage. More like The Art of Evil. It would have been so much easier to kill Lydia outside on the nearly pitch-black grounds. So why the elaborate orchestration, the intricate setup to murder?

The obvious was so frequently the answer. Maybe Ken was right. Was there anything sane about golf-ball diving among gators and water moccasins?

Passion. Lydia had a lover somewhere. I needed to find him. And I'd have to pursue that slip of the tongue by the Blonde from Marketing. She knew who was using the aerie. Although it seemed unlikely an illicit love affair on the fourth floor of an art museum had anything to do with Lydia's death, I would have to check it out. I sometimes wondered if anyone outside law enforcement had any idea how much of an investigator's time is spent chasing false leads, dead ends, deliberate misdirections.

My cell phone rang.

The usually ebullient Jody Tyler was hysterical. "She's gone! Mrs. Van Horne. I thought she was taking her nap, just like always, but when I went to take in her tea, she was gone. Bed looks like she was never in it. Mrs. Edmundson's got the whole hotel looking. You gotta come home. Right now."

I slammed out of the building so fast the visitors must have felt wind from my wake as I flew past. It was only as I was gritting my teeth, driving fifteen per through the crowded museum grounds, that I realized my cane had barely touched the ground. Not exactly a silver lining in the midst of all these storm clouds, but maybe just a light patch where the sun struggled to shine through.

I didn't bother to park in the garage beneath the hotel. If Aunt Hy had not been found, I was in for a long afternoon of driving the streets. I could tell by the look on the face of Fred, the doorman, that Aunt Hy was still missing. He had worse news.

"I'm so sorry, Miss Travis," he burst out. "I was on my break when she went missing. We just discovered that Lou, my relief, got her a taxi about three o'clock."

"To where?"

"I believe the manager is attempting to discover that now, Miss."

"Has anyone called the police?"

"Oh, no, Miss." Fred looked shocked. "We would never embarrass Mrs. Van Horne like that."

Of course not. I thanked Fred, told him to keep my car handy, and charged into the lobby.

I was whisked into the manager's office by a waiting minion with an aplomb that made me realize the staff of the Ritz-Carlton was accustomed to dealing with crises of every kind. To my relief, the manager was just hanging up the phone and she was smiling.

"I have it," she announced with triumph. "Your aunt went to a dance studio." She held out a slip of paper with the address.

My leg, which had performed so well only a short while ago, buckled. I grabbed at the chair in front of Miss Wayland's desk and sat. Abruptly. Karen Wayland was a very special lady. Not much more than ten years older than I, she ran this hotel with all the expertise and efficiency that had made it a star among Ritz-Carltons in its first year of operation. It wasn't surprising she had managed to track down Aunt Hy.

I stared at the slip of paper in my hand and groaned. "I suppose someone offered her free lessons. If I don't get up off this chair and find this place fast," I sighed, "she'll have signed a contract to the tune of ten thousand dollars."

"I hear the gowns run around five," Karen Wayland offered. With sympathy. "Not to worry," she added. "This is Florida. I believe there's a three-day right of recision."

I sat there with my head in my hands, my leg refusing to move. I wondered if Madame Celestine had recommended dance lessons.

"Rory," Karen said, more gently, "you don't suppose your aunt would *enjoy* dance lessons?"

"From what I've heard about my aunt, she could probably *teach* them. I doubt there's a dance invented before the last ten years that she isn't an expert on."

"Then perhaps she'd simply enjoy the dancing," Karen suggested.

I wondered if Martin danced. The picture of Aunt Hy in the arms of some young dance instructor out to make a bit extra on the side turned my stomach. Enough to put steel back in my leg and get me to my feet. I thanked Karen profusely and headed for my car.

"Good luck, Miss," Fred said, brown eyes alight with sincerity.

But when I found the dance studio, Aunt Hy had come and gone. The girl at the desk did not have the satisfied look of someone who had witnessed the signing of a pricey contract. No, she had not called a taxi for Mrs. Van Horne. Perhaps the old lady had found one outside. Perhaps she had decided to explore the many boutiques in the area.

I wondered if I should call in a favor with Ken Parrish. Call Martin. Or Josh. In the end, I did what Karen Wayland had done. I went back inside, asked for a phone book, and began calling the cab companies. I didn't hesitate to use those magic words, "FBI." On the third try: yes, a fare meeting Aunt Hy's description had been dropped off at a home on Pelican Key. I didn't need to listen to the address. I knew it by heart.

How long ago? Ten minutes. I thanked the dispatcher, thanked the girl who'd loaned me the phone book, and took off at a near run. It would take ten or fifteen minutes to get through the heavy traffic to Pelican Key. Nearly half an hour for a little old lady, lost in the past, to be turned away from the home that had been her own for most of her lifetime. To wander past mansions that hadn't existed in the time her mind had reverted to. Or—worse yet—to find herself wandering the congested streets around the central shopping area, with cars and pedestrians whizzing in every direction when she might well be reliving the slow and easy days of the forties or fifties, before Florida's most recent real estate boom.

I sat at the red light where the Tamiami Trail crossed the road to Pelican Key and wiped away a tear. Damn! She was a wonderful old lady. I'd love her even if she weren't my grandmother's sister.

It's impossible to speed on the way out to Pelican Key. The traffic is solid. Just choose a lane and hope it keeps moving. A high-speed chase it wasn't. I managed twenty-five past the new bridge construction, thirty as I passed the Sarasota Yacht Club. I hung a left and drove straight to Aunt Hy's old home, keeping a sharp eye left and right as I drove down the secluded streets, which exuded every evidence of the wildly wealthy. There was no sign of Aunt Hy.

I pulled up in front of monumental black wrought-iron gates and rang the bell. I explained my problem to a disembodied voice echoing from the speaker system. Slowly, the gates swung open.

Aunt Hy was having tea and ginger cookies at the old wooden table in the kitchen. She smiled when she saw me. "Aurora, my dear, you have come to my rescue. What a good child you are!" She threw open her arms, and we hugged, although my eyes were too misted to see her clearly.

"She was trying to remember her phone number, Miss," said the housekeeper, "but she had a bit of trouble."

"I'm so sorry," I apologized, "but she lived here so long . . ." The housekeeper and I exchanged a look that said it all. Thank God this perfect stranger understood. She introduced herself as Flora Evans. There was a trace of the Welsh lingering in her voice.

"The family hasn't come down for the winter yet," she explained. "I came ahead to hire staff and prepare the house."

"Thank God you did!" I told her about my visions of Aunt Hy wandering about lost and alone.

She nodded. "I was just about to call the police, but I hoped someone would think to look for her here. Such a lovely old lady. I couldn't see her go off in a patrol car, now could I?"

"I never spent much time in the kitchen," Aunt Hy interjected brightly. "It's really rather nice. I like it." She sighed. "I suppose I should have learned to cook, but I never had to, you know. My Edgar had such a lot of money." Her voice, with her mind, trailed off into the past.

Suddenly embarrassed, I faced up to discovering if I was dealing with old-school values or modern reality. I looked at Mrs. Evans. "Would you accept—"

I got no farther. "Oh, my no, Miss," she exclaimed. "I'm happy to be of help. It's not often a person gets a chance to do a good deed. Made my day, I can tell you. You just take the poor lady home where she can be comfortable with all her own things around her."

I wouldn't let it go at that, of course. A gift certificate inside a thank-you card would not be rejected, I thought. After another round of profound thanks from both Aunt Hy and myself, we made our way to the car. We were on the causeway, just before the drawbridge, when Aunt Hy said, "Madame Celestine was right. Those dance lessons were a scam, Aurora. Five thousand for the first round of lessons and they knew someone who could make a gown that would be absolutely perfect for me for only another four. Foolish children, I could have taught *them* how true ballroom dancing is done."

Although my mind wasn't quite keeping up with what she was saying, I managed to ask, "Then why did you go there?"

Aunt Hy heaved a sigh that went straight to my heart. "The first lesson was free, you see, and it had been so long since I'd danced. It brought back so many memories . . ."

Once again, I wondered if Martin Longstreet ever danced. "You say Madame Celestine warned you about scams?"

"Oh, yes, dear. And you're to be careful, too. Celestine says there's danger lurking where you least expect it. But," Aunt Hy added brightly, "your love life is definitely improving. *Two* young men, Aurora. Delightful. I am so pleased for you."

I had not mentioned a single word at home about Ken Parrish. Not one. The Sarasota City Police Department could stay out of my aunt's high-rise condo at the Ritz-Carlton, thank you very much. So either I was right that Martin and Aunt Hy were co-conspirators in matchmaking, or Martin shared all he knew with my aunt (highly unlikely), or Madame Celestine was not quite as much of a fraud as I thought. All three possibilities were abhorrent. I'd had months now of being jerked around like a puppet as outsiders—doctors, physical therapists, psychologists, my Uncle Sam employer, my family—dictated my life. I needed privacy. Independence. I would *not* be manipulated.

I was an ungrateful ass, and I should be ashamed of myself.

I was. Ashamed, that is. I'd barely cracked the chrysalis. I was so far from emerging as a gracefully mobile butterfly, physically or mentally, that the concept was downright laughable.

That evening, after supper, when Josh called, asking me to join him downstairs for a drink, I invited him up to the condo instead. Shaken by the afternoon's close call, I wasn't yet ready to allow Aunt Hy out of my sight. And, yes, I also wanted to challenge him just a little. To see how Josh Thomas would react to Aunt Hy's version of the palace at Versailles. And maybe, just maybe, he might seem more human if I saw him against a backdrop of home and hearth.

It didn't work, of course.

The Sarasota newspaper recently printed an update on the Big Bang theory, the one where astronomers tell us the entire universe was created 13.7 billion years ago in one gigantic explosion. I've always found the idea bizarre, but they may have got one thing right. They say the universe is four percent atoms, twenty-three percent dark matter and seventy-three percent some mysterious element called "dark energy." I'm inclined to believe them, because the description fits Josh Thomas to a T.

When I let him into Aunt Hy's condo, his dark presence permeated the spacious, well-lit rooms. I swear the polish dimmed on the gleaming exotic wood furniture, shadows filtered over the glazed ceramics and sparkling glass, even those in the subtly lit etagères. The sturdy Tang horse seemed to droop. Josh went straight to it, studying it for some moments before examining the other Oriental ceramics in the case. He wandered to the next etagère and on about the room, his eyes coming to rest at last on the Meissen shepherd and shepherdess on the mantel. "These just sit out here?" he asked at last, his back to the pink marble fireplace. "Without so much as a glass front and a lock?"

"I thought they were reproductions," I admitted, "until I saw the insurance premium."

"Insurance can't replace them," Josh snapped. "They ought to be in a museum."

"Aunt Hy has a right to enjoy her things!" I snapped right back, glaring. But he'd passed the test. His polish wasn't all on the outside. Josh Thomas recognized real art when he saw it.

"This is the most blatant burglary bait I've seen in years," he added, unnecessarily belaboring the point.

I told him in no uncertain terms that Aunt Hy's penthouse at the Ritz was probably more secure than most museums.

"*Probably?*" he huffed, throwing my words straight back. "I could clean this place out in ten minutes flat."

We stood there glaring at each other while I rearranged the neat little pigeonholes of my mind. Josh Thomas, art thief? Or merely Josh Thomas, know-it-all, expressing his superior male opinion?

I turned my back and stomped off to the kitchen. As I began to tumble ice into the first of two squat Waterford glasses, Josh's arms came round me from both sides and seized the glass. Ice tumbled over the edge of the door-front icemaker, spilled onto the floor. My body stung, as if I'd been encased in dry ice. I was frozen, going up in flames.

I jerked away, ending up across the room with my back against the wall of double ovens.

"Sorry," Josh murmured, after a few interesting moments as he juggled the Waterford glasses to keep them from shattering on the Italian tile floor. He shook his head. "Poor Rory. I didn't think you were that skittish."

I stalked off to the living room, leaving him to find the marquetry cabinet that held the liquor supply. By now Josh knew my taste, pouring out the Glenlivet without a word. After handing me my drink, he eased himself into an upholstered armchair five feet away from the couch where I was sitting. He took a hefty swallow of his drink, then simply stared at me, radiating blank suavity.

"Well," I said, "did you learn anything from Martin?"

"Didn't your mama ever tell you about all work and no play?"

"Didn't yours? I thought you told me this was your first vacation in years."

"Oh, very good," Josh mocked. "Rory Travis, the girl with

repartee for all occasions."

Correction. He was not as calm and cool as he appeared. "What did Martin say?"

"Martin, my dear Rory, is the original clam. Martin said absolutely nothing."

"Maybe you really are a burglar," I mused. "Surely a spook-type would have managed better."

Josh raised his glass in salute. To Martin, I was sure. Not to me. "Martin is the spook's spook," he said. "Even at his age the grass does not grow beneath his fast-shuffling feet. All I got out of him was that there was a member of the Board currently involved in a business problem that has absolutely nothing to do with the Bellman. It was not the kind of problem that could possibly be related to a dead girl, two effigies, or a mannequin covered in fingernail polish. It was the Board member's private business, and, therefore, he was not going to discuss it."

I thought about it. "Do you think he's right?" I asked.

"I think I'd like to know what he's concealing."

"I wonder . . . he may mean Parker St. Clair." I told Josh about our meeting with the St. Clairs in the Tea Room downstairs. And about the distinct impression of distaste I had gotten from Martin when he had introduced Aunt Hy and myself to Parker and Melinda St. Clair.

"Parker St. Clair," Josh said, savoring the name. "Let me check him out for you. I'm feeling remarkably useless at the moment."

I nodded, though I suddenly got the distinct impression he could have given me chapter and verse on Parker St. Clair without lifting a finger to a keyboard. And yet he was letting me take the lead, when I was quite certain it was many years since Josh Thomas had played second fiddle to anyone. He was backing off, professionally and emotionally. Giving me the time I needed to be me again.

He was, in essence, a wiser and better person than I was at the moment.

I resented him. His strength, his confidence. His power.

I feared him. If he touched me again, I'd drag him into the bedroom and keep him straight through 'til morning, and Devil take the hindmost. Which was probably exactly what was happening. And the hindmost was me.

I told him about my afternoon chasing down Aunt Hy. The depths of his black-hole eyes actually parted long enough to let out a ray of sympathy. And I caught the moment when he clamped his jaw over his tongue to refrain from offering advice.

For half an hour after that we rehashed the case from the Roman warrior to Lydia's death, ending up as mystified as when we'd begun. Neither of us took it well. When Josh left at close to midnight, he made no attempt to kiss me good night.

It wasn't just Aunt Hy's deteriorating health or Lydia's death that formed my depression as I went to bed that night. Josh Thomas loomed, like some dark, winged beast, over my every thought. I didn't even *like* him, for heaven's sake.

Then again, I doubted heaven had anything to do with Josh Thomas.

CHAPTER 14

At nine-fifteen the next morning, as I was driving to meet that sadist, my physical therapist, my cell phone rang. Ken Parrish's voice said, "I'm on my way to the Casa. Get over there now. I'll leave word to let you in."

"What?" I squawked. But he'd hung up. By the time I'd realized it, I was already doing a U-ey. With a smug satisfaction close to glee, I phoned the rehab center and told them not to expect me. Then I sobered as I realized only something serious could have triggered Ken's abrupt call.

Patrol cars, golf carts, Ken's SUV, other unmarked cop cars. The scene was all too familiar. The bay gleamed tropical blue under nearly cloudless skies. Giant banyans and graceful palms ringed the uneven mix of tarmac and crushed shell that passed for the Casa's parking lot. Birds twittered and small brown squirrels leaped across the green lawn. An ideal day in paradise. Yet blue uniforms stood guard at the top of the ramp to the mansion's entrance, interspersed with the burgundy-vested museum guards. Every face was grim.

Another murder. It had to be. Somehow the word *effigy* never crossed my mind.

The phalanx of guards parted, no need for explanations. Ken Parrish had done as promised, and, of course, the museum guards knew me. "Second floor," one of them told me. "Richard's bathroom."

When the elevator door opened on the second floor, I followed the low murmur of voices. (Somehow no one seems to shout in the face of death, although I've heard some really macabre black jokes.) I made my way through Richard Bellman's bedroom with its sumptuous reproduction of Napoleon the Third's furniture and the huge painting of a partially clad Pauline Bonaparte, hanging on the wall opposite the bed. (I once had a tram passenger ask me about that painting, wondering what Opal thought about her husband's taste in bedroom art. Happily, I was able to tell him that Richard Bellman thought the first Napoleon's sister resembled his Opal. He was, therefore, awaking each morning to a view of his *wife*. That, of course, is the official story. Frankly, I suspect the circus king–turned–art connoisseur simply had a genuine appreciation for a fine-looking, half-naked woman.)

Moving past Pauline Bonaparte, I found that death had indeed come to the Casa Bellissima. Not, as I had been told, in Richard's Bellman's bathroom, with its tub cut from a solid block of golden marble. No, this body was in a room on the bay side of the house. A room with an actual barber chair, set so it had a view of the water and of Pelican Key, where Richard Bellman had been the driving force in real estate development. Except, today, the circus magnate and business entrepreneur was not the one sitting there ready for his morning shave. But someone was. I could see fluffy white shaving cream puffing out his cheeks in stark contrast to the blood congealing on his slashed neck, on his teal blue polo shirt, and on his tan slacks. I could see the dark wavy hair, only lightly shot with gray, the round face, the ears that hugged his head, the broad shoulders of a sturdy body.

"Tell me that's not Rob Varney," I said.

Ken looked up. "Sorry," he muttered. "You got it in one."

Murder as art. There he was—the man who had said those words—artistically arranged with his head propped against the headrest of the barber chair, his feet flat on the metal supports. His right hand gripped the handle of a long, narrow straight razor.

As if anyone was going to believe this was a suicide! More likely, the razor was part of the artistic touch. Or a taunt. *See . . . I've left the murder weapon in plain sight, and you still can't find me.*

Talk about macabre jokes.

"I barely knew him," I murmured, "but I liked him. He was smart. Quick. He's the one who called all this the Art of Murder. A big, sick joke by some madman. And now . . . it begins to look as if he might have been right."

Ken started to reply, but the medical examiner arrived, still puffing from the staircase. As he and Ken exchanged a few terse words, I stepped back into Richard's bedroom. A team of forensic experts plus a medical examiner were about all the small shaving room could take. By the time Ken joined me, I had the essential question ready. "Has anyone checked on Billie?"

Ken swore softly. "Don't tell me you've come over to my side?"

"Of course not. I'm just hoping he has a damn good alibi."

"Until the ME gives us Time of Death we won't even know what hours to check. You know that, Travis."

I shrugged. "Guess I'm not accustomed to being first on scene, particularly twice in a row."

"That's the Feebs for you. A day late and a dollar short."

Someone called a question to Ken and he was off, back into the midst of the seeming chaos around the barber chair. I examined Richard Bellman's bedroom and bath with care, then thumped down the hall, past the stairs, following an alternate route to the room with the barber chair. Left along the gallery overlooking the vast living room below—the one where the mannequin had shattered onto the tile floor—then left again, down another short hallway. I stopped short at the doorway opposite the one I had used before. The shaving room was still overflowing with technical experts. From here I had a better look at Rob Varney's broad face. His eyes were open. Unsurprised. Blank.

Rohypnol?

When Ken looked my way, I gave him a nod. He was with me in ten seconds flat. I almost felt as if I were officially back at work, where my opinion counted for something. "My guess is that you'll find Rohypnol," I told him.

"Male date rape?" he threw back at me, eyebrows wiggling.

"Lydia wasn't a date rape. You told me yourself she hadn't been touched."

"Guess I did," he said with aw-shucks exaggeration.

I heaved a sigh. "Okay, once again I'm guilty of telling the Southern cop what he'd already figured out the minute he saw the body."

"Maybe two minutes."

I squirmed a bit, made an effort to look suitably put down. I mean, I like the guy. More than a little. There are times when a girl has to compromise.

And then I spoiled it. "There's no sign of a struggle. Not a drop of blood outside the room. So once again, we have someone drugged, brought to a predetermined location, killed in a particularly grisly manner, with lots of blood, then artistically arranged in an unusual setting."

"You got it. And now, Ms. Travis, would you care to tell me *why?* And while you're at it, I wouldn't mind *how.*"

I glared. He grinned. I grinned back, rather sheepishly. "Thanks for inviting me," I said, once again reminding myself Detective Parrish's invitation had been a major favor. "I'd appreciate a call later, when things finally simmer down." I turned away, heading for the elevator.

"Off to find Billie?" he challenged.

I stood with my back turned, head bowed, and cursed all smart city cops. "If I run into him," I said, "I'll give him your regards."

"Rory?"

"Don't worry," I grumbled, "I took an oath, remember? Being on leave doesn't break the chain."

"Sorry."

I walked away. I didn't look back. As I made my way to my car, tragedy threatened to shove the federal cop aside. I was feeling more and more like a jinx. First Eric. Now Lydia and Rob. I hadn't known them the way I knew Eric, of course, but they were both people I had looked forward to knowing better. And in a particularly bizarre and bloody manner they had been wiped away. Obliterated. As an insane joke? Revenge on the museum? But for what? Revenge on Richard Bellman personally for some ancient transgression?

It was all so elaborate, so stylized. Serial killers usually stick to one sex. All women or all men. And usually of one particular age. Yet Lydia was a twenty-something and female; Rob Varney, late-fifties and male. Nonsense. All nonsense. As were the two effigies and the shattered mannequin.

And then there was faceless Tim Mundell—whose body I had never seen—whispering softly, in unexpected moments. *Are you sure, sure, sure I killed myself? How can you be, when you never checked it out?*

Billie lived in an apartment complex whose stucco walls, tile roof, and scraggly landscaping stopped just short of seedy and rundown. But, as he had once explained to me, it had an actual backyard with a picnic table shaded by two tall slash pines, and a sizeable live oak. There was also a hose for the easy washing of golf balls. And his three rooms on the first floor rear—whose

169

walls were almost entirely composed of windows and doors—were less expensive as they were so easily accessible to passing strangers. A security guard from the museum—particularly a young, strong security guard—could get a good deal from the landlord. It was not an apartment any reasonably intelligent young woman would touch with a ten-foot pole.

"He ain't home," declared a female voice with a Brooklyn twang as I knocked on Billie's door.

It had been a long time since I'd seen a woman in a wraparound housecoat and hair done up in rollers, ill concealed by a kerchief. In fact, it was most likely I had only seen this particular look when watching old TV sitcoms. I wondered if this retiree from Up North had been looking like this every morning for the past fifty years or so.

"Any idea where I can find him?" I asked. "It's important." She looked me over, the fat sausages of silver gray crowning her forehead practically quivering with speculation. I could actually feel the heat rising in my cheeks. "It's business," I snapped, and wished I was wearing my Bellman T-shirt and ID.

"Thursday mornings he's at school. The Bellman Art School, y'know." Her eyes dropped, lingering on my cane.

I bristled. Since Billie's colorful jeep, a redecorated Postal Service breakdown, was not in the parking lot, I decided to accept her word. "Thanks." Then, swinging my cane more like a gandy dancer than a sane and sober Special Agent in recovery, I walked back to my car. Everything would have been fine if I hadn't been concentrating on head high, shoulders straight, pride flying like a flag. The toe of my weak leg encountered a live oak root thrusting up through the thin tarmac, and I went down hard on my hands and knees, the pain shooting through my left leg enough to make the world go away for a moment or two.

Mrs. Hair Rollers was saying something. I forced myself to

focus. Listen. Respond.

"I'm all right," I ground out. "Really. I should have been looking where I was going." I levered myself up to rest on my knees, shook off her helping hand. After another minute or so of deep breathing, I nodded, and with Hair Rollers on one side and my cane on the other, I managed to scramble to my feet. Very carefully, I slunk to the Caddy, ignoring the shell fragments imbedded in my palms and the blood I could feel running down my legs from scraped knees. *Damn, damn, and fucking damn!*

I let the blood drip. But by the time I arrived at the Bellman School of Art I was forced to mop up the evidence of damage with a whole slew of tissues. Unfortunately, my sneakers still tended to look as if they'd been at a murder scene (which, of course, they had, technically speaking), and, hopefully, I wouldn't be shaking hands with any new acquaintances.

My temper was distinctly unreliable. Among other things, on the short drive to the art school, I had remembered Josh Thomas's promised offer of a job and realized I'd actually allowed myself to fantasize a time or two about getting back into the game, traveling from Europe to Florida to Peru, as Josh had done. Rory Travis, International Agent. Sure. Right. Agent Triple-O. Zero, Nada, Zilch—that was me. Rory Travis, Agent Sit-at-a-Computer-all-day. That was the best I'd ever be able to do. Whatever had made me think, even for a few short weeks, that I'd ever be a field agent again?

Josh Thomas. Ken Parrish. Billie Ball Hamlin. With the connivance of Martin Longstreet?

Nice try, guys. But you're wrong.

Or was this all a setup? Had Martin, or Josh, paid Billie to throw a mystery in my face? Literally, in the case of the mannequin. And our murderer had simply taken advantage of the brouhaha?

The effigies certainly made a convenient excuse to throw Ken Parrish in my way.

Oh, shit!

Angry, now, with fingers that itched to grab hold of someone I could blame for all this, I wadded up the bloody tissues and squeezed them into the car's vinyl trash container. Time to find Billie. Who was not yet aware that at the moment my sympathies did not lie with any of the men involved in this case.

Except, of course, Rob Varney. Was it possible he had been murdered simply because his general appearance was so similar to Richard Bellman?

Murder as Art. Murder by a cold, calculating, evil bastard, maybe insane, maybe not.

As Lydia resembled the bronze Lygia. And had been the model, if all unknowing, for the Lygia effigy?

I was winging it now. As I had the day I associated Martin, Josh's father with the war in Vietnam and the CIA. I was running on instinct. Ken Parrish would laugh.

Josh Thomas would offer me a job.

Everything inside me was screaming, *No! Wrong. Stop!* Lydia and Rob weren't killed because a madman decided to stage a one-man show titled "The Art of Evil." There was a deeper reason for what was happening at the Bellman. Someone very clever, truly Machiavellian, was manipulating us all. Throwing up a grand smoke screen. Making us look as incompetent as I felt.

It was there. I could almost taste it. A concept dangling just out of reach. A juicy, meaty motive I hadn't found yet. One that might have nothing at all to do with Art.

I took one last look at my bloodstained sneakers, at the still dripping scrape peeking out through a tear in the left knee of my navy slacks, at the white shell dust I'd been unable to completely brush away. I curved my fingers so my lacerated palms wouldn't show. Gingerly, I opened the car door. Since there was no one nearby, I didn't bother to suppress my wince as my left foot hit the ground.

Billie was not sculpting. Billie was in Art History class. I sneaked into the back of the class, earning a glare from the professor that turned into a sharp once-over. For some reason my skin crawled. His was a type common to campuses everywhere. Fortyish, suavely good-looking, undoubtedly chalking up co-eds like they were the hottest sale item at the local discount store. Since this was an art school, he'd forsaken the professorial tweed jacket with leather patches in favor of the all-black look. Long-sleeved ribbed T, leather vest and black jeans. With a thick shock of wavy brown hair, wide brown eyes, and a tan almost as deep as Billie's, I had to admit he caught the eye. I recalled Josh Thomas's all black outfit the day he dropped out of nowhere into my tram. Josh Thomas in a tux. Josh Thomas as Zorro? My perception righted itself. Josh Thomas was a lot scarier than this small-time creep.

Unfortunately for Billie, class was almost over, and my temper was still up when he turned and saw me sitting in the back. "Rory?" He charged up the aisle, evidently sensing something was wrong.

"Where can we talk?"

"Here's fine. There's no class now." He searched my face. "Okay, Rory girl, what's happened?"

He looked so totally innocent. Grim, but clueless. I wanted to believe him, but things hadn't exactly been going well so far this morning. I lost it. I popped to my feet, my mouth on a level with his shoulder. I poked him in the chest with my index finger. "If there's something you haven't told me, Billie, I need to know it now! You're so close to a cell I can smell it. Did someone really pay you to make those effigies? If so, do you know who it was? Do you have any idea who killed Lydia? And why on earth would anyone kill Rob Varney?"

Sometimes temper works. If Billie was faking the astonishment that suffused his face, his performance was worthy of an Oscar. As his frown deepened, I could even see him processing my questions. Finally, he looked at me very oddly, as if maybe I was the one ready for the psych ward, and asked, "Who's Rob Whatsisname?"

I knuckled my fist over my mouth and thought about it. Then, "Okay, Billie, I hope you were someplace with a lot of witnesses last night. All night."

Have you ever seen someone with a heavy tan go pale? Well, Billie Ball Hamlin managed it. He slumped down onto a chair and stared up at me. "I was out on a course," he said, "from midnight to two. A half-hour drive each—"

"You were golf-ball diving after the police found out what you were doing!" I was close to screaming.

"Hell, Rory, that's the only place I can think. I'm at home on the courses at night. That's my territory. I didn't figure it mattered."

"Oh, Billie." Shaking my head, I sat down beside him. "I suppose you were at home, alone, the rest of the night?"

"Yeah."

"Billie," I groaned, "couldn't you have had a hot date with something besides an alligator?"

"Sorry," he muttered. "Am I screwed?"

"I wish you had been—at least you'd have an alibi." Silence hung while I thought it over. "Rob Varney's the new tram driver," I offered, "the one who looks—looked—like Richard Bellman."

"Didn't notice. Is he dead?" he ventured.

"Very. Nicely arranged in Richard's barber chair, shaving cream, strop razor and all."

Billie groaned. His head went down, his hands pulling at his hair.

"Okay," I said, "let's go back to Lydia. Who was her current boyfriend? You said something about a teacher?"

"Mel Corbin. Art History. You just saw him."

That made my day. There are certain types of people you just ache to take down. Mel Corbin was top of my list at the moment. But my surge of pleasure was short-lived. No matter how well acquainted he was with Lydia, I couldn't imagine how a professor from the Bellman School of Art would know a new retiree, now a tram volunteer, at the museum. The institutions were two miles apart, connected solely by the name Bellman.

"Did you tell me he was a consultant at the museum?"

"Yeah. In Conservancy."

Other than an accidental meeting in the lunch room, which was just outside Conservancy, I still could see no possible connection between Mel Corbin and Rob Varney. "Is he . . . strange?" I asked. "Corbin. I mean, can you see him—"

"Can't stand the guy. But, other than an eye for the women, he's as normal as you, me, or anyone else around here. 'Course that's not—"

"Point taken."

"I suppose I could say I spent the night at my mom's," Billie offered, raising his head and looking suddenly hopeful.

"Better the truth than getting caught in a lie."

"Mom would never tell!"

"Billie, do you really want your mother to perjure herself?"

His head dropped back into his hands. "Rory, what'm I gonna do? They're gonna come for me, aren't they?"

"They'll certainly question you. Hard." His shoulders drooped, while I felt more and more like Don Quixote. Expert in lost causes, that was Rory Travis. I fished in my purse and dug out my wallet badge. I dangled it in front of his nose. "Look,

Billie," I said. "I don't have official clout because I'm on disability leave, but I have enough credibility to get Detective Parrish to listen to me. I don't believe they have enough evidence to arrest you, particularly if there's no one who can connect you to Rob Varney. But you may be in for marathon questioning. If there's *anything,* anything at all, you haven't told me, now's the time. I can't help you if I'm going to come up with egg on my face."

"You're FBI?" Billie was staring at my badge as if it were pecan pie with ice cream.

"Was. I doubt I'll be going back. But the badge does tend to get people's attention."

Billie lifted his head. There were tears in his eyes. "Hell, Rory, I feel a thousand percent better already."

I wished I did.

CHAPTER 15

With Billie's help, I cornered Mel Corbin in his office. Even Billie's explanation that I was in law enforcement Up North and just trying to help a friend added only a slight edge of respect to what I presumed was his customary view of women—stark naked, and how would she rate in bed? (I was, by the way, expecting a call from the local FBI office any day now about what the bleep-bleep did I think I was doing mucking around in a Florida case? A Sarasota City case? So far, it hadn't happened. Maybe because, prior to today, only Ken Parrish had seen my badge, or maybe because I had friends with a surprising amount of influence. Meanwhile, I was almost beginning to enjoy myself. In spite of creeps like Professor Mel Corbin.)

After the obligatory buttering-up—"You have such an interesting face, Ms. Travis. You really should pose for the portrait class"—Mel Corbin folded his hands on his desk, fixed on a smarmy smile, and said, "Now tell me, my dear, how may I help you?"

Having Billie flatten him would have helped my mood considerably. I unclenched my teeth and said, "I was hoping you might be able tell us something about Lydia Hewitt. Give us some idea of who might have wanted to harm her."

"Poor dear child," Professor Corbin sighed. "So young, so lovely. But I've told the police all I know. She didn't have an enemy in the world. And, I assure you, I didn't do it. I was giving a lecture at a conference in Orlando that night. That's been thoroughly checked. Iron-clad alibi, Ms. Travis. Absolutely iron-clad."

Unfortunately, I believed him. Although I'd verify the alibi with Ken. My instincts are remarkably reliable, but no one's right every time. Josh Thomas was a case in point. For all I was inclined to think him some kind of spook, he could be the orchestrator of this whole sick scenario.

I pulled myself back to the problem at hand. Corbin was still wearing his unctuous smile. "There's a suite of rooms on the fourth floor of the museum," I said. "Did you ever go up there with Lydia?"

His smile faded a bit. He bent his head, then peered up at me with what I can only describe by using that old expression "bedroom eyes." Mel Corbin might not have killed Lydia, but it's likely his effect on some women was almost as lethal. I wasn't one of them. "Well, did you?" I persisted.

He shrugged. "Sure. It was convenient. We both had security clearance. The view, the whole ambiance thing was great. And we got a real charge out of having the whole museum to ourselves, after hours."

"And nobody knew?"

Corbin waggled his hand back and forth. "I'm not sure. The aerie was not exactly a secret. I'm sure you understand people of our kind don't pry." He looked so self-righteous, my temper flared another notch.

"Did you ever see anyone else when you were there after hours? Or did they see you?"

He threw back his head and actually laughed out loud. Surprised, I could only stare at him. Laughter was too natural an emotion for someone like Mel Corbin.

"Oh, my, yes." He leaned back in his chair, still chuckling. I could tell he was hoping to be able to disconcert the female cop who was attempting to be businesslike in spite of looking as if she'd just lost a battle with a pack of dogs. *"In delicto* and quite *flagrante,"* he said. "Them, not us," he added hastily.

Beside me, I heard Billie suck in his breath. The more people wandering around the Bellman after hours, the better for Billie Hamlin and his alibi, which consisted of nothing more than trespassing, theft, and a pile of golf balls.

"You found someone else in the aerie?" I prodded.

"And a great surprise it was, too," Corbin admitted. "And quite disappointing, actually. I mean, there was no place else with a bed—"

"Who was it?" I interjected.

"No idea. Lydia knew the girl, I believe. But the dear child was so embarrassed, I couldn't get anything more out of her."

"So you left?"

"What else?"

"How?" I asked. He stared at me blankly. "How did you get out? I presume the alarm systems were set?"

"Actually, no. It was still early, and a number of people work late. Actually, it was really only the front of the museum we had to ourselves. We simply walked out past Security, as usual."

"But there must have been times . . ." My voice trailed off. Even FBI agents can stumble over embarrassing questions.

Corbin grinned. Salaciously. "Well, if we wanted more than a quickie, we simply stayed through 'til morning. We kept supplies up there. Rather delicious, actually. Like camping out."

"So who was the man?"

"Really, Ms. Travis, I'm not a voyeur. One naked body's much like—" He stopped, considered. Nodded. "Very well. I didn't see much of the girl except short blond hair. Missionary," he explained with considerable scorn, "and she turned her head to the wall. But he was a large man, not young. Hair so blonde gray doesn't show. Good muscle tone. Not flabby. Still good-looking. Country club type."

So the Art History professor actually had an artist's eye. "Did Lydia ever mention the name Patricia?"

Corbin made a wry face. "You know how girls are. They'd die before peaching on another female. Sorry, I didn't mean that literally, of course."

The blond hair fit Patricia Arkwright, who was supposedly having an affair with a VIP. The man could have been Parker St. Clair, but I was reaching again. And even if I was right, it probably meant nothing more than two sets of couples were enjoying the unique comforts of the aerie.

Was I following another lead to nowhere? Looking for murderers or witnesses in entirely the wrong places? This case was seeming more and more like a banyan tree—twisted limbs extending in all directions, putting down roots, which expanded into thick trunks of information leading straight back into the ground. Dead end. Finis. Forgetaboutit!

I thanked Professor Corbin, managed not to wince as I forgot and offered my hand. Before I said good-bye to Billie, I once again—and more strongly—advised him to get an attorney. "When your only alibi is an illegal act—twice—you don't dare open your mouth," I lectured. "When the police find you—and they will be coming for you—the only words out of your mouth must be, 'I have to call my lawyer.' Do you understand? Promise me, Billie. If you can't afford—"

"Hey," he said, "I've piled up a lot of golf balls, girl. And I know who to call. I'll be fine. You just get out there and find the guy that did it, okay?"

He gave me a big hug. I had to sit in the Caddy for a few minutes before the mist cleared from my eyes. If only I could believe I was helping instead of spinning my wheels.

Time to go home and clean up. But, of course, my cell phone rang.

"I'm at the museum. Where are you?" Josh demanded,

without preliminaries. I told him I was at the Art School. "The murder was all over the news. Are you in the midst of it again?"

"I guess."

"Meet me in the Bellman parking lot. Trail side."

Such a gracious request. We Feebs don't do humble well. Or subservient. In fact, we don't take orders well at all. Not even from men like Josh Thomas.

Evidently, my seething silence tipped him off. "I've got info on Parker St. Clair," Josh offered in a slightly less dictatorial tone. "And I'll spring for lunch." Close to conciliatory now.

I'd never thought the man was stupid.

So I turned north, instead of south, and found Josh standing with his arms folded, leaning against his forest green rental car and managing to look as if he'd been waiting all morning, rather than five minutes. I pulled up next to him.

I opened the Caddy window. Josh bent down to talk to me. And in ten seconds—or maybe it was less—he'd taken in the shell dust, the rip in my slacks, the dried blood. When I tried to hide my hands in my lap, he grabbed one and pried my fingers open, revealing the rapidly reddening lacerations. "Taken up gator wrestling, have you?"

"I fell. It was bound to happen sometime."

"You left your cane in the car." It wasn't a question. He knew I'd done something stupid.

"It was pride I should have left in the car."

"So who were you trying to impress?"

"Would you believe a woman from Brooklyn—in hair rollers, and seventy, if she was a day?"

Josh groaned. He reached in, grabbed my keys, and scooped me out of the Caddy and into his rental. Twenty minutes later, we pulled up in front of a waterfront villa on Pelican Key, in an area of newer and more modest homes than the imposing mansions where Aunt Hy had once lived. In Florida, "villa" is used to distinguish free-standing homes that are part of a condominium association from high-rise apartment-style condos. It was a handsome house, with a red tile roof and lush landscaping. Its most striking feature, however, was its location on a canal, complete with dock and a boat of about sixteen feet, with a sturdy outboard, a blue canvas canopy, and a jaunty blue stripe just below the gunwale.

Boat. Shivers ran up my spine. Goosebumps rose on my arms. I'd spent considerable time analyzing how someone could come and go at the Bellman at night without being seen, and a small boat was at the top of my list.

Josh, stabbing Lydia, slitting Rob's throat? Impossible. For all the darkness in him, absolutely, utterly impossible. After a last lingering look at Josh's boat, rocking gently in the nearly current-less canal on the far side of the road, I followed him into the house.

I tried not to laugh, I swear I did. But Josh's current home was a typical Florida rental. The kind so many people buy, then rent out during the season to help pay for their future retirement home. They are almost always furnished with light-colored furniture, upholstered in bright floral prints. Inevitably, the pictures on the walls are also flowers, palm trees, and beaches, with perhaps a child or two dabbling in the sand. (Surefire appeal to grandparents everywhere.) In short, the villa was about as far from a bachelor pad as one could get. Although Josh wasn't wearing all black today, he looked about as at home in this setting as Aunt Hy would at a rock concert.

"Don't say it," he barked.

"I'm sure you're very grateful to Martin for finding this for you," I choked. But I was talking to his back. He'd disappeared into the kitchen.

Josh was back out in a moment, carrying a large mixing bowl. Empty. "This way," he said, and I followed blindly, without so much as a token protest. Josh is like that. If you don't consciously fight him every minute, he carries you along, with all the inevitability of a tidal wave. Besides, I wanted to see if the bedroom was as totally Florida as the living room.

It was. The bedspread and draperies were strewn with a mix of tropical flowers, mostly in hot pink and orange. Repressing a giggle, I followed Josh straight into the bathroom, where he was already running water and testing its warmth. He gave a curt nod toward the john on which he had thoughtfully lowered the lid. My giggles died in my throat. I don't care how sophisticated a woman might think herself, I challenge you not to be at least a teeny bit uncomfortable when confined in a bathroom with a man you really don't know very well, and you're sitting on the toilet. The lid, by the way, was soft and squishy, almost like sitting on someone's stomach. It was clear vinyl with a mix of seashells embedded in some sort of viscous liquid. It should have been comfortable, but I seemed to have gone into some kind of suspended animation. I sat ramrod stiff, my brain shut down, the Bellman totally forgotten.

I was as still as one of Billie's effigies, while I watched Josh work on my palms, recovering enough to make a feeble protest only as he finished fastening off the second gauze wrap. "I look like a burn victim," I said. "Aren't you overdoing it for a minor scrape?"

"Keeps the medicine on. Wiggle your fingers." I did. "See," Josh retorted, "you still have complete mobility. Now take off your pants."

I squeaked.

"You heard me," Josh said. "From what I can see, your knees are worse than your hands."

"I'll just pull up my pant legs."

"Jesus, woman, you think I've never seen a woman's panties before. Besides, I bet you're wearing twice as much cloth as the string bikinis at the beach."

I was. Aunt Hy had given me ten pairs of white cotton briefs. Suitable for the Florida climate, she'd said. And they were. They were also about as sexy as one of those old-fashioned voluminous cotton nightgowns. I thought of all the sexy silk undies I'd packed away, along with my previous life.

As if it mattered. There was no way my body could compete, no matter what I was (or wasn't) wearing. It was pride I was suffering from, that was all. It couldn't possibly matter if Josh Thomas saw me in white cotton Fruit of the Looms.

I didn't move.

"Off! Now!" he said. "Or I do it for you." He sounded like he meant it. Actually, I had never thought Josh Thomas the kind of man who bluffed.

I wiggled out of my slacks, the john lid huffing and puffing beneath me. It was unnerving. Or maybe it was just Josh.

My left knee, in particular, looked rather nasty when bared to the world. Speaking of bared, Josh took one swift glance at my white cotton panties, then ducked his head, and kept his eyes trained on my knees. I had the horrible feeling he actually felt sorry for catching me so totally unprepared for male eyes.

Not, of course, that Josh Thomas counted. I still had moments when I felt he wasn't quite human. He was not my type. Definitely not my type. But, no matter which side of the law he was on, he understood how the great underbelly of the world worked. And for that reason we had an empathy, albeit sometimes reluctant and wary. It was a mutual trait, I supposed. That *never trust anybody* learned in the school of hard knocks.

Way off in the living room, where I'd parked my purse on the coffee table, my cell phone rang. Josh had it in my hands before the third ring. I began to see how he had appeared in my tram out of nowhere. The man was *fast*.

"You told Billie to lawyer up!" Ken Parrish roared.

"How could I not?"

"Forgotten which side you're on, Travis? Two people dead, and you've shut down our chief suspect!"

"He didn't do it."

"Great, you've gone psychic now." His sarcasm practically leaped out of the phone.

"Think premeditation, Parrish," I snapped. Oh, lord, I'd planned to sit him down and discuss this in a reasonable manner, and, instead, I was yelling into a cell phone. Bad. Very bad. But I couldn't seem to stop. "You're thinking crime of passion with Lydia, but the guy had a knife. He used Rohypnol. He wore latex gloves. That's not a sudden 'I lost it.' That's premeditation. And Billie didn't even know Rob Varney—"

"That's what he told—"

I cut him off. "Rob's murder was premeditated as well. The strop razor, the shaving cream. And I bet you found Rohypnol, right?"

"Autopsy's just beginning."

"It's there. I'd bet on it. And, besides," I added righteously, "even if you could prove Billie knew Rob Varney—and I don't think he did—what possible motive could he have?"

"How about Varney saw him attach the effigy to the bull?"

My cell phone turned to ice. I had a feeling Ken hadn't planned to tell me that juicy bit, but, like me, he'd gotten carried away by our argument. "Did he?" I asked. Only a thread was left of my confident tone.

" 'Fraid so, Rory. Sorry."

"How long have you known?"

"Almost from the beginning. But since Hamlin confessed to the effigies, it didn't seem very important."

"Something's wrong," I muttered.

"No kidding. But women's intuition doesn't cut it, Travis."

I began to recover. "You know being caught for making the effigies is not sufficient motive for murder."

"But unrequited passion is. Maybe Varney made a habit of snooping. Maybe he saw something the night Hewitt was killed—"

"Did he tell you that?"

Ken sighed. "Hell, no. Don't I wish."

I remembered that I liked him. "You'll let me know about the autopsy?" I asked.

"I'll call you later. If it's not too damn late, maybe we can have coffee?"

"Sure," I said, "that would be great. 'Bye."

Josh's obsidian eyes were regarding me with considerable interest. "Have you made the Roman connection?" he asked. "You know, Roman chariot, Lygia's sacrifice similar to Christians being fed to the lions. Lydia Hewitt ending up in a lion cage?"

I widened my eyes. "And to think my office accuses *me* of making giant leaps instead of following a proper trail of hard facts."

"Those *are* hard facts."

"You're saying someone specified the Roman connection, or someone with a better than usual education took advantage of what Billie did?" Damn the man. It was difficult enough struggling back into my slacks without idiotic concepts like this to consider while I did it.

"Well, obviously, I wouldn't dare say Billie did it."

"Ha! Big macho spook scared of little old me?" Safe enough to say now, modesty restored.

Josh managed to look diffident. Not an easy feat. "Just scared of your displeasure, ma'am. Remember . . . I want you to work for me."

I grabbed my cane and levered myself off the john. Since

Josh had put away all the medical supplies while I was talking to Ken, he was right on my heels as I stalked out of the bathroom. "Had lunch?" he asked.

The tuna salad sandwich he made was so good he felt forced to admit it came out of a package. I didn't mind. It tasted great, and it had been a long morning. As I wiped the last crumbs from my fingers, Josh said, "I found out about Parker St. Clair, but I don't know if it means anything."

I put my elbows on the dining table, propped my bandaged hands under my chin. "Well?"

"About fifteen years ago he founded a company called Clairity, an obvious play on his name. He seems to have had a lot of government connections, because the company never struggled. It was off and running from Day One. It provides 'Services.' A wealthy citizen, a company, a government, a country wants something . . . Clairity finds a way for them to get it."

"That's a lot of bones," I whispered, my mind spinning with the possibilities.

"Oh, yeah. Clairity's still at it, but, lately, there's talk of watchdog committees, closer inspection of the government's connection to Clairity. Questions about Clairity's connections to other governments, some maybe not our friends. There's even talk of vast sums of money gone missing, maybe into personal bank accounts, such as Parker St. Clair's or his wife's."

"You didn't just find this out, did you?" I accused. "You recognized the name the minute I said it."

Josh took a long look out the window toward the dock and the boat. "I had to think about it a bit. Like Martin, I doubted there could be a connection to the troubles here."

"But it's possible, isn't it?" I prodded. "So why would Martin refuse to talk? Why would he—and you—protect someone like Parker St. Clair?"

"Martin protects everything," Josh returned with ease. "He's so used to *not* talking that revealing information, any kind of information, is practically against his religion."

"But we have to find out what he knows!" It occurred to me I was sounding as eager as a novice just out of Quantico.

"I like the *we* part," Josh said. He wasn't smiling.

I ignored him. Josh Thomas being nice wasn't an image I could handle. He was dangerous. I was weak. I couldn't ever let down my guard. "If Parker St. Clair feared someone," I said, "he'd hire a hit, right? He'd never stage an elaborate setup like this one. I mean, there's no reason to murder people at the Bellman. He's on the Board, for heaven's sake!"

"He's an arrogant son of a bitch."

"You know him?"

"Mostly by reputation, but Martin dragged me to a cocktail party at the St. Clair's last Saturday. Under all that polish, he struck me as a ruthless son of a bitch."

Takes one to know one, I thought. "And we probably want to nail him because we don't like him," I sighed. "There's nothing to connect him with Lydia—"

"Well?" Josh demanded as I sat, suddenly silent, among the sofa's fuschia flowers.

So I told him what I'd learned from Mel Corbin.

"Can't have been the first time St. Clair's been caught with his pants down," Josh said when I finished. "Hardly a motive for murder."

I couldn't disagree, but I told him I'd do my best to find out if the man in the aerie had been Parker St. Clair. "How about checking out Rob Varney?" I added.

Josh gave me a slow, wolfish, atta-girl smile that almost made me forget what we were talking about. He dragged me up out of the overly deep sofa and steered me into a small guest bedroom. I shouldn't have felt that teensy wave of disappointment when I saw we were headed toward a ridiculously fragile French

Provincial desk with a laptop taking up half its surface, instead of toward the bed. But for an instant—I admit it—my racing heart had nothing to do with the case at hand.

I was thoroughly ashamed of myself.

Josh knew databases even I had never heard of. I was impressed. And he didn't have to hack in. He already knew the way. But the only database that had ever heard of a Rob Varney was among the last we tried. The file came up labelled, "Classified."

Oh, great. That's all we needed in this case. Another spook.

CHAPTER 16

I turned down Josh's offer of a drive up to Cortez, one of the few Florida fishing villages that hasn't been flattened in favor of sport fishing marinas, condos, and bayside resorts. Not that I wouldn't have liked to opt out, to spend an afternoon being chauffeured around by the not-so-Sleeping Satyr, but I thought of Billie and Aunt Hy, of Lydia Hewitt and Rob Varney, and decided this wasn't the time to explore what made Josh Thomas tick. Or my own very mixed emotions in that direction. The wise move was to be hardheaded. Then again, I was seldom wise.

But this time I stuck stubbornly to *no*.

Josh's villa was on one of several streets with nearly identical homes, lined up side by side, daring their residents to find their way home on a dark night when three sheets to the wind. I use the nautical term advisedly, as each house has a dock, with boat, and each street dead-ends against Sarasota Bay. As Josh backed the car down the driveway, I waved my hand toward the waterfront end of the street. "Can we take a peek? I'd like to see if we can spot the museum from here."

I don't think I fooled him for a minute. Josh did a very nice version of a man not looking toward his dock and his boat, then he nodded and drove the two blocks to where the street ended in a sea wall on the bay. He turned off the engine, leaned back. "Glove compartment," he said.

I kept my wits sharp as I looked inside. Not that I really

expected a gun or a snake, but with Josh one could never be certain. But all that rested on top of a thin pile of local maps was a particularly fine pair of binoculars. The bay was broad. Without the binoculars only silhouettes were visible. With them, after a bit of adjustment and a careful sweep of the shoreline, I found what I was looking for. The Casa Bellissima, set on one thousand ninety feet of waterfront and sixty-six acres of lush plantings, did not exactly blend in with the other cheek-by-jowl mansions along the shore.

"You're almost directly across," I said, then wished I hadn't.

"Sure, I go over every night and prowl the grounds. How else does a spook amuse himself in this haven of senior citizens?"

"It was just a comment," I protested. Too strongly.

"Yeah, right."

"Where does Parker St. Clair live?"

Josh pointed to an area not far south of the Bellman museum grounds. "He was bragging he had to buy up four houses to acquire the land. Positively smug about pressuring the owners to sell. Guess one of them was really reluctant. Martin mentioned something about a dead dog."

"You're kidding, right?"

"No."

"And Martin doesn't think St. Clair capable of murder!"

"He never said that," Josh stated patiently. "He said he didn't see any motive for St. Clair to be involved in the murder of the girl. Or with the effigies. That was, of course," he added thoughtfully, "before Rob Varney turned up dead."

"You think Varney's connected to St. Clair?"

"Could be. If Varney was a government spook, he could have run into St. Clair on either side of the fence—as a colleague or maybe investigating Clairity's more questionable ops."

My spine was prickling again. "Can you find out?" Maybe my wits had been scrambled by the gentleness of Josh's hands as he bandaged mine, but at that moment any suspicions I might be asking the executioner to investigate his victim had vanished from my mind.

"I'd need to get into the Clairity database," Josh was saying, "which is about as easy as hacking the Department of Defense."

"Can you do it?"

He shrugged. "If not, I know someone who can."

I nodded. *Martin.* I had to talk to Martin. Though why I was so sure a man, long retired, would have important information had to be another of my odd intuitive leaps.

"Josh . . . there's something else. I'm probably wasting your time, but could you check on a Timothy Mundell from Tempe, Arizona—see if you can find something beyond the bare facts in the police report?"

Josh's frown deepened as I outlined the sad all-too-short story of the twenty-year-old found hanging in a banyan tree. I did not care for his initial reaction, which was an incredulous, "*Billie* found the body?"

"So?" I challenged, sparking righteous indignation straight at his satyr's head. "He works security."

"Some security," Josh scoffed.

"Damn it, Josh, not you, too!"

"How many people do you know who challenge gators and water moccasins for golf balls? Face it, Travis, Hamlin's certifiable. What's a lil' ol' murder here and there?"

Silence seethed as Josh drove me back to my car. And then he capped his demonstration of male pseudo-superiority by ordering me to stay home and nurse my scrapes. "And don't go off tilting with your City Cop, either. Everything will keep 'til tomorrow."

Oh, great. Even Josh Thomas thought of me as a deluded and ineffectual Don Quixote. Was absolutely everybody laughing at my feeble attempts at investigation? No pun intended.

You recall that old expression about "ready to chomp nails"? Well, that's how I must have looked as I stepped off the elevator to the penthouse. One glance at me, and Jody ran for the scotch. But an application of spirits wasn't going to work, I knew it. I managed a smile for Aunt Hy, who was, thank God, having one of her Perfectly Normal days. A second single malt didn't help, either, but it made it easier for me to say no when Ken Parrish called. Not that I didn't want to meet him for coffee—if for no other reason than because Josh had told me not to—but, truthfully, I needed to be by myself. To think. To make sense of the inexplicable.

To wonder if Martin Longstreet held the essential key. Or was Martin the person who had set me up for this snipe hunt?

And, yes—I confess—to wonder if maybe Billie really did it. An artistic temperament gone haywire. Weren't most serial killers described as personable, even charming? Tossing me a hint about the possibility of murder in Tim Mundell's death could have been the sheer bravado of a sick mind.

To wonder if it was Josh—so conveniently handy on all occasions. He could have made a swift visit to Sarasota to leave two thousand dollars under Billie's door. Or maybe the two thousand was a fabrication? Maybe Billie's "twenty Ben Franklins" was a cover story designed by a madman.

And, finally, to wonder if my desire to somehow blame it on Parker St. Clair was simply because I didn't want it to be Billie. Or Josh.

Had I gone totally soft? My skills, even the renowned Travis intuition, shown to be worthless?

I used my sore hands and knees as an excuse for not meeting Ken. He was suitably sympathetic. If I'd lived anywhere but a penthouse at the Ritz-Carlton, I think he would have jumped in his SUV and come straight over. As it was, I went to bed alone. Again. And every mistake I'd ever made—from an improper

Daryn Parke

pirouette in ballet class at age seven, to guzzling rum punch at a freshman college mixer, to the usual personal and business disasters we all encounter, to those last horrible moments with Eric on the fire escape—kaleidoscoped through my aching head. It was a bad night. With Lydia's and Rob's bloody bodies for a chaser. Not to mention a vision of myself kneeling amidst the shattered pieces of the mannequin, with that badly drawn gash across her throat, her white satin gown splashed with shiny red nail polish.

In the morning I once again climbed the two flights of Escher stairs to Marketing. The Blonde was Karen Woodley. She only confirmed what I already knew. Lydia had told her the story of walking in on the assignation in the aerie. It was, after all, too delicious a tale not to pass on. Yes, the girl had been Patricia Arkwright. The man Lydia didn't recognize. Her only description: he was "big" and "older."

"I asked, 'Big where?' " Karen confided, "and we both laughed so hard she never answered."

I thanked her and went in search of Patricia, waiting patiently while she finished a presentation on the circus to a busload of fifth graders. I told Pat, flat out, that if she had any lingering affection for Billie, she needed to answer my questions. We sat at one of the picnic tables near the Circus Museum. She might not have been one of my favorite people, but if my intuition wasn't totally screwed, I felt I had her attention. She was going to make an effort to tell me what she knew.

"I apologize for getting so personal," I said, "but was it you Lydia surprised up in the aerie?"

All I could see was blond hair as she hid her face in her hands. She nodded.

"Pat," I said as gently as I could, "I wouldn't ask this if I didn't believe it's important. Who was the man?"

"I wouldn't have minded so much if it was just Lydia," she

194

burst out, still not looking up. "But that awful creep, Mel Corbin. I mean, that man is slime!"

"I agree, but he didn't recognize you."

"Really?" Pat's head came up with a snap. Her eyes locked with mine.

"Really. I asked him."

"Oh, thank God!"

I truly felt sorry for her. Some things just aren't supposed to be made public. Like me sitting on a shell-covered john with Josh Thomas dabbing at my scarred and unclad legs.

"Uh, Pat . . . the man's name?"

"I can't," she gasped. "He's married. He's a VIP."

"Do you want Billie to have an intimate connection with Old Sparky?"

"That's horrible!" she snapped. "You know Billie would never murder anybody."

"*I* know. Believe me, Detective Sergeant Ken Parrish does not agree with me. Billie's in serious trouble."

She picked a live oak leaf off the picnic table, gazed up at the drooping Spanish moss high above, then allowed her eyes to drift down toward the riot of color that was Opal's Rose Garden. "Parker St. Clair," she mumbled at last.

"Where did you meet him?" I kept my voice low and steady, as if the identification hadn't sent a surge of blood pounding through my veins.

"At a fund-raiser last spring. He was gone for the summer, of course, but as soon as he came back, he seemed to want to take up where we left off." When I didn't come up with another question, Pat added defensively, "I'd never seen what wealth can do. Never had Cristal with a meal. Flown to Naples or Key West for a weekend. It was . . . Oh, shit! Are you going to tell his wife?" Pat wailed.

"Heavens, no!"

"There *is* a God!" Pat fished for a tissue, blew her nose. "Parker married money, you know. And now that his company's having problems, he'd really be in trouble if his wife left him."

Then he was damn stupid to be playing around. But, of course, I didn't say so. Yet I couldn't help wonder if I'd hit pay dirt. If Parker St. Clair was worried enough about Clairity to have mentioned it during pillow talk, then maybe the matter was serious. Rob Varney might have been here as an investigator. He might have been a whistle-blower. He also might have been exactly what he appeared to be—a retiree, keeping boredom away by becoming a volunteer. Even spooks retired. If they lived long enough. Look at Martin Longstreet.

And Lydia? Where did an artist's model without a serious thought in her head fit into all this? Except as a witness to Parker St. Clair's indiscretion? What about Mel Corbin? Didn't that make him a target also?

Or was it truly a case of Murder as Art? And all the rest was peripheral?

It was my afternoon to drive a tram, so I thanked Pat for being so honest, once again assured her Melinda St. Clair would hear nothing from me, and went off to find Tram 3.

The next morning Josh called to ask if I was free for an interview with Martin Longstreet late that afternoon. And would I have supper with him afterward?

I was back in skeptic mode. *Never trust anyone. Never trust anyone.* A woman with a shattered heart, as well as a shattered body, was most vulnerable of all.

I told Josh I had already arranged a private interview with Martin, and I had other plans for supper. To soften the blow, I added that I was sure he understood that any old spook would consider three a crowd.

The silence over the phone was so dense I could almost hear

the thoughts surging through Josh's brain. But were they the rage of a villain, the arrogant frustration of a man accustomed to being boss, the annoyance of a cop shut out of an investigation? Or—just perhaps—the hurt of a male whose help had been rejected, along with his interest in me as a female?

"Josh, I'm sorry," I mumbled and hung up. I had never felt more paranoid in my life. Outside the gilded womb at the top of the Ritz-Carlton, I had no friends. I had tried to adapt to this new life, really I had, but Lydia and Rob were gone, Billie compromised so badly only a fool would be blind to the possibility that he might be guilty. Ken Parrish was alienated because I clung stubbornly to Billie's cause. And Josh Thomas was too lethal to ignore as a possible suspect. And Martin? Dear old Martin had a thumb in this pie somewhere. He might, in fact, hold the key that had stayed so elusively out of reach since the day the Roman warrior had appeared in the chariot in the museum courtyard. And today at four-thirty when I would tackle the wily old boy in his lair, I was going to need every last bit of smarts I had.

Martin Longstreet lived in a villa similar to the one he had found for Josh, though it was a bit more homey, with begonias, geraniums, and petunias dripping from hanging baskets on either side of the front entrance. The primary difference between Josh's rented villa and his own, Martin explained as he ushered me inside, was that his home had three bedrooms and a deeper canal, suitable for his sailboat, which sat, bare poled, at its berth looking as sleek and expensive as it undoubtedly was.

And Martin, of course, had his own furniture. Leather, gleaming wood, glass tabletops. Antique Persian carpets. No garish prints of palms, flowers, beaches, or small children. Martin's taste in art was eclectic, ranging from Baroque to Impressionist to American Modern, but every painting was an original. I took the time to study his collection before finally taking a seat on the midnight-blue leather sofa.

Martin Longstreet had been married at some time. (I'd checked with Aunt Hy.) But to whom and how long ago, even she had no answer. He had come to Sarasota about twelve years earlier, unattached, and stayed that way. As attractive as his home was, it was wholly masculine. It was also a modest abode for a man of his wealth and influence. But this villa, I supposed, provided him with all the space he needed, freeing up whatever money he had to support the museum, and probably other local good causes as well.

"Atonement," Martin said, as if reading my thoughts. "I've spent my retirement trying to make up for things I wish had never happened." He ran a wrinkled hand over his face, slicked back his shock of white hair. He looked years older than on the night of the Gala. "One of my more recent regrets is failing to talk to you about Parker St. Clair."

"Martin," I said, sounding more severe than a feeble Feeb should when addressing an elder, and undoubtedly superior, officer, "there's a lot more to all this than Parker St. Clair. Suppose you start at the beginning."

He grinned at me, damn him. An old man of at least eighty, flashing me a grin as outrageously wolfish as Josh Thomas's. "No," he told me. "Some of this needs to wait until we've got past this case. Concentrate on the murders, Rory. That's all you should be doing right now."

"I have to know what right you have to tell me that," I said, determined to get around his steely control.

Martin steepled his fingers beneath his chin, gazed at a very fine painting of an old clipper ship sailing over a choppy sea. "Need to know, Rory," he murmured, "need to know. But in this case you certainly have a right to some of it."

I waited. Respectfully. I had to accept that Martin would tell me what he thought I ought to know. No more, no less. And nothing would budge him. I imagined a great many people had used a remarkable number of methods to pry information from Martin Longstreet. And failed. I would have to settle for what he was willing to give.

"Very well," he said, "as you seem to know, I worked for the CIA from the time it was still the OSS. Through the Cold War. Vietnam—where I worked with Josh's father. Something I believe you also figured out on your own, with very little to go on. You possess a remarkable gift, my dear."

I was inclined to think Martin had that special gift as well. I supposed that was how spooks got to be old spooks.

"Not really," I told him. "I knew about the CIA from Aunt Hy, and I overheard most of your conversation with Josh at the Gala."

"More than that, Rory. Your conclusion was a major leap. I'd heard about your gift, of course, but that was the first time I'd seen it. You heard a few minutes of conversation at a dinner party, and somehow you *knew.*"

"I guessed."

"Admit it, Rory. You hate Madame Celestine so much because she just might not be a fake."

"She's a scam artist!"

"Agreed. But sometimes she nails it, and you just won't admit it."

My chin was sticking out a mile. "Why," I demanded, "are we talking about Madame Celestine?"

We glared at each other. Finally, I shrugged. "If only my so-called gift was *useful*," I grumbled. "If only I could see what's going on at the Bellman. I mean, knowing you and Josh's father were CIA in 'Nam is hardly going to solve two murders here and now. If a person is going to have flashes of insight, they ought to be significant to the moment."

Martin chuckled and poured out two cups of Lapsang Souchong that had been steeping on the low table in front of the couch. "Rory," he said as he handed me a cup, "your insights wouldn't have become so well known if they were always useless."

I hid my face behind my tea cup. I took a sip. Damned if I wasn't more of a Lapsang Souchong type—smoky and mysterious—than China Rose Petal. I recalled thinking Josh, too, was Lapsang Souchong.

"That night at the Gala," I said, "your conversation with Josh, that was a Heads-Up, wasn't it? Time to give the poor girl a clue."

"You are a colleague, child, as well as my dear Hyacinth's niece. I was indeed attempting to give you a hint, though I admit I had not expected you to spring to such startlingly accurate conclusions."

So even that had been deliberate. Information spoon-fed, like baby cereal, into an infant's mouth. Pride dictated that I get up and stalk out, but I was stronger than that. I had come here for a reason. So I lifted my chin and stared at Martin in silent challenge.

"Very well," he said, after a deliberate sampling of tea, "you wish to know about Parker St. Clair."

"And Josh Thomas."

"You need not worry about Josh."

"That's what you said about Parker St. Clair!"

"You're a hard woman, Rory, my dear. You're quite right. I could not see how that poor girl's death had anything to do with Parker. But Varney—"

"Did you know him?"

"No. I did not encounter him here at the museum, and I would remember if I'd ever met anyone who looked like Richard Bellman elsewhere."

"So you have no idea if he has any connection to Parker St. Clair?"

"None—although Josh tells me he's working on it."

"Is it possible Varney was undercover, investigating St. Clair?"

"Of course. But it's also possible he was a retiree, driving a tram."

"Yes, I know," I sighed. "That hideous concept of Murder as Art hangs over all this like some ghastly shroud." Frustrated, I glared at Martin, who stared blandly back as if he were a sweet old man on the verge of senility. "So you won't talk about Josh?" He shook his head. Door closed, locked and bolted. "Okay," I groaned, "tell me about Parker St. Clair."

Martin took a long swallow of his tea. The tea cup clinked back onto its china saucer with the barest betrayal of shaking fingers. Martin Longstreet truly was an old man about to violate a code of silence as strict as the mafia's rule of *omerta*. It did not sit well with him.

"At one time Parker St. Clair was one of us," Martin said. "But he seemed to chafe at any kind of authority, and he never failed to announce to any and all that patriotism wasn't enough to augment his government salary. 'Cold hard cash,' he'd say. 'That's what it takes to live like a king.'

"So he left us." Martin paused, then skipped rather a lot of years. "Soon after Parker started Clairity, he found himself with enough power to have his records 'disappear' from an interesting variety of databases. On the World Wide Web we can find his family background, his date and place of birth, his schooling, his military service, even a job with an Import/Export company, for which he supposedly worked until creating Clairity." Martin shrugged. "But nowhere is there any mention of his being a merc. Nor of his climbing the dung heap to be head honcho in arms and drug dealing. Whatever it took to make enough money to start Clairity and become poster boy for Mr. American

Entrepreneur."

My view of a Country Club Parker St. Clair did a swift dive south. On this one, my intuition had failed me. Again. I didn't like St. Clair, but I had had trouble finding him dangerous. He might have hired the hits, I'd supposed, while speculating the worst case, but doing it himself? That I had not considered possible, until now.

"You think he did it," I said.

"I think he is capable of it," Martin replied, carefully precise.

"So is Josh."

"Possibly," Martin agreed, "but I should say that assassinating pretty young women really isn't in his line."

From Martin, a sterling bit of praise.

"And Billie?"

"My dear, you know Billie. I don't. Truly, I have no idea."

"Did you pay Billie to make those effigies?" I demanded.

"Rory, my child, why ever would I?" Martin's gray eyes were perfectly innocent. I bet he'd looked just like that before he shot someone. Nor had he vouched for Josh.

Not good.

"One more thing. Look at me, Rory," Martin demanded.

Dutifully, I looked him straight in the eye, even as I wondered what was so important.

"Parker St. Clair is dangerous," Martin emphasized. "He's bigger, tougher, and far more experienced than you are. He slits throats without an ounce of regret. Stay away from him, child. I'll speak to your detective, attempt to steer him away from Hamlin. Parrish is a good man. He'll listen. And handle it."

"But—"

"Leave it!" Martin barked. "This isn't your fight."

"You put me into the middle of this, I know you did!"

"I didn't know how far it was going to go." Martin—suddenly anguished, an old man. Unable to stop a ball he might well have started rolling.

I gathered my dignity. "I trust that one of these days someone is going to tell me the truth." My sarcasm was edgy. Nasty. Not the way to talk to an elderly gentleman who looked as if he might not be able to get up from his chair. My Aunt Hy's friend and escort. Her lover?

Good God! Did they really . . . ?

"I promise," Martin mumbled.

I took the tea things into the kitchen, then, after a long assessing look, I left him sitting there, head back, eyes closed. Quietly, I shut the door.

On the drive home my mind seethed with possibilities about Parker St. Clair, while my heart was heavy because Josh might be part of my worst-case scenario. I didn't want him to be the incarnation of Darkness. I didn't want him to be an assassin, a gun runner, a drug dealer, or anything else he might be when out from under Martin Longstreet's nose.

But with my luck . . .

My "other plans" for dinner, that I had so glibly tossed at Josh, were a ham and cheese casserole and salad of baby greens, shared with Aunt Hy and Marian Edmundson. We then watched three taped hours of *The Sopranos*. It occurred to me, not for the first time, that Josh Thomas could have walked onto that screen and been right at home.

CHAPTER 17

I was asleep when my cell phone rang the next morning. *Oh, no, not today!* I snarled as I groped for the phone. No tram driving, no matter how desperate Burt was. I had plans to spend Sunday sketching out what I knew, making a list of questions I needed to ask, a list of likely suspects, a list of improbable suspects . . .

My eyes were still shut, my hand flopping about. The phone went flying to the floor. Since the carpet was close to two inches thick, its stubborn ring continued. Expelling a word my mother never taught me, I pried my eyes open, peered over the edge of the bed, and grabbed the phone. "Travis," I grumped.

"Your pal Billie's just out of the ER," Ken Parrish said. "I thought you'd want to know."

"What?" I mumbled quite stupidly.

"A gator finally got him."

"What!" I was awake.

"He went down one time too many, but he was lucky. Fifty stitches, but he'll keep his arm . . . they think." Ken paused, then apologized. "Sorry, I've been up so long I didn't realize how early it was. Billie's name rang a bell at headquarters, and I got a call right after it happened."

"Where is he now?"

"Sarasota Memorial. They just took him up to a room. He'll be here a while."

I thanked Ken for calling, then staggered into the kitchen and made a large pot of coffee. After the night Billie had had, he didn't need me rushing down there and waking him up. So, first, a little effort to make sure he didn't move straight from hospital to jail.

Not wanting to intrude on Marian's kitchen, I decided to work on Aunt Hy's dining table, a creation of mosaic flowers handcrafted in Italy—a new treasure added to her collection when she moved into the Ritz-Carlton. I'd seen the bill. Eleven thousand and change. *Sans* chairs. It should, at the very least, be an inspiration for my creative thinking.

Dressed in the comfort of a navy corduroy caftan, I laid out a large pad of drawing paper, a brand-new yellow legal pad, sharpened a dozen pencils to a fine point, set three ballpoints down beside them. And then I stared at the mess I'd scattered over the intricate mosaic design and realized this case had just about as many pieces as the tabletop. And I had no access to the mind of the one person who carried the overall design in his head. Or how to maneuver the pieces to make it all fit.

How could I apply scientific method to the Art of Murder?

I was foolish even to try.

There were those who'd said the same about my walking again.

I picked up the large drawing pad and began to sketch the scene of each incident. I began with Tim Mundell, hanging from a banyan on the waterfront. Somehow I was certain he belonged in the picture. Next, the jaunty Roman Warrior, driving a Biga in the courtyard. The mannequin in white satin, in pieces on the tile floor at the Casa Bellissima, a crude slit painted on her throat with fingernail polish. The *papier mâché* Lygia strapped on top of her bronze counterpart, riding a bull prominently placed at the Art Museum's front entrance. (No wonder someone had seen Billie do it. Though surely the only significance about the person being Rob Varney was that he was a man who kept his eyes open at all times.)

Next came Lydia in the lion cage, far across the grounds at the Circus Museum. Lydia, who had massive knife wounds, as if the killer were attempting to duplicate her death by bull or by lion in the Roman Coliseum. Lydia, who had been Billie's model for the Lygia of *papier mâché*. Lydia who had seen Parker St. Clair and Patricia Arkwright in the aerie. But, if that mattered, why was Mel Corbin walking around as if he hadn't a care in the world?

Was Mel Corbin next? Or was he a murderer? Frankly, I didn't think he was smart enough to have orchestrated what was happening at the Bellman.

My sketch of Rob Varney in the barber chair was awkward, but it would have to do. Rob Varney. A bull of a man, who resembled Richard Bellman. Dead in Richard Bellman's barber chair at the Casa Bellissima, his throat slit by a strop razor, left tauntingly at the scene of the crime.

I started a fresh page, drawing a map of the Bellman grounds, with each of its major buildings: the Art Museum, the Circus Museum, the Casa Bellissima. Then I used an X to mark each incident. When I was finished, it was obvious the incidents had ranged over the full extent of the museum grounds. The waterfront, the inner courtyard of the Art Museum, the front entrance, the Circus, and one nasty incident and one murder at the House. The mannequin still bothered me. It wasn't artistic enough to fit. Almost as if it were part of someone else's scheme. Martin's, or Josh's, perhaps?

And yet I couldn't dismiss it. Professionally and personally, it stuck there, a sandspur clinging, prickling, refusing to let go. That mannequin had *hurt*. More than anyone could ever know. Those fractured fragments had gotten to me. Shown how vulnerable I was. How very far from recovery. It had taken every ounce of courage I had to continue on that evening, smiling, making polite conversation. Not even the Lygia effigy or my conversation later that night with Josh Thomas had seemed quite real. I had been holding myself together by a thread.

I shoved the map aside. Thoughtfully, I traced the outline of one of the table's mosaic flowers with my finger. That October night wasn't so long ago . . . but I'd changed. Physically, I was still struggling along, but inside . . . inside, shock had turned to anger and determination. As much as I hated to admit it, my frozen curiosity, my analytical mind had been jump-started by that damned mannequin.

I pulled the map back in front of me. The waterfront, the Roman charioteer, and *Lygia and the Bull* were about as far apart as two incidents could be on the Bellman grounds. Lydia's body was far across the Bellman grounds from all three. At the Casa, again, the only anomaly was the proximity of the mannequin and the barber chair. But if I eliminated the mannequin, the incidents were so perfectly spaced that they screamed premeditation. And not a fingerprint anywhere. Meticulous planning. Creative execution.

Evil as an art form.

I took up the yellow pad and listed the prime suspects. After a fierce battle with my inner self, I put Billie right after Parker St. Clair. Then Josh, because there was little doubt he was capable of murder, though I really couldn't see him murdering anyone for Art. Nor could I picture him carving up Lydia. I refused to believe it. But women can be incredible fools about men. His name stayed on the list.

Martin? I hesitated. Martin, I suspected, was ruthless enough, but he would have had to hire a hit man. He was past the age of do-it-yourself. Or was I being patronizing? Once a spook, always a spook.

Which brought me back to Josh Thomas. And motive. I was convinced neither Martin nor Josh were madmen. If they wanted someone dead, there had to be a very good reason. A motive to murder Rob Varney was not hard to imagine. But Lydia Hewitt? No way.

As for the Improbable Suspects, there were Mel Corbin and Patricia Arkwright. Frankly, they seemed about as likely as the descendants of the survivors of Sarasota's real estate bust—in which Richard Bellman had figured so prominently—or of the circus community, which had brought Bellman fame and fortune, only to find itself excluded from life at the Casa Bellissima.

My interviews with Sarasota County old-timers were about as productive as my interviews with circus people. The parents of Aunt Hy's husband, Edgar Van Horne, had bought their property on Pelican Key from Richard Bellman himself. Aunt Hy was well acquainted with almost all the old families. They all said the same thing. Bellman's real estate ventures had been hurt by the Florida building bust after a hurricane in 1926. So had every other real estate venture on both coasts, Gulf and Atlantic.

Yes, Bellman wasn't the greatest record keeper. Yes, he borrowed from Peter to pay Paul. There were some very lean years, particularly after Black Friday of 1929. Yes, Richard Bellman died owing money to nearly everyone. But even amidst the deepest days of the Great Depression, Bellman had other investments that had paid off, including the Circus and oil wells in the southwest. Although it took a good deal of maneuvering after his death, the debts had been paid. Descendants might have heard the tales of disgruntled ancestors, but no one, as far as they knew, still had an axe to grind. In fact, many were generous contributors to the museum.

So where the hell was I?

No farther along than when the phone rang this morning. But seeing it all on paper, the incident scenes so carefully spaced out (if I didn't count the mannequin), the effigies and victims so carefully arranged, emphasized Rob Varney's remark. Without a doubt, there was Art to these murders. They were the work of a cold-blooded madman or of an even more ruthless killer, bent on making us seek a madman and not himself.

I cleaned off Aunt Hy's marble mosaic table, dressed, and headed for the hospital. Beyond reinforcing my belief that a ruthless and skillful puppet master was pulling the strings, I had not made much progress.

I'd put three friends on my prime suspect list.

Way to go, Travis.

Billie was asleep, but when I laid my hand on his unbandaged arm, his eyes flew open. For a moment stark fear glazed his eyes.

"Hey," I said, "I know I don't look so great, but no one's mistaken me for a gator before."

He relaxed against the pillows and grinned, suddenly looking remarkably like the Billie Ball Hamlin I had first met. "Seven footer," he chortled. "Seven footer, and I wrestled him onto the bank. Not a soul around, y'know, so I had to do it myself. Punched him in the eye a couple of times and he let go. Managed to get back to my Jeep and dial 9-1-1."

Damn, but he actually looked pleased with himself.

"Y'know, Parrish isn't such a bad guy," Billie said. "He was here all night, down in the ER."

I couldn't say what I was thinking. *Billie, you're a sculptor. You darn near lost your arm. No more golf balls!* So I settled for platitudes: take it easy, be glad he was already on paid leave. Not to worry. We'd get this mess straightened out, get him off the hook before his bandages were off.

"Billie," I added, "there is one question I've been wanting to ask." He looked at me, expectantly, from guileless blue eyes. No way, absolutely no way was Billie running around out there killing people. "When you were given the two thousand dollars, were there any instructions about what kind of incidents to create? In other words, were you told to make a Roman charioteer? *Lygia on the Bull?*"

Billie shook his head. "My idea," he said. "I always thought the chariot needed a driver, and who could resist a naked lady on a bull? You know how I liked to tease Lydia about it."

"The Roman connection was all your idea?"

"Yeah."

"But you didn't do the mannequin?"

"Me? A mess like that? Rory, girl, that hurts worse'n' my arm."

"Sorry," I gulped. "I shouldn't be disturbing you." I kissed him on the cheek, tucked the stuffed panda I had bought in the Gift Shop under his good arm, and left. Rapidly.

Dear God, how I hate hospitals!

I did not hear from Josh. I presumed he was still sulking. He did not take rejection well. I met Ken at Mike's Place at five-thirty. "How about comparing notes over drinks?" he'd said, but naturally our "notes" extended to dinner and Jaeger on ice. And lots and lots of talk, speculation. And, once again, frustration.

Yet I remembered why I liked this solid detective with the sun-streaked hair and sharp gray eyes. We might not always agree. We might even fight like two strays over a bone, but he was a good man. Definitely not on my lists of suspects.

Somewhere, along about ten o'clock, I looked at Detective Sergeant Ken Parrish and said, "I have a feeling we're still waiting for the other shoe to drop."

"Oh, hell," he groaned. "I wish I didn't think you might be right."

"I don't know," I muttered. "When things simply won't make

sense, sometimes all we can do is wait."

"Wait for another body?" Ken snapped.

"Sorry, but I don't think the Art Show is over."

"You just want another body, so you can say, 'Look, look, Billie didn't do it!' "

I had to laugh. Truly I hadn't thought it, but he had a point. A definite point. "I'm sorry," I sighed. "Macabre cop humor." I peered at Ken's Everyman face and decided to prod him just a little more. "Maybe you should put me on your suspect list," I said. "Feeb, depressed over loss of lover and job, goes berserk, creates her own personal art show at the Bellman Museum." At the very strange look on his face—I swear his tan was turning purple, as if he were strangling—I added, very quietly, "Unless, of course, I'm already on your list."

He wouldn't look at me. My friend. My buddy. My informant. My macho cop, handpicked for Rory Travis by Hyacinth Van Horne and Martin Longstreet, had put me on his suspect list. Well, hot shit!

I threw two twenties on the table and thumped my way out of Mike's Place. Quite a few people didn't bother to veil their stares. I heard Ken's chair scrape back, but, evidently, he thought better of it. He did not come after me.

Well, fuck! I hoped he choked on his suspicions.

I sat on the edge of my bed, quivering with a rage and hurt no amount of common sense seemed able to assuage. Ken was a cop. I was on his list for the same reason Billie was on mine. It was necessary.

It didn't help.

After eyeing the phone for several minutes, almost as if it were a poisonous snake, I dug out the card with Josh's cell phone number. Telling him about Billie and the alligator was my excuse.

His cell phone was off. I left no message. Caller ID would be enough.

Sure, I go over every night and prowl the grounds. How else does a spook amuse himself in this haven of senior citizens?

I must have sat there for half an hour, hoping he'd call back. Hoping he wasn't the killer I was looking for. Hoping he and Martin weren't playing at some deeper game than I'd been able to unearth. Hoping Josh was one of the Good Guys.

I undressed, put on my nightgown, brushed my teeth. Stared at my phone.

It didn't ring.

I should take out the sketches and notes I'd made that morning, study them once again before bed. But I couldn't. All I wanted was to talk to Josh. Try to mend our silent quarrel. Tell him about Billie, about my list of suspects.

Compare the Martin Longstreet he knew to the old, and possibly broken, man I had interviewed yesterday afternoon.

The phone never rang.

I went to bed, feeling more alone than I had at any time since Josh Thomas and Ken Parrish came into my life.

Monday was quiet. It's possible I participated in rehab with a bit more cooperation that morning. My therapist, who had finally learned not to be so damned cheerful, merely rocked back on his heels, looked thoughtful and muttered, "Not bad, Travis. Not bad."

After therapy, I stopped at the local newspaper and spent so long fighting my way through articles on old real estate developments, debts, scandals, and bankruptcies, with a few juicy bits of social gossip thrown in to keep me from terminal boredom, that my stomach was protesting loudly. Two-thirty, and I'd had nothing but coffee for breakfast.

Fortunately, I wasn't too far from my favorite deli on Main

Street, where I squeaked into a booth just shortly before their closing time at three. While I waited for my food, I realized that the only old news article that had really stuck in my mind was one about Opal Bellman. She had carried a gun while walking her acres. Evidently, rattlesnakes had been enjoying the Bellman grounds since long before Richard Bellman began to build on it. I suppose I should have felt sorry for the snakes, now driven from their habitat, but a picture of those sixty-plus lush acres of heavy landscaping flashed before me, and I began to realize why there was so little low-growing greenery. I shuddered. And thought about my Glock, back in its case in the closet. Maybe it was time to start carrying it again.

With the marvel of a stomach filled with a Mufaletta and Amberbock, it was easier to face the fact that Josh had never returned my call. Evidently, I'd stepped on his toes big-time. It wasn't just that I was female. *No one* pushed Josh Thomas aside. I'd also made it clear I didn't completely trust him.

My energy restored, if not my spirits, I went to visit Billie. He had a little more color. There was guarded optimism that he might regain full function in his alligator-torn arm. I smiled a lot and made assurances that had little logical basis. I was determined Billie Ball Hamlin wasn't going to jail for murders he didn't commit, but anyone crazy enough to dive, night after night, into alligator-infested ponds, just might have a few other hidden quirks.

So what next? My instincts told me my research at the newspaper had been fruitless. Whatever was going on had nothing to do with Richard Bellman's ancient history.

I wasn't speaking to Ken Parrish. Josh Thomas wasn't speaking to me. I feared prodding Martin Longstreet into a heart attack or stroke. So I went home and re-examined my sketches of the crime scenes, my list of suspects . . . and got absolutely nowhere. My much-vaunted intuition cried, "Parker St. Clair."

Daryn Parke

My common sense countered with, "But you *want* it to be Parker St. Clair." I gathered, from what had been said, that Clairity teetered on the knife edge of black ops; its client list, anyone with money. Martin didn't like Parker. I didn't like Parker's wife.

Scarcely enough to hang a man.

Nor did I want it to be Billie or Josh or dear old Martin, who probably had a string of bodies behind him, going back fifty years or more.

I didn't want to be one of those cops who protected his friends, no matter what. Or ran with gut instincts, and to hell with the facts. Too many innocent people had ended up in jail, or the death chamber, that way.

Yet uncertainty, lack of decision, could be the death of me. As had already come so close, once before.

Billie. Billie was a gifted artist, and artists were notoriously given to eccentricities, if not madness itself. Billie was young, strong, and agile. Billie was smart. Billie's art had not made its mark in the professional art community. As much as I liked Billie, he could well be staging a one-man show of protest. *The Art of Murder.*

Billie kill Lydia? Psychologists prated about love–hate relationships. I supposed, reluctantly, that it was possible.

Josh. Josh Thomas was as sane as any man who chose danger as a profession could be. No matter which side of the legal fence he was on, he was capable of killing. All he needed was a reason. Which made Lydia Hewitt's death the stumbling block. I could not see Josh killing a girl who seemed to be truly innocent of any wrongdoing except a bit of sleeping around.

Martin. I suspected Martin still had his hand in a few sticky pies. He might even have been involved in Clairity. An investor? Or had he not liked Parker St. Clair using his old CIA connections to create a hugely profitable private business? And if Martin had wanted St. Clair shut down—or dead?—on whom would he call?

His old friend's armed and dangerous son, Josh Thomas.

Josh. Who would not kill Rob Varney if he were the good guy he appeared to be. Who would never stage artistic murders on the grounds of the Bellman. He'd shoot his victims and be done with it. Men like Josh Thomas left their victims lying where they fell, or, if absolutely necessary, dumped their bodies in the woods somewhere. They did not fill them full of Rohypnol and slit their throats in lion cages and barber chairs.

Parker. Parker St. Clair ran a company that provided "services." Swiftly, discreetly, with little regard to legality. Once helpful only to our side, Clairity had branched out, providing services to anyone with the money to pay for it. Which could lead to doing odd jobs for both sides of a situation. Tricky. Very tricky. It was possible a lot of different people wanted Parker St. Clair dead . . .

Good God! I sat up straight. (I'd been lounging on my bed with all my papers scattered around me.) Was it possible Parker was not the killer, but the next *victim,* instead?

Was Josh Thomas here because of Parker St. Clair? Was his vacation a sham? Were he and Martin putting together evidence against St. Clair?

As was Rob Varney, probably for a different government alphabet soup?

But not Lydia. Never Lydia. She'd been born and raised here. Never went farther than graduating from the local performing arts high school.

I called Ken. (I may have been angry with him, but I was still a cop.)

CHAPTER 18

Ken Parrish listened with so much patience I could almost feel his long-suffering through the air waves. Parker St. Clair, prominent member of the Bellman Board, a possible serial killer? Pardon me, scratch that. It's Parker St. Clair, potential victim.

"Rory, do you hear yourself?" Ken asked. "You've been deep-sixed by your obsession over Billie."

"I am not—"

"Yes, you are! I'm not about to bring in a member of the Bellman Board for questioning, just because you think I should."

"Then check his alibis for both times. You can do that, can't you?"

"Believe me, Travis, his alibi's gonna be his wife, or he was in a roomful of people at the Yacht Club, the University Club, some place old-boy and iron-clad."

"His wife's not iron-clad. And, besides, he's got a mistress."

Ken groaned. "That's not a crime, Travis."

"I told you—Lydia Hewitt saw him with her. At the museum. *In flagrante.*"

Pregnant pause. "Pretty thin, Rory, but I'll check his alibis. Okay?"

"Thanks."

Silence. "Look, Rory, I'm sorry—"

"It's okay. I'm over it. You were just doing your job."

Longer silence. "Rory . . . do you want to talk to me about

Josh Thomas? I mean, have you checked the man out?"

"My current clearance doesn't run that high."

"Neither does ours. He's either exactly what he appears to be, an international businessman on vacation or—"

"He's a crook or a spook. Most likely, a spook."

"Uh . . . right."

"It's a problem," I inserted an elaborate sigh. No way was I going to discuss Josh Thomas with Ken Parrish. "So promise you'll check on Parker St. Clair."

"I promise. Take care, Rory. Tell you the truth, I'm beginning to agree with you about Billie." He hung up.

Well, I'll be damned. I was still sitting there, staring at my cell phone, when Jody brought me a drink before she went home for the day. At supper, Aunt Hy and Marian Edmundson were unusually quiet, each giving me surreptitious little glances before hastily turning back to Marian's onion-laced meatloaf. It's a very good meatloaf, by the way, always served with mashed potatoes and gravy. But that night I didn't taste it. My mind was firmly planted in the world of intrigue, my hands grabbing madly for elusive details that spun just out of reach, that refused to coalesce into a solid fact that could be laid at any one person's feet.

We were so close.

We hadn't a clue.

So who was *We?* Ken and I? Josh and I? The old Rory, the paralyzed Rory, the resurrected Rory? The Rory-to-be?

Thank God tomorrow was one of my tram days. I would be much too busy to think. Almost—for a moment or two—I thought longingly of the lost-in-limbo Rory who hadn't given a damn about anything but feeling sorry for herself.

On this particular Tuesday, the loggia, which provided welcome shelter from Florida's hot summer sun, was several shades too cool. As I laid my mini-cooler on the wooden bench before taking my usual peek at *David*, it finally occurred to me that lunches with my favorite hunk of bronze might have to go on hiatus for the winter. I clung to the terra-cotta balustrade above the courtyard and took a good long look. I swear all seventeen feet of Michelangelo's muscled marvel had goose bumps.

It wasn't supposed to be that way, of course. Aunt Hy, Marian, Jody, and the old-timers among the tram drivers were all complaining about the weather. It looked as if, this year, Florida might actually have a Winter. Reluctantly, I picked up my cooler and hiked to the east end of the courtyard where I found a table in full sun. *David*, at the far end of the courtyard, was like a distant memory, the dark silhouette of someone I'd known in another lifetime. I unwrapped my grilled cheese with avocado and bacon on sourdough bread, custom-made at a restaurant I passed on the way to the museum, and tried not to think about the significance of my now-distant male surrogate. Yet the thought wouldn't go away.

David, my stalwart bronze hero, was no longer the linchpin of my life. I didn't have to cling to him for support. I even occasionally wondered what certain other bodies would look like in the buff. Starkers, as the Brits say. The visions (definitely plural) conjured by this aberrant notion were so delicious I nearly choked on a crisp chunk of bacon. Obviously, my mind wasn't the only part of my anatomy that was coming back to life. Sternly, I chewed, swallowed, drank my soda, and tried not to think at all. I disposed of my trash and headed out to the tram run.

But turning off a reawakened mind is almost an impossibility. When, in the midst of all the recent chaos, had I started to live again? When had I decided that, no matter how vulnerable I was, I was going to rejoin the human race? That bronze statues, even driving a tram, weren't enough?

The answer was multiple choice. Josh Thomas's arrival on a clap of thunder had jolted me into forward motion. Then came Billie's problems and the arrival of Detective Sergeant Ken Parrish on the scene. But it had taken the shock of the shattered mannequin to catapult my numbed emotions into anger, into cold determination mounting to burning fury. I would find out who did this. To the Bellman . . . and to *me*.

I waved good-bye to George, who didn't mind walking to his car on such a cool day, and set off on Tram 3 with a full load of passengers. Four got off at the Circus Museum and restaurant stop; the remainder were going to the Casa Bellissima. Between the Circus and the Casa my tour guide routine is constant: rose garden, banyan trees, sausage tree, the swimming pool, the Bellmans' burial site, Sarasota Bay, and Pelican Key. I was so busy talking I almost missed it. Nearly every day there are fishermen in the bay just north of the Casa. The water is so shallow they walk, wearing hip waders, to the sandbar about a hundred feet offshore. Occasionally, fishermen arrive by shallow-bottom boat. I was unloading my passengers, my view cut off by the bulk of the House, before I realized what I had just seen.

There was a larger boat than usual out there, perhaps as long as sixteen feet. It had a blue stripe just below the gunwale, a blue canvas canopy, and a powerful outboard engine. It looked, in fact, remarkably similar to the boat I had seen tied up at Josh Thomas's dock. And it appeared to be empty. Nor was there a single fisherman anywhere in the vicinity. Fortunately, I had no passengers, so I circled around the Casa's drive and took another look. I pulled to the side of the driveway to allow another tram to pass, then I dug out my cell phone. Fortunately, Josh was not doing one of his disappearing acts.

"Are you at home?" I demanded without preliminaries.

"Yeah. Computer digging," he drawled. "Why?"

"Is your boat where it's supposed to be?"

"Well, of course . . . Hang on . . ." Since he was such a fast mover, the pause was short. "Fuck!" he breathed into the phone, probably more stunned that the great Josh Thomas could have missed something like that than by the actual loss of the boat. "Have you seen it?" he demanded, making the obvious leap.

When I told him about the empty boat in front of the Casa, Josh surprised me. He made another leap, one that hadn't yet occurred to me. "Call your boyfriend," he snapped. "Right now. I doubt that boat's really empty, and damned if I'm going to take the rap for this one. Play it by the book, Rory. No pussyfooting on this one."

"You think there's a body—"

"Hell, yes. I'll be there as fast as traffic will allow. Call Parrish now!"

He was right, of course. I'd let myself be distracted by personal issues, by the demands of my tram job. I was the one with the much-vaunted super intuition, and I'd missed it. Were Josh's leaps truly faster than mine? Or did he *know* there was a body in his boat?

But if Josh was guiltless, someone was trying to implicate him. Why . . . ?

Josh, himself, confirmed my speculation on that question, when he arrived ahead of Ken Parrish and yet another round of city patrol cars. "Want to bet our guy had a dead body on his hands before he discovered Billie Hamlin spent the last two nights in the hospital?"

"So he needed another patsy?"

"A reasonable guess. I'd go out there," Josh added, "but Parrish would have my hide. Getting involved, even peripherally, isn't good. I like to keep a low profile."

I bet he did.

Ken's silver SUV could be seen far up the long drive, wending its way through the usual crowd of people meandering down the middle of the road. Sure enough, by the time he parked and made his way to where Josh and I were standing on the grass north of the Casa Bellissima, looking out at the boat, Ken resembled a lightning bolt on the verge of piercing any great black cloud one could name, even one with The Sleeping Satyr's name on it.

I had, of course, forgotten they'd never met. These two new men in my life. They stood four feet apart, bodies tense, and glared at each other, the air crackling with waves of hostility and belligerence. Darkness and Light, squaring off for confrontation on so many different levels I was momentarily speechless, wondering if I was going to have to step in and separate them.

"So you think there's a body out there?" Ken challenged.

"Just a guess," Josh shrugged, and explained his conjecture about the killer not realizing Billie had been removed from the equation.

Ken turned to me. "Guess *you're* happy," he growled.

"It does seem to get Billie off the hook."

"*If* there's a body in there," Ken said. "And if we're sure the TOD wasn't prior to Billie's accident."

"This is Tuesday," I pointed out with exaggerated patience. "The boat wasn't there yesterday. Therefore it *can't* be Billie."

"We're all going to look foolish if the damn boat's empty," Josh pointed out.

"Maybe it isn't even yours," I offered, just to be contrary.

"It isn't. I rented it."

Ken pounced on that. "Why?" he snapped. "Why rent a boat?"

"Exploring." Josh put on a wicked grin, his body slouching into sexy satyr mode. "And I was hoping to have some company. You know, anchor behind a mangrove island, a loaf of bread, a jug of wine . . ."

An explanation that might have been acceptable if he hadn't

looked straight at me as he said it. Ken's tan darkened by a couple of shades; his body language moved from hostile to on-the-brink-of-attack.

"So why are we all standing here?" I asked. Briskly.

"I would have checked it out," Josh tossed at Ken like a challenge, "but I figured you'd want to do it yourself. Or are you passing the job to a uniform?" he added sweetly.

I saw Ken's fists clench. So did Josh's, but he never moved. It was almost as if he stuck out his chin and dared Ken to hit him. Darkness and Light, with a Great Divide between.

Ken peeled off his jacket and handed it to me, gun, shoulder holster and all. He emptied his pants pockets—wallet, car keys, coins. I tucked them into his jacket. He took off his shoes and socks. Josh and I followed him across the lawn until he jumped down from the seawall into the shallows below.

I felt guilty. Ken was probably waiting for the harbor patrol, and I'd let Josh taunt him into going out there by himself. Not smart. For all we knew . . .

He was almost to the sandbar, the water up to his thighs, when one of my nastier moments of intuition hit me so hard I was nauseous. "Tell him to come back," I gasped to Josh as I doubled over. "Now!"

I give Josh credit, he didn't stop for questions. He yelled, waved his arms in the universal signal of "Come back!" He then semaphored the crossed-hands wave of "Abort, Abort!" Ken was moving onto the sandbar, now in water only up to his ankles. I recovered enough to add my own shouts of warning and waving arms.

Stupid, stupid overreaction. The boat was empty. It had drifted away from Josh's dock.

And anchored itself just off the sandbar.

Sure it had.

Ken, hands on hips, turned to stare at us. I could practically hear him thinking, *What the hell?*

The boat blew up. Debris shot in all directions as a plume of black smoke rose from the center of the cockpit that remained afloat. Ken pitched forward into the water, and didn't move. Josh, flinging aside his shoes, hit the water on the run. As he splashed and plowed his way across that hundred feet of bay, whatever was in the bottom of the boat continued to burn with the intensity only an accelerant could provide. Ken was still lying in the water, facedown.

By the time Josh had hauled Ken out and applied a little rough and ready emergency treatment, while kneeling on the now almost completely exposed sandbar, there was nothing left of the boat. That ominous canvas mound that had been burning so fiercely in the cockpit had sunk in the deeper water beyond the sandbar. Vanishing in something more lethal than a Viking funeral. Was it a body? Only divers would be able to find out.

Ken Parrish, as stalwart as his looks implied, was able to make it back to shore on his own two feet. The handshake he offered Josh Thomas wasn't even grudging. I hoped his gratitude would count for something when he got around to questioning Josh about whatever was in the boat.

Needless to say, by this time a large crowd had gathered. Even the Bellman museums and mansion couldn't compete with an explosion on Sarasota Bay. The terrace and lawn in front of the Casa Bellissima looked rather like the mass of spectators at a golf tournament. Since Burt, the tram boss, had been taking my shift for the last hour, I very reluctantly went back to work. Though not before offering Josh the most sincere words we'd exchanged since we met. If I'd tried to rescue Ken, he might have drowned. Josh had moved like lightning. It was not a moment when I cared to recall that he was Number Three on my suspect list. Correction. Number Two. This latest incident had moved Billie to the bottom, if not off the list altogether.

Would Josh have saved Ken if I hadn't been there?

Nasty, insidious thought.

I drove my tram, shamelessly craning my neck each time I passed the salvage operations. But the crowd remained a dense curtain that occasionally shifted, but never enough for me to see. My passengers, however, were eager to share their news. An unidentifiable something had surfaced with the divers, only to be discreetly body-bagged on the far side of the harbor patrol boat. Josh and Ken, of course, were somewhere in the middle of it all, probably back out on the sandbar, watching every move. While Rory drove her blasted tram and railed against the inequities of the world.

I didn't snap at my passengers, but it was hard.

Not surprisingly, by the time the patrol boat chugged off, the crowd dispersed, and the bevy of patrol cars crept back out of the Bellman grounds, Josh and Ken sloshed up from the beach, apparently the best of friends. I could feel them getting ready to give the long-suffering little woman a nice pat on the head. I might have refrained from snapping at the museum visitors, but nothing was guaranteed with these two.

But, of course, Ken—brown hair stiff and tousled, trailing water with every barefoot step—swooped down and planted a very satisfactory kiss on my lips, even if Sarasota Bay doesn't taste quite as fresh and tangy as the Gulf of Mexico. "A few steps closer and that body bag would have been for me," he said. "How about dinner?"

"The three of us," Josh qualified. "Say, eight o'clock, when we've had time to change."

Slowly, Ken unfolded from tram height to his full five-eleven. He did his best to look down on Josh who was at least an inch taller. Camaraderie vanished on the instant. "What makes you think I had a trio in mind?" he bristled.

"You didn't. I did," Josh returned with deliberate insouciance. "There are a lot of questions that need discussion." He offered his satyr smile. "And, besides, don't you want to talk to me? It was my boat."

"Mike's Place, eight o'clock," I interjected before the crackling atmosphere could deteriorate any further. "Josh's right," I said, wrapping my hand around one of Ken's clenched fists, "we're all three professionals, and maybe if we put our heads together . . ."

"Yeah, sure," Ken growled. "Professional *what?*"

"Believe me," Josh retorted, stung into a rare display of emotion, "if I had a dead body on my hands, I wouldn't have blown it up in my own boat."

Professional *what?* A question that fit me as well. Agent *ex officio,* that was Rory Travis. Blithely out on a limb, tackling simple pranks that had turned into murder and plunged me way beyond my present capabilities. Yet what had I been before? A great lump, as dead in the water as Josh's boat.

And I wasn't operating solo. My collaborators were, in fact, rather stunningly competent. If Josh was one of the Good Guys, we might actually make some progress on this case. If he wasn't . . . then maybe Ken and I could find the scratch on his perfect façade, the peephole into the soul of the satyr, who seemed to be playing us for all he was worth.

Oh, shit! That was a thought I didn't want to have.

"Are we agreed?" I asked too brightly. "Mike's at eight?"

"I'll pick you up at—" They both spoke at once.

I should have insisted on independence, but I heard myself say to Ken, "Josh has to drive right by the Ritz. We'll meet you there."

I had not thought anyone could look more poker-faced than Josh Thomas, but Ken Parrish managed it. Unthinkingly, I'd made it Us vs. Him. Which hadn't been my intention at all. Ken was my Rock of Gibraltar, the one perfectly reliable person in this whole darn mess. I liked him. I liked Josh, too, but I was too smart to trust him.

"Mike's at eight," Ken growled and strode off toward his SUV.

"I'll ride out with you," Josh said. "I'm parked in the lot across the street." He came round to the passenger side of my tram and climbed in. *Déjà vu.* No lightning or thunder, but the sun, partially obscured by clouds, was close to setting, and the entire Bellman grounds seemed shrouded in gloom. The crowds were gone, the docents were gone; even the daytime security guards were heading out. The palms swayed in the sea breeze, as did the sausages on the sausage tree. The giant banyans, which cast welcome shade in the sunlight, took on a sinister cast.

I was halfway back to the Art Museum before I found my voice. "Josh—"

"I didn't do it, Rory. Have I killed people? Yes. Have I always been on the right side of the law? No. Did I come here because of Parker St. Clair's problems? Partly. Did I kill that poor kid in the lion cage? No. Did I slit Rob Varney's throat? No. Hell, I don't even know whose body was in that boat. Do you hear me, Travis? *I didn't do it.*"

"Sorry, but lying through your teeth is also part and parcel of your job."

As always when I was stubborn, Josh retreated into himself, not saying another word. When I stopped at the Art Museum, he loped off up the sidewalk without a backward glance.

It was going to be an interesting dinner. I wondered if an upscale restaurant like Mike's Place had a bouncer.

CHAPTER 19

They cleaned up well, the two of them. Heads turned as the three of us walked the length of the dining room to our table. I rather enjoyed the glimpses of envy I saw on a number of female faces, even some gray-haired seniors. Men like Josh Thomas and Ken Parrish are few and far between. I rather suspected it had taken considerable connivance by certain octogenarians of my acquaintance to place me smack-dab between them.

With Thanksgiving less than a week away, the Sarasota population was increasing by leaps and bounds. Mike's Place was crowded, serious conversation impossible, so we settled for social chitchat. Ken had a younger sister, who was married and had made him an uncle to a boy and a girl of less than school age. He had a younger brother still in college in Gainesville. His parents lived where they always had, on one of Sarasota's quiet older streets. The whole family would be home for Thanksgiving.

I looked expectantly at Josh. Both men looked at me. I admitted to an older brother, still unmarried, and parents living on the Connecticut shoreline. We deviated briefly into colleges. Ken, too, had attended the University of Florida in Gainesville. "Brown, then Yale law," I muttered. Ken whistled. Josh just looked mysterious. I suspected there was very little about me he didn't already know.

Ken and I both turned to Josh. I put my elbows on the table, rested my chin on my locked fingers. "Well?" I said.

Our reply was Josh signaling the waiter for the bill. "How about the Cà d'Zan bar?" he said. "We can talk there."

Eager to get to the true meat of the evening—and maybe learn something about Josh Thomas as well—we were back at the hotel in less than fifteen minutes. Ken took one of the tall leather wing chairs in a corner of the room, leaving Josh and me to arrange ourselves on the comfortable sofa set at a right angle to the chair. I had to give the City Detective credit. There was little doubt that, un-intimidated by a federal agent or an international spook, he was setting himself up as Chairman of the Board.

"You were saying?" I challenged Josh.

His reply was postponed yet again by the arrival of the waiter. But his response, when it came, wasn't very satisfactory. "How about Stanford, Oxford, and the Sorbonne?" he said.

"Nice choice," I commended dryly, wondering if any of the three had ever heard of him, by the name Josh Thomas or any other.

Ken leaned forward and, keeping his voice low, brought the meeting of our ad hoc Bellman Investigation Committee to order. "You should know," he said, "that Parker St. Clair doesn't like you two."

"I scarcely know him," I protested.

"Ah, but his girlfriend has been telling him all about your inquiries into their romance. Of course, he didn't mention your campaign to save Hamlin's neck, but it may be that's the real reason he'd like to see you hung by your toes."

"At least you talked to him," I grumbled.

"And his wife," Ken supplied. For just a moment his poker face wavered. His talk with Melinda St. Clair had not been without fruit, I'd almost bet on it.

"And *you*," Ken said oh-so-smoothly to Josh. "St. Clair really hates someone named Anthony Johns. Does that name sound familiar?"

"I assume you know damn well it does."

"Would you care to tell us about it?" Ken made a show of looking around. Our corner of the Cà d'Zan bar was completely secluded. "I believe we are sufficiently private now."

I found myself a spectator at a duel. Josh and Ken were locked eyeball to eyeball, except that Ken had managed to seat himself where he could look down on his adversary. A clever move. I, however, might as well have been upstairs, watching television with Aunt Hy. Or at least it seemed that way.

"Josh Thomas is just a name, one of many," said the black-haired satyr sitting beside me so close I could feel the warmth of his body.

"And Anthony Johns?"

"I was christened Anthony."

"Anthony what?"

Josh—Anthony—hesitated, then did the unexpected. He took my hand and held it as he said, "Gianelli. Yes, *that* Gianelli. But my father got bitten by the patriotic bug and went off to 'Nam. He ended up working for the CIA. Long story you don't need to know."

"But grandpa was a don, right?"

"*The* don," said the man beside me. "I loved the old boy," he added with an edge to his voice. "He was quite a character."

Ken bent his blond head, a single finger tapping the tan leather arm of the chair. "I'm not stupid enough to get into ancient history," he said at last. "But right now, at this moment, Anthony Johns is how you sign your checks. Right?"

"Yes."

"And Parker St. Clair seems to consider you some kind of rival who's out to get him." It wasn't really a question.

"Yes." Josh's slash of a mouth stopped moving.

I squeezed his hand hard. "You can't stop now," I protested. "Tell us what's going on." At that moment his magic was working well. Simple hand contact had frizzed my brain. Once again, I'd completely forgotten the man once known as Josh Thomas was second on my suspect list.

"Believe me, I would if I could," Josh said. "But it makes no more sense to me than it does to you. I did actually come here on vacation, although I admit I intended to keep an eye on St. Clair while I was here. The organization I work for would like to contribute to the investigation to bring him down. He's definitely not one of the good guys."

"And you are?" Ken scoffed.

"I'm not as bad as St. Clair," Josh qualified carefully.

"Why here for vacation?" Ken demanded.

Josh shrugged. "Why not?"

Martin had sent for him. Of that I was certain. And I suspected the reason was personal. Job-making for poor Rory? Or was it matchmaking?

"So, tell me," Ken said, "how did the damn boat blow up just as I got there?"

"Someone had to be watching," I said. "Someone who only had to wait for the right moment and press a button."

"But I'd stopped."

"Yes, and anyone could also see Josh and I were signaling 'Danger, come back.' The odds were, that was as close as you were going to get. So—boom!—he set it off."

"Madame Celestine wins the day," Josh drawled.

I jerked my hand from his grasp and put six inches between us on the sofa, while regretting I'd ever told him the tale of Aunt Hy and her obsession with the television psychic.

"Rory doesn't appreciate her gift," Josh said, ignoring me and talking man-to-man with Detective Ken Parrish, "but the demo was truly impressive." He held up his hand, palm out. "I'm now a true believer."

"Well, believe it doesn't happen on cue," I snapped with considerable bitterness. "I hadn't a clue the night my partner was killed."

Josh grabbed my hand back. We wrestled, briefly, before I gave in.

"In any event, I'm grateful," Ken said. "To both of you. Otherwise, we wouldn't be sitting here having this conversation."

Understood. Josh and I nodded.

"So you think somebody watched the boat all day, waiting for the right moment?" Ken asked.

"Looks like it," I said. "Josh, didn't you say Parker St. Clair lives near there? Could he see the boat from his house?"

"Wouldn't even need binoculars."

"You know," I said, "I seem to recall that Richard Bellman lost a couple of big yachts. One sank and the other burned."

"Another artful murder?" Even Josh sounded surprised. Or was it all another big put-on? Had the man whose touch was raising my blood pressure reverted to his dubious ancestry? Was he, after all, capable of the cold-blooded murders of Lydia Hewitt, Rob Varney, possibly Tim Mundell . . . and whoever had been in that boat today? If he had enough reason, I was very much afraid he was. Sicilian blood can run as cold and deep as it could be hot and passionate.

"So it all ties in," Ken murmured.

"And is just as damned much of a mystery," said Josh, "as it's been all a—"

Ken's cell phone rang. Josh and I waited, our bodies tensing into eager alert as Ken's poker face crumbled to surprise, dismay . . . and guilt.

He snapped the phone closed, staring off into space for a moment before turning back to his impatient audience. "When

I interviewed Melinda St. Clair," he told us, "I had the feeling she was on the verge of telling me a good deal more. I talked to her at her house, very informally. I didn't feel I had cause to press her, so I let it go for another time." For a moment Ken steepled his fingers in front of his face. "It was a mistake," he said at last. "They've identified the body. It was Melinda St. Clair."

Beside me, I heard Josh catch his breath. "Martin's going to have a major guilt attack," he said.

"That makes two of us," Ken said. "I could almost swear she was going to talk, and yet I never thought he'd kill her. I mean, the man's a pillar of the community. I'm sorry," he added on a rush. "I deal with domestic violence and drug dealers, some pretty bad stuff, but true evil caught me with my pants down."

"It's like the night Eric died," I told him. "No matter how good we think we are, no matter how careful, or how intuitive, sometimes we get blindsided. For months now, everyone's been telling me Eric's death wasn't my fault, and I simply wouldn't believe them. Now that I find myself saying the same to you . . . well, I begin to get a broader picture."

I leaned in, speaking in short, sharp bursts. "You went on an initial interview. An interview with a very wealthy society matron in her own home. You had only the vaguest suspicion her husband might be involved in the murders. Absolutely no evidence. You were there only because I urged you to check her husband's alibis. Your gut instinct told you she knew something. Gut instinct said she might be willing to talk. But about what? You were there in your official position as a detective. You could have been in serious trouble if you pressed her—a well-connected lady in the sanctuary of her own home. So you filed it all away for future reference. You had absolutely no reason to suspect St. Clair, even if he was guilty, would turn on her."

"He had a mistress."

"And I bet he's had twenty or a hundred others in the past."

"She's right," Josh interjected. "It's not your fault, Parrish. I know a lot more than you do about what a bastard St. Clair is, yet it never even occurred to me he'd kill his wife. She'd stuck with him through a lot worse than this."

"Are we so sure he did it?" I asked, just to be difficult.

"Who else?" Josh retorted. "Me?"

"It was your boat." I knew I sounded ridiculous, even as I said it.

"Travis," Ken sighed, "you can't really think Mr. Anthony Johns, a.k.a. Josh Thomas, would be stupid enough to put the body in his own boat?"

"He would if he thought it would be the perfect twist on the obvious: You know . . . *he'd never be stupid enough to put the body in his own boat.*"

"Excuse me," Josh said, "but I'm still here. And I assure you I haven't murdered anybody lately. Not a single soul in Sarasota County, as best I can recall. Of course . . . I may have been hit over the head one too many times. Perhaps I'm suffering from blackouts. Murderous rages in the middle of the night—"

"Enough!" Ken decreed. "What good is having all this high-powered talent around if the two of you are going to squabble instead of help?"

Josh and I subsided into the sofa's cushions, pouting. Separately.

"Parker St. Clair's alibis for the nights of the murders—the first two, anyway—" Ken said, "were being at home with his wife, with social events earlier each evening. Therefore, it seems pretty odd he'd do away with his alibi."

"Maybe she was tired of covering for him," I said. "Maybe, as you said, she changed her mind and was going to tell all."

"Believe me," Ken said, "I'll be talking to him again first thing in the morning."

"He's slippery," Josh said, "but maybe you can find where he bought his bomb-making supplies."

"And a strop razor," I added. "And did he take two thousand in cash from the bank to pay Billie? And is there a local Rohypnol dealer who might recognize him?"

"Pillars of the community tend to be Teflon coated," Ken sighed, "but I'll try."

"Ten minutes," I heard Josh mutter. "Give me ten minutes."

"Just don't tell me about it," Ken growled.

I stared at my squeaky-clean City Cop and realized just how desperate he was to end this mess.

And Josh—this stranger named Anthony—was he as vengeful as he appeared to be? Or was it all an act? Was Melinda St. Clair's murder designed to be the final nail in Parker's coffin? The final piece in Josh's precisely orchestrated trap to get rid of a business rival? I didn't really think Josh or Martin would go that far, yet I had to consider it.

"And now," Josh said, "if Miz Travis is finished demolishing my character, I've some intel to pass along."

He had our full attention.

"For what it's worth," Josh said, "after retiring early from government service, Rob Varney went to work for Clairity. He could easily have been involved in things St. Clair didn't care for a watchdog committee to discover." Josh glanced at me out of the corner of his eye, gave an infinitesimal nod. "And Rory could be right about Tim Mundell. Tempe may have been listed on the police report as his hometown, but the last two summers he was an intern in the computer department at Clairity."

Oh, my God! Even my toes prickled.

Ken swore, softly but fiercely. No cop likes to discover his department missed a possible murder.

Of course, Josh could be making the whole thing up. Anything to trail red herring across the investigation. Anything so Anthony

Gianelli of the infamous Gianelli Family would come up smelling of roses.

"Watch your back," Ken was saying. "Both of you. St. Clair has you on his short list."

If he was guilty. "Is Billie off the hook?" I asked.

Ken patted his thumb against his lips and favored me with his most enigmatic gaze. "If I let him off on trespassing and theft."

"Aw, come on."

Ken grinned. "Okay, I'm ninety-five percent certain your favorite gator wrestler was only guilty of being stupid. And not being able to resist two thousand dollars to show off his sculpting talent."

"Thank you, thank you!" My raised eyes strayed higher than the top of Detective Sergeant Ken Parrish's head.

"Rory," Josh said sternly, turning to grasp both my shoulders, his onyx gaze fixed on my face, "take my word for it, Parker St. Clair is a very dangerous man. If asked a month ago, I would have said he'd never go this far, but since I know I didn't do it, he's the only game left. Do *not* think he won't turn on you."

"I haven't done anything!"

"In trying to save Billie, you stirred up an enormous amount of trouble. Basically, you threw a monkey wrench into his well-laid charade. I would guess he had to get rid of Mundell because the kid stumbled onto something he shouldn't have. Probably hacking around through the Clairity system for the hell of it. When Billie discovered the body, St. Clair did a bit of what he does so well and found out Billie was a sculptor—"

"And set him up," Ken finished. "Hell, that actually makes sense."

"Until Rory came along," Josh said, giving my hand a quick squeeze. "Billie was the perfect patsy for a serial killer. His only nighttime alibi was an illegal date with gators and golf balls."

"An alligator saved Billie," I pointed out.

"You laid a lot of groundwork before that. Parker's scheme was already in serious trouble before Billie ended up in the hospital."

"I guess," I said. *Damn!* My two Macho Men were trying to make me feel good.

"I believed you, Travis," Ken said. "You'd convinced me Billie didn't do it."

Josh gave my shoulders a shake. "Listen to him, dammit, and stop looking like a lost soul."

I shoved Josh's hands away. "And when I saw the boat, who told me to call Ken?" I demanded. "Who set him up to take the blast? Well?"

One moment Josh was sitting; the next, he was on his feet, throwing a hundred-dollar bill onto the long narrow table. He stalked out, his shiny black shoes practically burning holes in the thick carpet.

"So why *did* he save my life?" Ken drawled, breaking the ringing silence.

"Because I had one of my freaking fits, which he couldn't possibly ignore."

"So he blew up the boat, then ran out and kept me from drowning?"

"What else could he do with a crowd gathering fast, let alone me standing there watching?" I knew my jaw must be jutted out so far that I looked like some cocky kid spoiling for a fight.

Ken came over and sat down beside me. I didn't flinch when he put his arms around my shoulders. "Listen, Rory," he said, "you saved my life today. Since I don't believe in psychic gifts, the obvious explanation is that you knew the bomb was there and decided at the last minute you didn't want to see me dead."

I have no idea what my face looked like, but my expression must have been a beaut. Ken tossed me a quizzical look. "Do I really think you're a murderer? Hell, no. But I've got to tell you that as much as I dislike our *mafioso*'s guts, I think you're being a bit hard on him. Basically, I dislike him less for what he is than because he has the hots for you. And the feeling is mutual, by the way. For equal cause."

Really? My head swam. And it wasn't from that second glass of Jaeger on the rocks.

Ken Parrish, Boy Scout to the end. The modern-day embodiment of *noblesse oblige*.

Shakily, leaning heavily on my purple-flowered cane and Ken's strong right arm, I got to my feet. He walked me to the elevator, and he wasn't any more hesitant about a kiss in full view of the security guard than Josh had been. But with Ken Parrish I felt wrapped in security and a surprising tenderness. Warmth and comfort. For a moment I was reluctant to let him go. And then I remembered what had brought us here tonight, the three of us. And that for all the elegance and wealth that surrounded my life at the Ritz-Carlton and at the Bellman Museum, there was no protection against evil. Not for Lydia, or Rob. Most of all, not for Melinda St. Clair, who had had it all. And lost it. Had she appreciated the Viking farewell? I could only hope so. Perhaps, somewhere deep down, Parker had cared just a bit.

Or was Melinda's immolation just another artful murder?

I stepped into the elevator. *My God, it was all coming together.* At last. No matter who the killer was, we were going to get him. Perhaps I had a Sicilian ancestor somewhere on the family tree, because Lydia's senseless death cried out for vengeance. As did Rob's death and Billie's anguish. Even Melinda's, though I still couldn't like her.

Sicilian. Anthony Gianelli. The Godfather's grandson.

Josh. My personal enigma. I wanted to cry, but my eyes refused to tear.

Exhaustion and confusion disappeared. I was empowered. Somehow, in spite of two men brought up on too many Westerns where the hero patted the heroine on the head with, "Aw, shucks, little lady,"—not to mention the notoriously protective attitude of *mafiosi* toward their women—I, Rory Travis, was going to bring in whoever killed Lydia, Rob, and Melinda, and made Billie's life a living hell. So I sat at the kitchen table and cleaned my Glock. I got out my shoulder holster and used some of Marian's leather balm to shine it and get it back into supple condition. How fortunate that the Florida weather had turned nippy enough to warrant my wearing a jacket.

I even gave my badge a polish. I wouldn't call the local office, of course. I knew what they'd say. Which was all right, as I didn't think I'd ever be going back to work for the Death Star. (That, by the way, is what we younger graduates of Quantico call the head office in Washington.)

It was two a.m. before I was done. But I felt good.

Even if Ken Parrish turned out to be the villain, I could handle it.

CHAPTER 20

The next morning the Bellman murders took the whole top half of the front page of the newspaper. The local TV channel could talk of little else. Lawrence Kent, the Museum Director, was seen, looking grim, while responding to such questions as, "Are you hiring extra security guards?" and "Do you plan to close the Museum?" A few terse words were dragged from Ken Parrish about his close call. And, no, sorry, he couldn't comment on an on-going investigation. Yes, he knew the person who rescued him, and he was very grateful.

Nor did the bereaved widower escape the camera's glare. Parker St. Clair, looking suitably devastated, spoke of his wife's many fine qualities, her work as a docent at the museum, his terrible shock, how much he would miss her.

I was so quiet at rehab my therapist actually looked concerned. "Comin' along well, Rory. Real well," he cajoled, for the thousandth patronizing time. He was frowning when I left, obviously puzzled by why I hadn't snapped at him. On the way home I stopped to see Billie. He high-fived me and told me I was the greatest, while I tried to remind him that he really owed his deliverance to an alligator now on its way to becoming shoes and handbags. I abandoned driving around Sarasota, carrying concealed, and spent the rest of the day helping Marian prepare for Thanksgiving. Although the turkey and all the fixin's would be sent up from the hotel's kitchen, along with a waitress, we were preparing the hors d'oeuvres ourselves, not to mention making sure that Aunt Hy's immaculate condominium was even more immaculate than usual. After all, it isn't every day we had two spooks to dinner.

Yes, that's right. Martin and Josh had been invited to something so mom and apple pie as Thanksgiving dinner. So I allowed Josh his sulk all day on Wednesday. He was bound to show up tomorrow. Not even a soulless, villainous satyr would miss Thanksgiving, right?

Ken called about nine o'clock that night. Nothing new. Parker St. Clair put on the same façade at the police station that he had on television. Double-coated Teflon. Anthony Johns, born Gianelli, had fallen back on Martin Longstreet as a character reference. And since gainsaying Martin is rather like calling the Governor or the President a liar—maybe even the Pope—Josh, too, was covered in Teflon. So, no, Ken said, he hadn't called about business. He just wanted to wish me Happy Thanksgiving and he'd stop by the tram run on Friday afternoon to give me an update. Meanwhile, everyone stayed out of jail, and the spirits of Tim, Lydia, Rob, and Melinda St. Clair remained restless.

No, I'm not into the supernatural. It didn't take a séance to tell me they deserved better than they'd gotten from law enforcement so far. Thanksgiving was a pause, a refueling of the soul. Time for me to take a deep breath and say, "Okay, I can do this."

For Thanksgiving dinner I wore an ankle-length dress, pantyhose and brand-new shoes with one-inch heels. I inaugurated my walking stick of twisted sassafras. It was handsome, and I didn't look so bad myself. Naturally, Aunt Hy seated me next to Josh. We made polite conversation, but, after all, not much is needed when there is so much to eat. I asked the fresh-faced young woman who was serving us—a Ritz-Carlton employee—if she minded working on Thanksgiving. Her reply was typical of the Sarasota area. Oh, no, she was delighted to help out. I thought of all the other people working this day, in hospitals, nursing homes, police and fire departments, EMS, and was humbled. I thought of Ken in the midst of his large family gathering. Of Martin and Josh, who for all the mysterious power they wielded, might have been alone today if we had not invited them to dinner. Our family celebration might be a bit alternative, I conceded, but it was a day from which it was impossible to erase sentiment.

Josh and I said little to each other, but he was always there, beside me, his essence so strong it penetrated all the way to places I didn't want to acknowledge. We sat down to the table, hostile, and got up, family.

Not that I wouldn't put him away for murder, just as I would my own brother, if I had to. But the last link in the chain between Anthony Gianelli and me had been forged. I was unsure if he had become a brother, kissin' cousin, or something more, but I knew he was in my life to stay.

Truthfully, if my physical reactions counted as we lingered sipping liqueurs amidst Aunt Hy's collection of treasures, I didn't think of Josh as a brother, even though we tended to squabble like spoiled siblings. There'd been disturbing emotions arcing between us from the moment we met. Something frightening, intriguing. And always dangerous.

"You're driving tomorrow, right?" Josh said as I walked him to the door. "I'll come by. We need to talk."

We certainly did. Yet how could I ever believe anything Josh Thomas, a.k.a. Anthony Johns, a.k.a. Tony Gianelli, told me?

"I'm so sorry, Rory," Martin said, the bonhomie displayed at dinner, disappearing on the instant. "None of this was supposed to happen. None of it. I fear I've grown old and careless."

Josh grasped his arm and had him out the door in under five

seconds. I was left standing, eyes wide, head awhirl, readjusting my theories, like a juggler switching from round rubber balls to fragile eggs.

Na-aw. No way. I'd just decided Josh was family. And so was Martin. They had to be numbered among the Good Guys. Even if I couldn't believe a word they said.

I went to bed early and brooded.

Ken didn't call.

We had miscalculated. I wouldn't be discussing sensitive information with anyone on my Friday afternoon tram run. Every household in Sarasota had brought its Thanksgiving guests to the Bellman on the day after the holiday. Or so it seemed. The line for tickets snaked past the *Lygia and the Bull,* all the way out to the street. The trams ran harder and faster than worker ants trying to save eggs from a ravening anteater. Detective Sergeant Ken Parrish stood in line at the Tram Stop like everyone else, neatly outmaneuvering a little old blue-haired lady to plop down into the seat beside me. He leaned close and spoke in my ear. My tram-wide bank of mirrors reflected looks, both knowing and indulgent, from my six passengers behind. ("Oo-o, she's got a boyfriend. Isn't that sweet?") We were lucky I didn't veer off the road and twist us all up in the arms of a gi-ant banyan.

The gist of Ken's words was, there was no evidence against Parker St. Clair. No red hand caught buying bomb supplies. No scarlet credit card, either. (Of course, what else could we expect from an ex-spook?) The Roofie dealers were, naturally, elusive— hard to find, let alone pin down for information. And antique strop razors? All they'd been able to discover was that neither Parker St. Clair, nor anyone else, had bought one on eBay. They were still canvassing local antique dealers.

Ken made the full tram circle, earning dirty looks from waiting visitors when he didn't get off at the Casa Bellissima. He strode off up the sidewalk, Detective Sergeant Ken Parrish, the Boy Scout who had parked across the street rather than use his badge to park on the Bellman grounds. But there was no time to think; my tram was already full. I put the pedal to the metal and started my next circle.

An hour or so later, I saw Josh leaning against a banyan trunk down by the Casa. He gave me one of those barely-a-flip waves and that was it. Obviously, he could see it would be hours before there would be an opportunity for that talk he'd promised. The next time I passed that spot, he was gone.

As I've said, I'm thirty or forty years younger than most of the tram drivers, but by closing time I was exhausted. The crowd had turned out to be the biggest one-day attendance in the Bellman's history. Every last volunteer and security guard was on the ropes before we shooed the final visitors out the front gate at closer to six than the scheduled five-thirty. Since the other drivers go home at five, I had done the last forty-five minutes on my own, scrambling back and forth between the Art Museum, the Circus Museum, and the Casa until my poor little Tram 3 was bucking and jumping, and I was afraid its batteries were so low my last passengers might have to get out and push.

After I sat and quivered for a moment or two, watching the last batch head up the sidewalk to the front gate, I headed for the tram barn. And promptly dropped into another world. The sun had just set, and shadows were everywhere. Even the old live oak that sheltered my car from the sun reminded me of one of those claw-like tree creatures in the more ghoulish fairy tales. And the banyans? I took one glance at those looming twisted shapes and concentrated on parking, shifting into neutral, removing the key, and plugging in my baby for its much-needed overnight fix of electricity. I threw my empty water bottle into the trash and took a last look around. It was always quiet back here behind the museum after closing time, but tonight, as Florida's short dusk settled into darkness, I felt . . . more than abandoned. I felt the touch of Evil.

And, as on that night when Eric and I had plunged off the fire escape, my spark of intuition came too late. I was caught, dumb and flat-footed, when a shadow stepped out of the doorway of the building where I'd just parked my tram.

"You're so easy, Travis," a voice said from out of the darkness behind Tram 3. "Did you think the law of averages favored you? Just because you'd been smashed up once, no one was going to go after you again?"

The oddest thing was, I was swept, not by fear but by relief. And triumph. The voice wasn't Josh's. It was the smarmy baritone of Parker St. Clair.

I didn't make a run for the car, grab for my cell phone, or reach for the solid bulk of what rested inside the left front of my jacket. I waited. This man was mine.

He came out from behind Tram 3, the gun in his hand almost invisible against his three-piece, navy pinstripe suit. Interesting. He was dressed for the boardroom. Or a funeral. He came in real close, so we could see each other in the gloom.

"You fucking bitch," he said, quite conversationally, "why couldn't you have stayed out of it? That dumb city cop would have locked Hamlin up and thrown away the key."

"No, he wouldn't," I declared, loyal to Ken, even though St. Clair might well be right.

"I suppose you're carrying," St. Clair sighed, moving his solid bulk another step closer, so close I could smell his designer cologne and feel his hatred. "Two fingers, girl. Take it out and drop it."

So much for my vow to shoot next time instead of try to wrestle the perp into handcuffs. I did as I was told. While acknowledging to myself that Parker St. Clair outweighed me by a hundred pounds.

Josh, damn you, did you go home?

"Why?" I begged. "Just tell me why—"

He waved his gun toward the path through the rose garden. "Move. We're going to the House."

As I walked very carefully across the humped and broken pavement behind the museum, I remembered that I had one weapon left. The sassafras cane I was using to keep from falling flat on my face in the treacherous gloom. I also had brains and a lot of training in hand-to-hand combat. Oddly enough, I wasn't even worried. I should have been, but I was so damn glad to know the Bellman serial killer was Parker St. Clair that little else seemed to matter.

As we moved onto the relatively smooth path through the rose garden, I asked, "So why Lydia Hewitt? What had she ever done to you?"

"Besides catching me in the buff?"

"Big deal," I scoffed. "What's the matter—your equipment doesn't match the rest of you?"

The gun barrel bit into my back. "And here I thought you were a lady," St. Clair breathed down my neck. He gave me a vicious shove forward. "Lydia was convenient," he added.

Ah-h. I'd suspected he would want to brag about it. A man doesn't go to all the trouble to arrange so many artful murders and not want to take credit for it.

"I wanted it to look like a deranged serial killer," he said. "So with Lydia I was killing two birds with one stone—setting up Billie and getting rid of a nasty little peek."

I maneuvered around the columns in the center of the rose garden. The light was nearly gone. "And Rob?" I asked.

"Varney worked for me. And retired a bit too suddenly a few months back. A definite risk if a watchdog committee started asking questions."

"So Varney was another double-header. Scratch one witness and put another nail in Billie's coffin. Clever." And I meant it. Whatever Parker St. Clair was, he was good at his job. "And Tim Mundell?"

"Stupid little fuck. Guess his mama never told him about curiosity killing the cat. All those brains and he didn't know shit about reality. *Blackmail*. That half-pint nerd tried to blackmail me. *Me!* Can you believe it?"

Yeah, I could believe it. High intelligence frequently does not go hand in hand with common sense.

"Had me meet him here, right over there at the picnic table under the banyan. An easy walk along the seawall for both of us. When I arranged a second meet, told him I was anteing up, the little idiot thought he had me." By some silent agreement St. Clair and I stopped walking as we looked toward the dark twisted mass where Tim Mundell had lost his life. "But I'd come equipped with more than the wad of cash I dangled under his stupid nose. I had scotch laced with Roofies and a plain white bed sheet. Unidentifiable. We had quite a party. Kid never had a chance."

There was nothing I could say to that, although my determination to get this arrogant son of a bitch spiked even higher.

As we moved forward once again, we passed the banyan tree I'd been sheltering under the afternoon Josh Thomas made his sudden appearance in my tram. The day The Sleeping Satyr disappeared. Had it really gone to Tallahassee?

Josh, where the hell are you? Sulking again? Tucked up in your villa, surfing databases?

"And what about your wife?" I asked.

Ignoring my question, St. Clair prodded me toward a narrow set of stairs leading down to the Casa's cellar. At the bottom of the steps he backed me against the stucco wall and, with his left hand, put the gun to my chest. With his right, he punched a series of numbers into a key pad. So much for expecting the wail of a klaxon. Blast, but the man was slick. He'd probably been the consultant when the alarm system was installed.

Back at the Art Museum, far up on the top floor at Main Security, there wouldn't be so much as a blip on the computer screen or the first squeal of an alarm going off at the Casa Bellissima.

St. Clair produced a pencil flash, and we made our way through the maze of the basement with its segmented compartments to prevent flooding. Then up the stairs to the kitchen, a room with western windows where, thankfully, there was some last lingering light. "Your wife," I asked, "was she your real goal?"

"Poor Linnie," he mused. "She wanted a divorce. After all we'd been through together, she wanted out. She even had a pre-nup that would let her take all that lovely money with her. Oh, yeah," Parker added softly, "she slit her own throat, believe me. She was dead long before she decided to talk to your city cop."

For that, Ken would be eternally grateful. "The setup was very clever," I said.

He grabbed me by the arm, turning me to face him, a great hulking menace backed by all the dainty and luxurious gifts sold at the Casa Bellissima. He preened, I swear he did. The giant peacock, spreading his tail feathers to impress the drab little peahen.

"It was, wasn't it?" Parker said. "Even before the kid tried to blackmail me, I figured I needed several deaths prior to Linnie's to make it look like a serial killer, but I never dreamed they'd be so . . . satisfactory. So double-edged."

"The Viking funeral was a great touch," I said, trying to keep him talking. Stalling for time.

He waved me down the hallway. "I liked her, you know. Classy woman. And she tolerated my wandering ways." St. Clair came to a halt in front of the elevator, producing a key with his now-expected efficiency. "But you sicced that city cop on her, and damned if she wasn't charmed. I could tell she was going to spill it all. Couldn't give her another moment."

"You really are a cold-blooded son of a bitch," I breathed.

"Oh, yeah, believe it, Ms. Travis. I surely am." He punched the button, slid open the gate; the elevator door opened. Transferring his gun to his left hand, he hauled open the old-fashioned metal gate.

I knew where we were going now. I'd known it ever since we reached the elevator. This was a man who was as creatively intelligent as he was lethally dangerous.

We were going to the tower. Sixty feet up. Twice the distance Eric and I had fallen. The tower, which was guaranteed to turn me into a slathering, mindless wreck. Parker St. Clair could do any damn thing he pleased, and I wouldn't be able to stop him. Not all the shrinks in the world could have prepared me for this moment. I was done for.

Failed again. Only this time my suffering would be over. Permanently.

CHAPTER 21

As the elevator rose, I leaned on my walking stick and shut my eyes.

Josh! Anthony! Tony. Friend.

I tried to tell myself to stand on my own two feet and take care of the bastard, as I had planned so blithely such a short time ago, but my knees had turned to jelly, and my heart rate was powered up to launch speed. The same nausea I'd felt when kneeling amidst the splintered pieces of the satin-clad mannequin nearly took me to the floor.

The elevator stopped. Parker shoved me out. I was in such bad shape he gave me only a scornful glance before he took out yet another key and opened the door to the outside staircase that led up to the tower. When the door swung open, letting in a rush of cool sea breeze and a faint glow of light from the security spotlights surrounding the Casa, he turned and gave me a wonderfully smug little smile.

"What a shame you never recovered from your loss, Ms. Travis. Your lover dead, your career as messed up as your body. Everyone tried, but you shoved them all away. Cut yourself off. Just couldn't get your act together. No wonder you lost it, scattering bodies about so little Miss Feeb could step right up, show she still had what it takes to solve a crime. But you were too far gone, poor girl, though not too mad to realize the end was near. So what better way to end it than a leap from the Casa tower? So dramatic. Romantic even. Dashing yourself to the pavement to be with your lover forever."

The sea breeze helped, penetrating my near total funk. I was Special Agent Rory Travis. Josh Thomas—or whoever he was—respected me enough to offer me a job.

I looked straight into the depths of St. Clair's all-too-sharp blue eyes. "No one will believe you," I told him.

"Oh, my dear girl, of course they will. I typed your farewell myself. It's quite poignant, I assure you. After all, it isn't as if it's my first. You'd be surprised how many suicides have had my assistance. And no one the wiser. Not a one."

Like Tim Mundell's.

It didn't look good. I tried to remember what that outside staircase was like. While doing the docent tour, I'd stood well back and watched while the others climbed. The staircase was steep and curved, swirling in a graceful one-eighty to the square Renaissance-style tower above. To the right, at the bottom of the stairs, it was only a one-story leap to the red-tiled roof of the bulk of the house. The slanted red-tile roof. Could I do it?

Deliberately go over a railing? No way.

Not even to save my life?

I shouldn't have told that shrink what he could do with his damned psychobabble.

Josh! A silent scream, but very real.

Once again, Parker grabbed my arm and pushed me toward the stairs. I sagged, my back sliding down the wall. He slugged me, hard enough to snap my head around, but not hard enough to make me lose consciousness. "Move! Or I'll knock you out and splatter you all over the pavement before you've had a chance to fight back."

He smiled at me, and I wondered how I could ever have thought Josh the face of Evil. It was Parker St. Clair who was the reincarnation of my missing satyr.

"And you don't want that, do you, Travis? Scared as you are, you hate my guts. You want me so bad, you're willing to climb those stairs just to see what'll happen. Poor little wimp, you want to find out if you've still got it. Even with your teeth chattering and your panties wet, you'll follow me to the end, won't you? And then I'll make you look down . . . and like that guy in Philly, while you're frozen in fear, I'll just tip you over." He leered, thrusting his face within an inch of my mouth. "Too bad Tony Johns isn't here, or your city cop. We could have restaged the whole thing." His lips brushed against mine, breathing the fires of hell into my mouth. "Except this time it would be a clean sweep. Two dead. Sixty feet, Travis. You'll be as broken as if you'd been dropped from a plane."

Some things are worse than a fall from a great height. I bolted up the stairs, with St. Clair pounding behind. Surely, surely, there had to be something up there I could use for a weapon. Maybe Zorro's escape rope was still there . . .

But the tower was empty. A space, at least twenty by twenty, with a terra-cotta balustrade. Above our heads the sky was obscured by a red-tiled roof. If we weren't sixty feet up, the structure might have been considered a rather elaborate gazebo. I looked for signs of deteriorated stucco or concrete, a chunk I might break off for a weapon. But, of course, the Casa Bellissima's renovations had included every last little detail. Even in near darkness, I could see the place was in perfect shape.

Parker St. Clair had stopped at the top of the staircase. He was simply watching, enjoying my frantic dash around the tower, looking for a weapon. The rope, of course, was long gone. He waved a hand toward the east railing. "Take a look," he invited. "Sixty feet straight down to the driveway."

"No thanks." I planted my feet in the center of the floor and waited for him to come at me. When he did, he sauntered. He was *so* enjoying my torture.

He took a piece of paper out of his inside jacket pocket and waved it in my face. "Your suicide note," he said. "It's beautiful. Want to read it?"

I stared at it, considering. With my left hand I reached for it. With my right I brought up my walking stick and jabbed it straight into his eye. He screamed and grabbed his face. I ran for the stairs. But he was not only big, he was tough. And at the moment I was *numero uno* on his hate list. Just as I reached the top step, he tackled me, and we both went down hard. I threw myself aside as I fell, saving my head from the balustrade at the same time I tried to fall on top of Parker's head, driving him into the hard Italian tile floor. I heard the breath *whoosh* out of him, but his swearing scarcely paused. So far, not so good. But I had time to roll off and retrieve my stick. He staggered to his feet, and we circled each other. A ridiculously uneven match. Holding my twisted sassafras in both hands, I felt like a Medieval Little John catapulted into a future with guns and—

Guns. Gun. Parker had lost his gun. Although it hadn't registered at the time, I'd heard it slither away after I'd struck him in the eye. Where? If I could find it, the odds would take an abrupt turn in my favor. But if I looked away for so much as a second . . .

I backed up, sliding my right leg in an arc, hoping to hit something solid. All I was doing was getting closer to the railing. The east railing. No wonder Parker's smile was inching back, even though blood was running down his face.

Out of the corner of my eye I thought I saw a shadow behind Parker, something tall and black in the north corner on the staircase side of the tower. Something far too big for a gun. But no time to think about that shadow now. With my sassafras stick horizontal in front of me, I circled slowly, watching Parker, who moved with me, his lips now twisting in a feral grimace as he savored the thought of the final rush that would send me flying over the long drop on the east side of the tower.

My foot hit something. What if it wasn't Parker's gun? But it had to be, for as I stopped, he glanced down, his eyes went wide. Could I do it? Could I move with Josh's lightning speed? Or would I fall flat on my face? Would St. Clair get to me before I could pull the trigger?

I toed the gun. Solid metal scraped against the slick tile. *Now or never, Rory. This is it.*

I went down on one knee, grabbed the gun and shot him, catching him in mid-leap, not more than eighteen inches from my chest. He slammed me into the floor. And lay still.

A moment later, when his body moved, only my absolute certainty that I had killed him kept me from despair. For, truthfully, I'd reached my limit. The invalid still had a ways to go.

"You okay?" Josh drawled as he heaved Parker St. Clair aside.

"Oh, sure," I said. "I kill men in three-piece suits in tall towers every day before supper just for the hell of it."

Josh picked me up, putting his hands in a few interesting places, ostensibly while dusting me off.

"Did you have to just stand there?" I fumed as I let him hold me.

He rested his chin on the top of my head. "Well, now . . . I figured you wanted to do it yourself. I had your back, Rory. You know that, don't you?"

Yes, I knew it. Now . . . when it was almost too late.

"Your city cop's on the way, probably with half the patrol cars in town. So let's get out of here and let him clean up the mess. He knows how to find you."

His arms felt so good, so right, but I pushed him away. I walked to the east balustrade, took a firm grip and looked down. My head swam, my breath *whoosh*ed out. I swayed. Josh pulled me away.

Stubbornly, I went back and did it again. This time my vision cleared, and I could see straight down to the driveway, which was now clearly lit by at least six pairs of headlights from Sarasota's finest, with museum golf carts closing in fast from the rear.

"Rory? Time to go."

"Is he dead?"

A brief pause, then a terse, "Yes."

"Then let's go home," I said.

We popped into the elevator and were out of there while the phalanx of cops climbed the stairs.

We did all the right things, of course, even while escaping the law. I called Aunt Hy and told her Josh was taking me out to supper. I apologized for the last-minute notice.

Supper. I almost gagged as I said it. I was covered with Parker St. Clair's blood and other bits of matter I won't try to name. I'd never shot anyone before, let alone shot someone dead.

Josh called Ken and filled him in, promising we'd both be in in the morning to make statements. No, the gun we'd left lying beside the body wasn't mine, Josh replied to Ken's question. It was Parker St. Clair's, but the last prints on it would be mine.

Josh took me back to his villa, where we both showered. (No, not together.) He loaned me a slinky silk robe. I carefully folded the clothes I'd been wearing and stuffed them in a plastic grocery bag to hand over to Ken in the morning. We drank supper while watching old movies on TV. (No, I have no recollection what they were.) Along about three in the morning we had scrambled eggs and toast. And then I fell into bed. In the guestroom. But I wasn't so far gone I didn't visualize the smiles of delight I would have to face from Aunt Hy, Marian, and Jody when I returned to the penthouse. Dear Rory had stayed out all night with Josh Thomas.

Whoopee!

They would be so disappointed.

Not that I had to tell them the truth, of course.

Naturally, the morning was mostly gone before Josh and I made it to Cop Central. (I will not describe walking through the lobby of the Ritz-Carlton wearing Josh's shorts and polo shirt.) By the time Ken showed us into a conference room, he was glowering. Or maybe it was not our tardiness that distressed him. It was possible he had a pretty good idea of where I had spent the night and was simply glowering at Josh. Fortunately, being the good cop he was, Detective Sergeant Ken Parrish finally assured me that it didn't look like I was in danger of being added to the list of America's Most Wanted. And since Josh and I had picked up *my* gun on our way out last night, there wasn't going to be a flap about that, either.

It was two in the afternoon before Josh and I stopped at Mike's Place for some much-needed food. Then, in spite of my aching head, I asked him to drive to the park way out at the south end of Pelican Key. In the last few weeks I'd faced a lot of the demons in my life, but there was one left. I couldn't let it go.

We sat at the same picnic table, but the sea breeze was stronger, cooler, than the other times I'd been there. An omen, I feared. This was a conversation I wasn't going to like.

I sneaked a peek at the man sitting next to me. The strikingly handsome face, the oddly pale skin, black hair, black eyes. The ever-alert stance of his super fit body. The strength, the utter reliability I wanted to believe in . . . and couldn't. He'd backed me up this time, but would our interests always coincide? Was he "family"? Or was I plunging down a rabbit hole far worse than Alice's?

"Are you really on vacation?" I asked. "Or was that a cover for investigating Parker St. Clair?"

"Both. Martin sent for me, and since I knew St. Clair was in Sarasota, I wasn't averse to killing two birds with one stone. Sorry. Tripped over my clichés," he added apologetically.

"Was I the other bird?"

He actually had the grace to squirm, his black-hole eyes fixed on the current racing between Pelican Key and the barrier island to the south. "Martin and your Aunt Hy concocted the scheme. Job-generating, matchmaking—whatever it was, I swear I had nothing to do with it. They love you, you know. I guess they thought I might be able to pry you out of the doldrums." Josh's gaze followed a fisherman who was reeling in a violently flopping fish. "To be honest, if it hadn't been a good opportunity to keep an eye on St. Clair, I might not have come. Like you, I'm inclined to balk at being manipulated."

I nodded. That I could understand.

"But Martin founded the company I work for. Which, oddly enough, isn't so different from Parker St. Clair's. He was my father's mentor and friend, then mine. I owed him. So I came to Sarasota and did what I was told. I looked up a girl named Rory Travis."

"Tell me about the mannequin," I said.

Into the sudden silence, Josh sighed. "Martin was truly pissed about that," he said, "but you were a tough nut to crack. More armor plating than a tank. I thought shock tactics were warranted. As it happened, Martin didn't agree with me."

"So it *was* you?"

"Oh, yeah. I'd heard about the Roman chariot stunt, and the mannequin seemed like a good idea at the time. I mean, why shouldn't we cloak-and-dagger types get to wear an actual cape on occasion?" Josh looked at me, hopefully, as if he could cajole his way out of this mess.

And then he made his biggest mistake of all. Taking my silence for forgiveness, he picked that particular moment to offer me a job. Working with him in his Clairity-like company that operated on the shady side of legality. And maybe of honor as well.

"Rory?"

"I'll call a cab," I said.

"*What?*"

"Do you know how I felt that night," I hissed, "kneeling on the floor in the midst of all those shattered pieces? Can you even imagine the horror as the nightmare came rushing back?"

Josh's eyes snapped. He bent his face to mine. "And then you got angry," he said. "You got angry, and you set out to find the person who did it. You set out to help Billie. You set out to find a murderer. And you did. So don't look down your nose at me, Travis. What I did is called tough love, and, by God, if I had to, I'd do it again."

I told him what he could do with tough love. And the job as well. I called a cab.

Josh scribbled an international phone number on a card and thrust it into my hand. I was tempted to tear the card into tiny pieces and throw it at his feet. I left him sitting there, at the picnic table, staring out over the sun-sparkled channel, looking into a world only Tony Gianelli could see. He was alone. And, as far as I was concerned, he could stay that way.

A month or so later, Ken Parrish and I spent a long weekend in Key West. I am happy to report he has skills that go way beyond Eagle Scout.

I didn't call Josh Thomas/Anthony Johns/Tony Gianelli.

But even though I had long since memorized the phone number, I sometimes took his card out of my wallet and fingered it, remembering . . .

I didn't call.

But I would. Someday—maybe soon—I would.

ABOUT THE AUTHOR

Daryn Parke recalls people looking at her strangely as she walked home from school at age six, lips moving as she told herself stories. Little has changed—she still loves to create stories, while including background material from travels that have taken her from Siberia to Peru. Daryn is the author of numerous books of romance and suspense under the pen name, Blair Bancroft, but *The Art of Evil* is her first mystery. She likes the first-person style and hopes to add to her mystery list in the near future. Daryn lives with a feral cat called Ghostie. She can be contacted at her Web site, www.darynparke.com.